The
Dressmaker's
Gift

The
Dressmaker's
Gift

Fiona Valpy

Published by Lake Union Publishing, Seattle

www.apub.com

Amazon, the Amazon logo, and Lake Union Publishing are trademarks of Amazon.com, Inc., or its affiliates.

ISBN-13: 9781542005135
ISBN-10: 1542005132

Cover design by Emma Rogers

Printed and bound by CPI Group (UK) Ltd, Croydon, CR0 4YY

Dedicated to the memory of the female Special Operations Executive (SOE) agents, who worked with the French Resistance movement in World War Two and lost their lives in the concentration camps of Natzweiler-Struthof, Dachau and Ravensbrück:

Yolande Beekman, Denise Bloch, Andrée Borrell, Madeleine Damerment, Noor Inayat Khan, Cecily Lefort, Vera Leigh, Sonia Olchanezky, Eliane Plewman, Lilian Rolfe, Diana Rowden, Yvonne Rudelatt and Violette Szabo.

And their sisters-in-arms whose names were not recorded and whose fate remains unknown to this day.

2017

From a distance, the midnight blue dress looks as though it has been cut from one single piece of silk. Its graceful lines drape and flow, skimming the form of the mannequin on which it is displayed.

But if you look more closely, you will see that this is an illusion. The dress has been pieced together from scraps and off-cuts, sewn edge to edge so cleverly that they have been transformed into something else.

The years that have passed have aged the gown, making it so fragile that it must be protected if it is to tell its story in the years that are to come, and so the museum staff have placed it in a glass cabinet for the exhibition. On one side, the display case is made of magnifying glass to enable the viewer to study the detail of the seamstress's handiwork. Each fragment of material has been hand-sewn with invisible stitches, as tiny and regular as any modern-day machine could manage. The people who come to see it will marvel at its complexity, and at the time and patience it must have taken to create it.

There is a history displayed in this glass case. It's a part of all our shared histories, and it's a part of my own personal history.

The museum director comes in to check that all is in order for the opening. He nods his approval and the rest of the team head off for drinks at the bar round the corner to celebrate.

But I hang back and, just before I finally close the cabinet, I run my fingertips over the delicate silver beads that draw the eye to the neckline of the dress. They are another clever distraction from the patchwork pieces, a scattering of stars against a midnight sky. I can imagine how they would have caught the light and how the eye of the beholder would then have been drawn upwards, to the sweep of the neck, the line of the cheekbones, the eyes of the wearer of this gown; eyes which would have held that same light in their depths.

I shut the display cabinet and I know that everything is ready. Tomorrow, the gallery doors will open and people will come here to look at the dress whose image is displayed on the posters on the walls of the Métro.

And from a distance they will think it's been cut from one single piece of silk. It's only when they look more closely that they will see the truth.

Harriet

A gust of hot, stale air, belched from the tangle of tunnels below ground, buffets my legs and snatches at my hair as I wrestle my heavy suitcase up the steps of the Métro and emerge into the light of the Paris afternoon. The pavement is busy with tourists, who amble and dawdle, consulting maps and phones as they work out which direction to go next. With quicker, more purposeful steps, smartly dressed locals who have recently returned to reclaim their city, having spent the month of August by the sea, weave their way in and out of the crowds.

The river of traffic streams by – a continual blur of colour and noise – and for a moment I feel dizzy, light-headed with the mixture of all that movement and the nervous excitement of being in the city that will be my home for the next twelve months. I may look like a tourist right now, but soon, I hope I might be mistaken for a native Parisienne.

To give myself a moment to regain my composure, I pull my case to the railings alongside the entrance to Saint-Germain-des-Prés station and consult the email on my phone, rechecking the details. Not that I need to – I know the words off by heart . . .

Dear Ms Shaw,

Further to my phone call, I am pleased to confirm that your application for a one-year internship at the Agence Guillemet has been successful. Congratulations!

As discussed, whilst we are only able to offer the minimum wage for the position of intern, we are pleased to be able to offer you accommodation in an apartment above the office.

Once you have finalised your travel arrangements, please confirm the date and time of your arrival. I look forward to welcoming you to the company.

Yours sincerely,

Florence Guillemet

Directrice

Agence Guillemet, Relations Publiques

12 Rue Cardinale, Paris 75000.

I still can't quite believe that I managed to talk Florence into taking me on. She runs a PR agency specialising in the fashion sector, focusing on a client list of smaller companies and start-ups who can't afford their own in-house communications personnel. She doesn't usually take on interns but my letter and CV were persuasive enough to make her call me at last (after I'd resent them twice, that is, and she'd realised I wasn't going to leave her alone until I'd had an answer). The fact that I was prepared to do the job for a whole year on minimal pay, coupled with my fluency in French, led to a more formal Skype interview. And a glowing reference from my university tutor, emphasising my interest in the fashion industry and my commitment to hard work, finally convinced her to take me on.

I'd been prepared to look for a place to rent in one of the less salubrious suburbs of the city, eking out the small inheritance which had been left in trust for me in my mother's will. So the offer of a room above the office was a fantastic bonus as far as I was concerned. I'd be living in the very building that had led me to find the Agence Guillemet in the first place.

I don't usually believe in fate, but it felt as if a force was at work, drawing me to Paris. Leading me to the Boulevard Saint-Germain. Bringing me here.

To the building in the photograph.

❧

I'd found the photo in a cardboard box of my mother's things which had been pushed to the back of the highest shelf of the wardrobe in my bedroom, presumably by my father. Perhaps he'd wanted to hide it away up there so that I'd only find it when I'd grown up enough to be ready to see its contents, once the passing years had softened the edges of my grief so that they could no longer inflict such pain. Or perhaps it was guilt that made him push the taped-up box out of sight and out of reach, so that he and his new wife wouldn't have to see this pathetically meagre reminder of the part they'd played in the unbearable sadness which finally led my mother to take her own life.

I'd discovered it one damp day when I was in my teens, home from boarding school for the Easter holidays. Despite the trouble they'd gone to – making sure I had my own room, letting me choose the colour for the walls and allowing me to arrange the books, ornaments and posters I'd brought with me however I liked – my father and stepmother's house never really felt like 'home' at all. It was always *their* house, never mine. It was the place where I had to come and live when my own home had suddenly ceased to exist.

I'd been bored that wet April day. My two younger stepsisters were bored too, which meant they were niggling at one another, and the niggling had inevitably escalated into name-calling, a full-blown argument and then a good deal of loud screeching and door-slamming.

I retreated to my room and plugged my earbuds into my ears, using my music to block out the noise. Sitting cross-legged on my bed, I began to turn the pages of the latest copy of *Vogue*. At my request, my stepmother had given me a subscription for my Christmas present. I always savoured the moment when I opened the latest edition of the magazine, poring over each of the glossy pages, expensively scented with samples of the latest perfumes and lotions, a portal into the glamorous world of high fashion. That day, there was a picture of a model in a primrose-yellow T-shirt heading up a feature entitled 'Early Summer Pastels'. It reminded me that I had one quite like it somewhere in my wardrobe among the summer clothes that I'd washed and folded carefully last autumn, swapping them over on the top shelf for the warmer tops and jumpers that were stashed there.

I laid the magazine aside and dragged the chair from my desk over to the wardrobe. As I reached for the pile of summery tops, my fingertips brushed against the age-softened cardboard of the box pushed to the back of the shelf.

I'd never paid any attention to it before that day – probably because I hadn't been tall enough to see the writing – but now, standing on tiptoes, I pulled the box towards me and saw my mother's name written in thick black marker pen on the parcel tape that sealed the top shut.

All thoughts of early summer pastels forgotten for the moment, I lifted the box down. Alongside her name – Felicity – was scrawled 'papers/photos etc. for Harriet' in my father's handwriting.

I ran my fingers over the words and my eyes filled with tears at the sight of her name, and mine, written there. The wide brown tape had lost its stickiness over the years and it lifted away from the cardboard as I touched it, crackling softly. I brushed away my tears with my sleeve and opened the box.

The pile of papers within looked as though they'd been hastily – and somewhat randomly – thrown in in no particular order, the roughly sorted remnants of my mother's life that had made it on to the 'keep for Harriet' pile landing in a brown box instead of a black bin bag.

I spread them out across my bedroom floor, sorting official documents – her out-of-date driving licence and passport – from copies of my old school reports and the handmade birthday cards that I'd given her over the years. I cried again at the sight of the clumsy, childish drawings of the two of us hand in hand, alone together. But I smiled through my tears as I realised that even at that early age I'd added fashionable touches in the form of large buttons down the front of our dresses and brightly coloured handbags to match. The handwriting inside the cards ranged from laborious nursery school printing to a rounded primary school script, heartfelt messages of love that she'd treasured enough to hold on to for safekeeping. Maybe I imagined it but it seemed to me that, even after all these years, those pictures were scented – very faintly – with the perfume that she'd always worn. The sweetly floral smell brought back a vivid memory of the black bottle with a silver top sitting on her dressing table, a French perfume called Arpège.

And yet, my pictures and messages hadn't been enough. They hadn't been able to pull her out of the quicksand of loneliness and sorrow that had eventually overwhelmed her, dragging her down so deep that the only escape she could find was death. Her name was one of the ultimate ironies in a life that had been anything but felicitous. The only time she had seemed really happy was when she played her piano, losing herself in the music she made as her hands floated effortlessly across the keys. My throat closed around a lump of grief as solid as a stone as I sorted the cards into a careful pile: the evidence that my mother had loved me so much, but that love, ultimately, hadn't been able to save her.

When, at last, I was able to set the other papers aside and dry my eyes, I turned my attention to a bundle of photographs at the bottom of the box.

At the top of the pile there was one which made me catch my breath. It was a picture of her cradling me in her arms, my baby hair a halo of thistledown, catching the sunlight which streamed in from the window alongside us. The light, which made her look like a Renaissance Madonna, bathed my baby features in gold as well and it was as if I was illuminated by the love that shone from her eyes as she gazed at me. On her wrist, clearly visible, was the gold charm bracelet that I now wear. My father gave it to me on my sixteenth birthday, explaining that it had belonged to my mother and to her mother before her. I've worn it every day since. In the photograph, I could make out some of the charms that hang round my own wrist today – the tiny Eiffel Tower, the bobbin of thread and the thimble.

My father must have taken the picture, I realised, once upon a time when it was just the three of us and we were enough. When we were everything.

I set the print aside. I'd find a frame for it and take it back to school with me so that it could sit on the windowsill by my bed and I could see it each day without having to worry about it upsetting my father or irritating my stepmother, this reminder of a Before which they would prefer to forget. As if my presence in their house wasn't already enough.

There were several school photos in the box too: pictures of me in my white blouse and navy jumper, sitting stiffly in front of the photographer's sky blue backcloth, smiling my cautious smile. She'd kept them all, one year after the next, my strawberry blonde hair pulled back from my face by a dark blue hairband in one, and drawn into a neat ponytail in another, but my expression of wary watchfulness never changing.

I picked the last of these school photos from the very bottom of the box. As I opened the cream card cover, another photo fell into my lap. It was an old black and white print, curling and yellowed with age. Probably long forgotten, it must have got stuck beneath the mount by mistake.

Something about the picture – the smiles of the three girls it depicted perhaps, or the elegantly cut lines of the suits they wore – caught my attention. There was an air of continental chic about them. As I looked more closely, I realised that I was right. They were standing in front of a shop window above which was painted the number of the building – 12 – and the words *Delavigne, Couturier*. When I carried the photo to the window to examine it in the better light, I could make out the words on the enamelled sign affixed to the building, unmistakeably French, which read *Rue Cardinale – 6e arrondissement*.

I recognised the girl on the left. With her delicate features, fair hair and gentle smile she bore more than a passing resemblance to my mother. I was sure this must be my grandmother, Claire. I vaguely remembered her image from looking through old family albums (where were those albums now?) and my mother telling me that her mother had been born in France. She never said much more about her though, and it only now struck me as strange that she had changed the subject whenever I asked questions about this French grandmother.

Sure enough, when I turned the picture over, written on the back in a looping hand were three names: *Claire, Vivienne, Mireille*, and the words *Paris, Mai 1941*.

❦

I knew I was clutching at straws, but somehow that old photograph – a fragment of my mother's family history – became an important part of my heritage. There was so little left of that side of my family that this tenuous link to one of my ancestors took on huge significance for me. It had sat in a frame, alongside the mother-and-baby photo, and it then kept me company through the remainder of my school days and on to university. And even though I'd already begun to take a keen interest in the fashion business before I'd discovered the forgotten photo in the cardboard box, the picture of those three elegant young women standing on that street corner more than forty years ago certainly played its part in piquing my fascination. Maybe the love of fashion was already in my blood, but the photograph helped to shape my dreams. It had seemed like fate when I tracked down the address – 12 Rue Cardinale – on a school trip to Paris and found myself standing in front of a plate glass window bearing the name *Agence Guillemet, Relations Publiques (spécialiste Mode)*. In that moment, my future was decided. That sign opened up a whole career path that I'd never imagined existed, and drove me on to apply for an internship in fashion PR once I'd finished my degree in Business Studies with French.

I'd hesitated before contacting the agency, lacking the confidence to make an approach out of the blue, and receiving no encouragement from my father. If anything, Dad had always tried to discourage my interest in fashion, seeming to disapprove of my choice of career. But, as if egging me on, my grandmother Claire and her two friends had smiled at me from the black and white photo propped on the desk beside my laptop, as if to say, '*At last! What are you waiting for? Come and find us!*'

And so here I am, in Paris on a September afternoon, straightening my jacket and smoothing my hair into place before I wheel my suitcase along the busy pavement and press the buzzer on the door of the office. The plate glass windows, half-covered by blinds bearing the Agence Guillemet logo that have been pulled down to keep the glare of the afternoon sun at bay, reflect my anxiety back at me and I realise my heart is beating fast.

With a click, the door unlocks itself and I push it open, stepping into a softly lit reception area.

French grey walls are hung with framed copies of magazine covers – *Vogue, Paris Match, Elle* – and fashion shots. Even at first glance, I can tell they bear the trademark styles of photographers like Mario Testino, Patrick Demarchelier and Annie Leibovitz. A pair of minimalist sofas, upholstered in a highly impractical ivory linen, face one another across a low table upon which sits a selection of the latest fashion publications in a variety of languages. For a moment, I imagine sinking down on to one of them and kicking off the shoes that are pinching my travel-swollen feet.

Instead, I step forward to shake the hand of the receptionist who has come around from behind her desk to greet me. The first thing I notice about her is the mass of dark curls which frame her face and tumble over her shoulders. And the second thing is her effortlessly chic style. The little black dress she wears hugs the curves of her figure and the flat ballerina pumps on her feet add very little to her diminutive height. I immediately feel awkwardly tall and ungainly in my high heels, and stuffily formal in my tailored suit and tight-fitting white blouse, now creased from my journey and the heat.

Thankfully, though, the third thing I notice is her friendly smile, which lights up her dark eyes as she welcomes me, saying, 'Hello, you must be Harriet Shaw. I'm Simone Thibault. Very pleased to meet you. I've been looking forward to having the company – we're going to be flatmates, sharing the apartment upstairs.' She nods toward the ornate cornicing on the ceiling above our heads as she says this, making her curls dance. I warm to her immediately and am secretly relieved that she isn't one of the snooty, skinny French fashionistas I'd imagined my colleagues might be.

Simone stashes my suitcase behind her desk and then ushers me through a door at the back of the reception area. I am immediately aware of the discreet chirping of telephones and the low murmur of voices in the busy PR office. One of the half-dozen or so employees – the account managers and their assistants – stands up to shake my hand, but the others in the room are completely absorbed in their work and only have time to nod briefly as we walk past. Simone pauses before a panelled door at the far end of the room and knocks. After a moment, a voice calls, '*Entrez!*' and I find myself standing in front of a wide mahogany desk, behind which sits Florence Guillemet, the director of the agency.

She raises her eyes from her computer screen and removes the dark-rimmed glasses she's been wearing. She is immaculately dressed in the most elegant trouser suit I have ever seen. Chanel, maybe? Or Yves Saint Laurent? Her streaked blonde hair is cut in a way that shows off the height of her cheekbones whilst flattering a jawline that is just starting to show the first signs of softening with age. Her eyes are a warm amber-brown and they seem to see right through me.

'Harriet?' she asks.

I nod, struck dumb momentarily as the magnitude of what I've done hits me. A year? In this professional, A-list public relations agency? In the fashion capital of the world? What am I doing here? And how long will it take them to discover how ill-equipped I am – fresh out of university – to contribute anything of any value to the work they do here?

And then she smiles. 'You remind me of myself, many years ago when I started out in the industry. You have demonstrated both courage and determination in getting yourself here. Although, maybe it feels a bit overwhelming just at this moment?'

I nod again, still unable to find the words . . .

'Well, that is only natural. You've had a long journey and you must be tired. For today, Simone will show you up to the apartment and leave you to settle in. You have the weekend to find your feet. Work starts on Monday. It will be good to have an extra pair of hands. We're so busy with preparations for Fashion Week.'

The anxiety that I'm feeling, which the mention of Paris Fashion Week – one of the most important events in the couture calendar – only serves to deepen, must show in my expression, because she adds, 'Don't worry. You're going to do just fine.'

I manage to find my voice again and blurt out, '*Merci*, Madame Guillemet.' But then the phone on her desk rings and she dismisses us with another smile and a wave of her hand as she turns to answer it.

Simone helps me lug my suitcase up five flights of steep and nar-row stairs. The first floor, she explains, is used as a photographic studio, rented out on a freelance basis. We poke our heads around the door to take a look. It's one vast room with clean white walls, empty save for a pair of folding screens in one corner. With its tall windows and high ceiling it's the perfect space for fashion shoots.

The next three floors are sublet as offices. The brass nameplates on their doors announce that the rooms are occupied by an accounting firm and a photographer. 'Florence needs to make the building pay its way,' Simone says. 'And there are always people looking to rent a little office space in Saint-Germain. It's a condition of the lease, though, that the top floor rooms cannot be rented out, so that they can be a perk of the job. Luckily for you and me!'

The top floor of the building, tucked in under the eaves, consists of a series of small rooms, a couple of which are used as storage, filled with filing cabinets, boxes of old office materials, defunct computers and piles of magazines. Simone shows me the cramped galley kitchen where there's just enough space for a fridge, cooker and sink, and the living room, which has a round, bistro-style table with two chairs in one corner and a small sofa pushed against the far wall. Its compact size is more than compensated for by the sloping roof light set into the low ceiling which allows sunshine to pour in. If I stand on tiptoes and crane my neck a little, I can see the Parisian skyline and glimpse the roof of the church from which the Boulevard Saint-Germain takes its name.

'And this is your room,' Simone says, pushing open another door. It's tiny – there's just enough space for a single iron bedstead, a chest of drawers and a utilitarian, free-standing clothes rail which looks like it may have been salvaged from a warehouse at some point in the distant past.

If I stoop beneath the sloping ceiling, from the small square of the dormer window I can see an ocean of slate rooftops, across which a flotilla of chimney pots and television aerials are scattered, under a clear blue September sky.

I turn to smile at Simone.

She shrugs apologetically. 'It's small, but . . .'

'It's perfect,' I say. And I mean it. Because this tiny room is mine. My own space, for the next twelve months. And somehow, even though I've never seen it before in my life, I have a sense of belonging here: it feels like home.

An old, long-forgotten photograph, discovered by accident in a box of fading memories, is my only tenuous link to this place. But then I don't really have any other strong connections in life and so this most fragile of threads, as fine as a strand of age-worn silk, has become the only lifeline I know, binding me to this tiny bedroom in an unknown building in a foreign city. It has drawn me here and I feel a strong compulsion to see where it takes me, following it back through the years, back through the generations, to its source.

'Well, I'd better get back to work.' Simone glances at her watch. 'Another hour to go before the weekend can officially begin. I'll leave you to unpack. See you later.' She leaves, closing the door of the apartment behind her, and I hear her footsteps fade away down the stairs.

I open my suitcase and dig beneath the layers of carefully folded clothes until my fingertips connect with the hard edges of the frame, wrapped for safe-keeping in the folds of a woollen jumper.

The eyes of the three young women in the photograph seem to be fixed upon mine as I search their faces for the thousandth time for clues about their lives. As I set the picture on top of the chest of drawers beside my narrow bed, I am more conscious than ever of how rootless I am and of how vital it is for me to find out more about them.

I'm not just searching for who they are. I'm trying to find out who I am, too.

⁓❧⁓

The purposeful sounds of people who are homeward bound at the end of another working week float in through my window from the street below. I'm just hanging the last of my clothes on the rail when I hear the apartment door open. Simone sings out, '*Coucou!*' She appears in the doorway of my room and holds up a bottle, the glass beaded with dew from the chilled white wine within. 'Would you like a drink? I thought we should celebrate your first evening in Paris.' She lifts the shopping bag she holds in her other hand and says, 'I got a few bits and pieces to accompany it, too, as you haven't had time to explore the shops yet. I can show you where things are tomorrow.'

She looks around the room, taking in the few personal touches that I've added – a couple of books sit by the bed alongside my bottle of perfume and a painted china trinket box of my mother's that contains the few items of jewellery that I own: some pairs of earrings and a string of pearls. I keep the charm bracelet in it, too, when I take it off at night.

Noticing the photograph, she sets down her bag of shopping and stoops to look at it more closely.

I point at the blonde on the left of the group. 'That's my grandmother, Claire, outside this very building. She's the reason I'm here.'

Simone glances up at me, a look of incredulity on her face. 'And that,' she says, pointing at the figure on the right of the trio, is *my* grandmother, Mireille. Standing outside this very building with your grandmother Claire.'

She laughs, as my jaw drops in amazement.

'You're joking!' I exclaim. 'That's an incredible coincidence.'

Simone nods, but then shakes her head. 'Or maybe it's no coincidence at all. I'm here because my grandmother inspired me with the stories of her life in Paris during the war, and it's because of her links with the world of couture that I'm working here at Agence Guillemet. It seems you and I have both been led here by a shared history.'

I nod slowly, pondering this, then pick up the framed picture, bringing it closer to examine Mireille's face in detail. With her laughing eyes and the tendrils of hair that refuse to be tamed by the band which draws them back from her forehead, I imagine that I can make out a resemblance between her and Simone.

I point at the third figure, the young woman in the centre of the group. 'I wonder who she was? Her name is written on the back of the picture: Vivienne.'

Simone's expression grows serious suddenly and I glimpse something I can't quite identify, a flicker of sadness, or fear, or pain perhaps? A wariness in her eyes. But then she recomposes her features and says, with careful insouciance, 'I believe their friend, Vivienne, lived and worked with them here too. Isn't it astounding to imagine the three of them working right here for Delavigne?'

Am I imagining it, or is she trying to divert the subject away from Vivienne?

Simone continues, 'My *mamie* Mireille told me that they slept in these little rooms, above the *atelier*, during the war years.'

For a moment, I seem to hear the sound of laughter echoing from the walls of the cramped apartment as I imagine Claire, Mireille and Vivienne here.

'Can you tell me more about your grandmother's time here in the 1940s?' I ask eagerly. 'It may hold clues to some of the questions I have about my own family history.'

Simone glances at the photograph, her expression thoughtful. Then she raises her eyes to meet mine and she says, 'I can tell you what I know of Mireille's story. And it is inextricably linked with the stories of Claire and Vivienne. But Harriet, perhaps you should only ask those questions if you are absolutely certain that you want to know the answers.'

I meet her gaze steadily. Should I deny myself this opportunity of finding out about the only family to which I have any feeling of connection? At the thought, a flash of disappointment passes through me, so strong it makes my breath catch in my chest.

I think of the fragile thread, weaving its way back through the years, binding me to my mother, Felicity, and binding her to her own mother, Claire.

And then I nod my head. Whatever the story – whoever I really am – I need to know.

1940

Paris was a very different city.

Of course, some things looked the same: the exclamation mark of the Eiffel Tower still punctuated the skyline; Sacré-Coeur still sat on top of its hill at Montmartre watching over the city's inhabitants as they went about their business; and the silver ribbon of the Seine continued to wind its way past palaces, churches and public gardens, looping around the buttressed flanks of Notre-Dame on the Île de la Cité and churning beneath the bridges that linked the river's right and left banks.

But something had changed. Not just the obvious signs, such as the groups of German soldiers who marched along the boulevard, and the flags that unfurled themselves in the wind from the facades of buildings with languorous menace – as she walked beneath them, the whisper of the fabric emblazoned with stark black and white swastikas on a blood-red background seemed to Mireille as loud as any bombardment. No, she could sense something else that was different, something less tangible, as she made her way from the Gare Montparnasse back to Saint-Germain. It was there in the look of defeat in the downcast eyes of the people who hurried past; she heard it in the harsh monotone of German voices from the tables outside the cafes and bars, and it was driven home by the sight of military vehicles bearing more Nazi insignia – those grim emblems which seemed to be everywhere now – as they sped past her through the streets.

The message was clear. Her country's capital no longer belonged to France. It had been abandoned by its government, handed over by the country's politicians like a bartered bride in a hastily arranged marriage.

And although many of those, like Mireille, who had fled in the face of the German advance a few months earlier were now returning, they were coming home to a city transformed. Like its citizens, the city seemed to be hanging its head in shame at the brutal reminders that were everywhere: Paris was in German hands now.

~❧~

As the afternoon light began to stretch the shadows cast by the window frames across the broad expanse of the cutting table, Claire hunched a little closer to the skirt upon which she was stitching a decorative braid. Finishing it off with a few quick over-stitches, she used the scissors which hung from a ribbon around her neck to snip the thread. Unable to help herself, she yawned and then stretched, rubbing the ache of a day's work from the back of her neck.

It was so boring in the *atelier* these days, with many of the girls gone and no one to gossip and laugh with at break times. The supervisor, Mademoiselle Vannier, was in an even worse mood than usual as the work mounted up, cajoling the seamstresses to sew faster but then pouncing on the slightest slip in quality which, in Claire's eyes, was usually imagined.

She hoped some of the other girls would return soon, now that the new administration was organising special trains to bring workers back to their jobs in Paris, and then it wouldn't be so lonely at night in the bedrooms under the eaves. The sounds of the city beyond the windows seemed to Claire to be muted nowadays, and an eerie silence fell as soon as the ten o'clock curfew arrived. But in the quiet darkness the building creaked and muttered to itself and sometimes Claire fancied she heard footsteps in the night, so she pulled the blankets over her head as she imagined German soldiers breaking in and searching for more people to arrest.

She might have been one of the youngest of the seamstresses but Claire hadn't fled, as so many others had done, that day in June when France fell to the Nazis. It was simply not an option to run back home to Brittany with her tail between her legs, when she'd only recently managed to escape the little fishing village of Port Meilhon, where nobody had the slightest sense of style and where the only men left were either ancient or stank of sardines, or both. With the recklessness of youth, she'd decided to take her chances and stay in Paris. And it had turned out to have been a good choice, since the government had surrendered so that the Germans would allow the city to remain intact. The departure of several of her more senior colleagues meant that she had been allowed to work on some of the more interesting orders to be sent up from the *salon* on the ground floor. At this rate, perhaps she'd catch Monsieur Delavigne's attention and fulfil her dream of becoming an assistant in the *salon* and then a *vendeuse* before she had to serve too many more years of drudgery in the sewing room.

She could picture herself dressed in an immaculately tailored suit, her hair swept into an elegant chignon, advising Delavigne's top clients on the latest fashions. She would have her own desk with a little gilt chair, and a team of assistants who would call her Mademoiselle Meynardier and jump to her every command.

The supervisor flicked on the electric lights, illuminating the room where several of the girls were starting to put away their things for the day, stowing their scissors and pincushions and thimbles in their bags and hanging up their white coats on the row of pegs beside the door. Unlike Claire, most of them had homes in the city to go to and they were in a hurry to get back to their families and their evening meals.

Mademoiselle Vannier paused as she passed behind Claire's chair, reaching out a hand for the skirt. She held it up to the harsh glare of the bare bulbs overhead so that she could inspect the garment closely. Her lips, which were already pleated with deep lines – the inevitable consequence of her age and her twenty-a-day cigarette habit – concertinaed into even deeper creases as she pursed her mouth in concentration. Finally, she gave an abrupt nod and handed the skirt back to Claire. 'Press it and hang it up, then you may pack up your things too.'

Mademoiselle Vannier had always made it clear that those who enjoyed the privilege of being accommodated in the apartment upstairs at the couture house were at her beck and call until she decided that their work was over for the day, even if sometimes that meant working late into the evenings on important commissions. Claire was annoyed at being made, as usual, to stay later than the other seamstresses and, in the haste born of her irritation, she caught the soft skin on the inside of her wrist against the edge of the hot iron. She bit her lip to stop herself from crying out at the searing pain of the burn. Any fuss would only attract the attention of Mademoiselle Vannier again and then her departure would be delayed by yet another scolding for not taking proper care over her work.

She hung the skirt on the clothes rail for the night, smoothing the softly stippled texture of the tweed over its russet silk lining and admiring the way the contrasting braid flattered the waistline. It was a beautifully classic design, typical of Delavigne's work, and her own tiny, neat stitches were as good as invisible, befitting the elegance of the garment. The matching jacket was being finished off by the tailor and the new suit would soon be ready for delivery to its owner.

The sound of footsteps on the stairs and the door opening made Claire turn to see who it was, thinking it must be one of the other dressmakers who had forgotten something and come back to fetch it.

But the figure standing in the doorway wasn't one of the seamstresses. It was another girl, whose dark curls surrounded a face grown so thin and pale that it took Claire a few moments to recognise who it was.

Mademoiselle Vannier spoke first. 'Mireille!' she exclaimed. 'You've returned!' She took a step towards the figure in the doorway, but then stopped and regained her usual formal demeanour. 'So you decided to come back, did you? Very well, we shall be pleased to have another pair of hands. Your room upstairs is empty. Claire can help you make up your bed. And has Esther also returned with you?'

Mireille shook her head, pressing one hand against the door frame as if she needed the support. And then she spoke, her voice rough with sorrow. 'Esther is dead.'

She swayed slightly and the harsh light in the sewing room made the dark circles beneath her eyes look like tender bruises.

There was a shocked silence as Claire and the supervisor absorbed Mireille's words, and then Mademoiselle Vannier pulled herself together again.

'Alright, Mireille. You are tired after your journey. This is not the time to talk. Go upstairs now with Claire. Get a night's sleep and tomorrow you can take your place on the team once more.' Her tone softened slightly as she added, 'It is good to have you back.'

Only then did Claire, who had been frozen by the unexpected, altered appearance of her friend and by the shocking words she had uttered, move swiftly to Mireille's side and wrap an arm around her in a brief hug. 'Come,' she said, taking the bag from Mireille's hand. 'There's some bread and cheese in the kitchen. You must be hungry.' With quick, light steps she led the way, and Mireille followed her more slowly up the stairs.

Sensing that Mireille needed a little time to readjust to being back in the apartment, Claire busied herself with making up the bed for her and then setting out a meagre supper for the two of them. Sharing her week's rations, Claire wondered for a moment how they would eat tomorrow, but she shrugged the thought aside. It was more important that Mireille should eat properly tonight. Perhaps she'd be able to find some vegetables for a soup. And with Mireille here now too, they'd be able to get double the rations, which would help make things go further.

'*A table!*' she called. But when Mireille did not immediately appear, she went to find her.

Mireille had opened the door to the room that Esther had occupied when she'd arrived in Paris as a refugee from Poland, pregnant and desperate to protect her unborn child. A few months later, her baby had been delivered in the tiny attic room, and given the name Blanche. Claire remembered the awe she'd felt on seeing Esther propped against her pillows, holding her newborn daughter in her arms. She would never forget the look of exhausted elation on Esther's face as she gazed into her baby's dark blue eyes, the strength of her love seeming to be both instantaneous and visceral.

As Mireille stood in the doorway of Esther's old room, Claire slipped an arm around her shoulders. 'What happened to her?' she asked, quietly.

Staring at the iron bedstead with its mattress stripped bare, Mireille's face was expressionless as she told Claire in a low voice how they'd got caught up in the flood of refugees fleeing Paris as the German forces broke through the Maginot Line and advanced on the capital. The road south had been choked with the tide of civilians when the lone plane attacked, diving again and again to strafe the crowd with machine-gun fire. 'Esther had gone to try to find some food for Blanche. When I found her, her face looked so peaceful. But the blood was everywhere, Claire. Everywhere.'

The expression of wide-eyed horror on Claire's face crumpled as her tears began to flow. 'And Blanche?' she whispered. 'Did she die too?'

Mireille shook her head. And then she turned to look at Claire, meeting her eyes at last, with a flash of defiance. 'No. They didn't get Blanche. She is safe with my family in the Sud-Ouest. My mother and sister are caring for her there. But, for her own safety, her origins must remain a secret as long as the Nazis continue their barbaric persecution of the Jewish people. Do you understand, Claire? If anyone asks, just say that Esther and Blanche are both dead.'

Claire nodded as she tried, ineffectually, to stem the flow of her tears with her sleeve.

Mireille reached out and grasped Claire by the shoulders with a fierceness in her grip that commanded attention. 'Save your tears, Claire. There will be a time for grieving when all this is over, but now is not that time. Now we must do all that we can to fight back, to resist this living nightmare.'

'But how, Mireille? The Germans are everywhere. There's nothing to be done when our own government has given up on France.'

'There's always something to be done, no matter how small and insignificant our efforts may seem. We have to *resist*.' She repeated the word again, with an emphasis that made Claire's eyes widen in fear.

'Do you mean . . .? Would you get involved . . .?'

Mireille's dark curls danced with something of their old determination and there was defiance written across her features as she nodded. Then she asked, 'And you, Claire? What will you do?'

Claire shook her head. 'I'm not sure . . . I don't know, Mireille. Surely there's nothing ordinary people like you and I *can* do.'

'But if the "ordinary people" do nothing then who is going to step forward and take a stand against the Nazis? Not the politicians in Vichy who are puppets of the new regime; and not the French army whose battalions lie rotting in shallow graves along the Eastern Front. We are all that is left, Claire. Ordinary people like you and me.'

After a pause, Claire replied. 'But aren't you afraid, Mireille? To get involved in such a dangerous way . . . and right under the nose of the German army? Paris is theirs now. They are everywhere.'

'I was afraid, once. But I have seen what they did to Esther, and to so many others who were on the road that day. More "ordinary people". And now I am angry. And anger is stronger than fear.'

Claire shrugged, causing Mireille to relinquish her grip on her shoulders. 'It's too late, Mireille. We have to accept that things have changed. France is not the only country to have fallen to the Germans. Let the Allies do the fighting. It's enough of a battle to stay alive these days without going looking for trouble elsewhere.'

Stepping backwards into the narrow hallway, Mireille reached for the handle of the door to Esther's room and pulled it firmly shut.

Claire tugged nervously at the hem of her shirt, uncertain what to say next. 'There's a bit of supper . . .' she began.

'That's alright,' Mireille replied, with a smile that couldn't erase the sadness in her eyes. 'I'm not hungry tonight. I think I'll just unpack my things and get some sleep.'

She turned towards her own bedroom, but then paused, without looking back. Her voice was calm and low as she said, 'But you're wrong, Claire. It is never too late.'

Harriet

As I lie in the unfamiliar darkness of my new bedroom, listening to the sounds of Paris by night wafting up from the streets down below, I mull over what Simone has told me of my grandmother's story so far. It seems important to capture her words, so I've begun to write them down in the journal that I've brought with me. I'd intended to use it to record my year working in Paris, but Claire and Mireille's story seems so connected to me, such a vital part of who I am, that I want to remember every detail.

As I read back over the first few pages, I have to admit to feeling a little disappointed that it was Mireille who wanted to join the Resistance and not Claire, who quite frankly seems to have been a bit of a wimp in comparison. But she was young, I remind myself, and hadn't experienced the horrors of the war in the way that Mireille had.

The background sounds of the traffic a couple of streets away on the Boulevard Saint-Germain are interrupted by the urgent wail of police sirens. Their sudden noise makes my heartbeat race. As I listen to them fade, the city lights cast a dull orange glow through my attic window and I reach out a hand to steady myself, touching the bars of the bedstead behind my head. The metal feels cool, despite the mugginess of the city night. The mattress on my bed is clearly a recent addition and is comfortable enough, but could this be one of the original bed frames that was in the apartment all those years ago? Did Claire sleep here? Or Esther and her baby, Blanche?

I roll on to my side, willing sleep to come. In the dim light, the photograph on the chest of drawers gleams faintly in its frame. I can just make out the three figures, although I can't see their faces in the darkness.

I recall Simone's words of warning from earlier, that I should only ask questions if I am absolutely certain that I want to know the answers. Which is worse, I wonder: knowing the horrors of war like Mireille, or choosing to remain as unaware as possible like Claire?

Simone must have realised I'd feel a bit let down by my grandmother's passivity and her reluctance to join the struggle against the Occupation. Maybe that was why she didn't want to tell me the story. But how could any of us nowadays know what it feels like to have your country invaded? What it feels like to live with deprivation and fear, in the grip of foreign control, with the ever-present threat of casual acts of brutality? How could any of us know how we'd respond?

I fall asleep at last. And I dream of rows of girls in white coats, their heads bowed over their work as they stitch together an endless river of blood-red silk.

1940

Mireille shivered as she waited outside the tobacconist on the Rue Buffon, pretending to wait for a bus. It was bitterly cold and her feet were frozen. She knew that later on, when she washed them in a bowl of warmed water back at the apartment, her toes would itch and burn as the chilblains that pierced them thawed out.

To take her mind off the cold, she ran through her instructions in her head once again, making sure she'd got them straight. Wait here until a man in a grey homburg with a green band goes into the shop. He will come out carrying a copy of *Le Temps*. Go into the shop and buy a copy of the newspaper, asking the tobacconist whether he has any of yesterday's edition left over. He will hand you a folded copy from under the counter. Keep it safe in your bag. Walk to the Métro at the Gare d'Austerlitz and catch a train back to Saint-Germain-des-Prés. Sitting at a table in the back corner of the Café de Flore, you will see a man with sandy-coloured hair wearing a silk tie with a paisley pattern. Join him as if greeting a friend, and he will order you a coffee. Put the folded copy of the newspaper on the table while you drink your coffee. When you leave, do not pick it up.

This was not the first time she'd passed messages on for the network. Shortly after she'd returned to Paris, when she was dropping off some silk at the dyer's to be matched as a lining for an evening dress, she'd spoken to a contact there whom she'd guessed might be involved in

Resistance activities. Through him, she'd been introduced to a member of the network and had soon been given assignments like this one. She was aware that they were testing her at first, making sure she was who she said she was and that she was a reliable courier. She wasn't even certain whether the messages she'd been passing on had been real so far. But today's assignment was a little different from the usual, and she guessed that the proximity of the pick-up point to the Gare d'Austerlitz, which was one of the arrival points in Paris for trains from the east and the south as well as a point of departure for transports to the work camps, held an important significance. So she tried to ignore the cold, which seeped through the soles of her shoes, worn thin by the miles she'd walked in them, and pretended to study a bus timetable as, out of the corner of her eye, she glimpsed the customer in the homburg hat entering the *tabac*.

❧

A cloud of warmth, noise and cigarette smoke engulfed Mireille as she pushed open the door and stepped across the threshold of the Café de Flore. She picked her way around the pillars, making for the back corner of the room by the wood-panelled bar, as directed. At a banquette near the door, a group of soldiers in Nazi uniform laughed uproariously and one clicked his fingers in the air, summoning the waiter and ordering another bottle of wine. As Mireille passed, one of the soldiers leapt to his feet, blocking her passage. Her heart thumped against her ribs at the thought that he might demand to see what she was carrying in her bag and discover whatever message was concealed within the pages of the newspaper. But instead he made an elaborate bow and pretended to offer her his seat, to the raucous cheers of his comrades.

Suppressing her first instinct to spit in his face, and her second instinct to turn and run, Mireille managed to summon a polite smile and, with a diplomatic shake of her head, she stepped past the soldier and headed for the table in the back corner where a sandy-haired man wearing a paisley-patterned silk tie sat sipping a *café-crème*, reading his own copy of *Le Temps*.

The man set down his paper and rose to his feet as she approached, and they embraced as if they knew each other well. For a second, she breathed in the expensive scent of his cologne – a subtle blend of cedarwood and limes – and then she settled herself on the banquette opposite him.

A waiter appeared and the man ordered her a coffee while she casually pulled the folded newspaper out of her bag and laid it on top of the one on the table. The man ignored it completely, pushing both papers to one side so that he could lean towards her as a lover would do.

'I'm Monsieur Leroux,' he said. 'And you, I think, must be Mireille? It's a pleasure to meet a new friend of our cause.'

She nodded, feeling awkward and self-conscious, unsure what to say to this man about whom she knew absolutely nothing, even though he clearly knew a bit about her.

She had fulfilled her task and now she wanted nothing more than to push her way out of the café and hurry back to the peace and safety of her attic room. But she forced herself to stay seated and to smile and nod, playing out the charade.

There was a momentary silence between them as the waiter appeared and set a cup of coffee down in front of Mireille, slipping a scribbled note of the price under the ashtray in the centre of the table. Monsieur Leroux used the opportunity of the arrival of the coffee to move the two newspapers, tucking them casually into the pocket of his overcoat which was draped over the back of his chair.

He watched her as she picked up the thick china cup and blew cautiously on the contents to cool them down enough to take a sip. The coffee wasn't too bad – a little watery but not overly tainted with the bitterness of chicory.

'So, you are one of Delavigne's seamstresses? How is the world of couture faring these days? I hear special licences have been granted to all the major fashion houses to enable them to continue trading. It appears our German friends like to dress their wives and mistresses in the best French finery.'

He spoke evenly, his tone pleasantly conversational, but she detected the undercurrent of scorn for the occupying enemy in his words.

'We're busier than ever,' she agreed. 'Even with two teams back up to full strength, we can scarcely keep up with the demand. Every well-dressed woman in Paris still wants her new suit and her evening dress for the season. And it's true, even though the government rations the food we eat and the fuel to heat our homes, it has ensured that buttons and braid are not rationed. It can be hard to get enough material sometimes though, and the prices are extortionate, naturally.'

Monsieur Leroux nodded. 'What a bizarre playground for the Germans Paris has become. While her citizens starve and freeze, her newest inhabitants parade around in world-class designs in the finest of fabrics, drinking vintage wines and entertaining themselves at the Moulin Rouge.'

Again, Mireille was struck by his facade of equanimity as he spoke; only the bitterness of his words belied the air of pleasant social conversation with which they were delivered.

As she sipped her cooling coffee, Monsieur Leroux asked her a series of questions about the *atelier*. What did her work involve? How many seamstresses were there? And how many lived above the shop?

When she set her empty cup back on its saucer, he reached across and put his hand over hers. To the casual observer, it would simply look like a gesture of romantic intimacy. 'Thank you for helping, Mireille,' he said. 'I wonder, might you be interested in helping us a bit more? Although I must warn you, the dangers are very real and very serious.'

She smiled at him and withdrew her hand from his, the picture of bashful propriety. 'I wish to do all that I can to help, m'sieur.'

'Then there may well be a further role for you. Our mutual friend, the dyer, will let you know. Thank you for coming today, Mireille. Take care.'

She stood, pushing back her chair, gathering up her coat and bag. 'You too, Monsieur Leroux.'

As she left the café, she glanced back to where the man with the sandy hair and the paisley print tie was paying the waiter.

He stood and shrugged on his overcoat. And she could just make out the corner of a folded newspaper, barely visible, where it protruded from the pocket.

⁂

Outside the tall windows of the sewing room, the December sky had taken on the same dull gunmetal-grey colour as the uniforms of the Nazi occupiers, as if it, too, had surrendered all hope and capitulated with the new order. The glare of the lightbulbs overhead seemed to Claire as bright as the searchlights sweeping the darkness for Allied aircraft, whose beams could be seen in the distance if one peeped out from behind the blackout which covered the attic windows at night. She held the bodice of the scarlet crêpe de Chine evening gown that she was working on a little closer to her face as the stitches blurred and swam, her eyes having been strained in focused concentration for hours on end. It was draughty in her seat by the window, but she wouldn't have exchanged it with any of the other seamstresses for a chair closer to the cast-iron radiators on the far wall. She needed the light to work by. And those radiators didn't give out that much heat anyway nowadays, since coal for the furnace in the basement was so strictly rationed. It would often go out and not be relit for days on end, although there was always enough coal to keep the fireplace in the salon blazing so that clients would be warm enough when they came in for fittings.

Claire and the other seamstresses were all thinner now, surviving on the measly rations that they had to queue for at the weekends. But, glancing around the table, she realised that it only showed in their faces where the lights cast dark shadows beneath sunken cheekbones and eyes. Their bodies looked bloated, well-padded under their white coats, and on some of the girls the buttons strained and gaped. In reality, this illusion was down to the layers of clothes that they wore to try to keep out the cold while they sat at work in the *atelier*.

Delavigne Couture was busier than ever and the run-up to Christmas was proving, if anything, even more hectic than in the years before the war. Paris had become an oasis of luxurious escapism in war-torn Europe, and the Germans flocked in to spend their pay on black market food, wine and designer gowns for their wives and mistresses. And their money went a long way now that the exchange rate had soared to almost twenty francs to the Reichsmark.

Even the German women who had been assigned to Paris to help run the new administration could afford to have couture creations made for themselves. The saleswomen in the salon scathingly referred to them as 'grey mice' behind their backs, because they looked so frumpy and dowdy in their uniforms when they came in for their fittings.

Mademoiselle Vannier left the room for a few minutes to go and fetch another bolt of the thin, unbleached muslin that was used to make the mock-ups of the more complex garments. Once they'd been cut out and tacked together, these *toiles* were then taken apart again and used as templates to make sure the more expensive fabrics used for the finished garments were cut accurately and with minimal wastage.

Taking advantage of Mademoiselle Vannier's absence, Claire joined in the chatter and gossip with the other seamstresses around the table: one of the models from the salon was rumoured to have taken up with a German soldier and opinion amongst the girls was divided. Some were shocked and disgusted, but others asked what a girl was supposed to do? With so few Frenchmen left now that any able-bodied males of working age who had survived thus far were being sent to work in the factories and camps in Germany, young French women were faced with the choice of becoming old maids or being spoiled and pampered by a rich German lover.

From beneath her lashes, Claire glanced at Mireille in the seat next to her. She seemed so distant these days. Mireille didn't join in the chatter any more, remaining studiously focused on her work. She was always preoccupied now, a far cry from the vivacious, fun-loving friend she had been before the Occupation, and she seemed lost in her thoughts most of the time. She kept to herself more, too, in the evenings and at weekends, often disappearing without inviting Claire to come along. And there was no point asking questions, Claire had learnt, as Mireille simply smiled her sad-eyed smile and shook her head, refusing to answer. Maybe she really was playing at her 'Resistance' games, as she'd threatened to do when she first came back to Paris, but Claire couldn't see what earthly good any of that sort of thing might do. However, if Mireille wanted to be all cloak-and-dagger and keep her own company then so be it.

But Claire did miss the friendship they'd once shared. There were only two other girls sleeping in the rooms above the shop at the moment and they were in the other team of seamstresses, so they tended to exclude Claire from their weekend outings, probably assuming that she'd be spending time with Mireille.

Claire cut a thread and smoothed out the scarlet fabric, relishing the vicarious sense of luxury. Her fingers, roughened with cold and work, caught slightly on the crêpe.

Rubbing her thumb against the chapped skin of her fingertips, the sensation transported Claire back to the years spent growing up in Port Meilhon. After her mother had died of pneumonia, brought on by the damp and chill and exhaustion, leaving her only daughter a silver thimble and a pincushion stuffed with coffee grounds, Claire had been responsible for darning socks and mending the clothes of her father and four older brothers. The pins and needles would quickly grow rusty in the sea air and she had to pause frequently to rub them down with emery paper to stop them becoming blunt and staining the fabric of her father's and brothers' shirts with little brown marks like dried-on droplets of blood. As she'd sat at her sewing beside the range in the kitchen of the cottage that had been her home, her chapped fingers cracking open in places with painful fissures, a quiet determination had grown within her: her mother's legacy of needles and pins would become her passport out of there. It was all she had. She would use it to change her path, refusing to follow in her mother's footsteps. Instead of her grief at losing her mother lessening over time, the thought of the grave in the churchyard up on the hill had become more than Claire could bear. She preferred to think instead about the possibility of a life elsewhere filled with elegance and sophistication. And so she had concentrated on making her stitches smaller and neater, sewing quickly but fastidiously.

Her longing for pretty things was a form of escapism from Claire's rough and ready upbringing in a cottage full of men who spent their days wrestling creels from the grip of the cold Atlantic waters. When her father and brothers were off in the boats, she offered to take in mending for her village neighbours, charging them a few *sous* a time, saving the coins in an old sock stuffed into the bottom of her mending basket. Slowly, the sock became heavier, the toe weighted down as the coins accumulated. And then one day she counted her money and discovered that she had enough for the train fare to Paris.

Her father had scarcely reacted when she told him she was leaving. She suspected it would be more of a relief to him than anything else – one less mouth to feed. And Claire sensed, too, that increasingly she reminded him of his dead wife, her mother, a reminder which probably stabbed his heart with guilt each time he looked at her. He must know that this was no place for her to live so, she said to herself, he couldn't blame her for wanting to leave. He'd driven her to the station at Quimper and given her a gruff pat on the shoulder as the train pulled in, picking up her bag and handing it up to her once she'd climbed the steps into the carriage, which was about as much of a blessing as she could have expected.

Setting aside the bodice of the red evening gown, she sighed. Well, she'd made it to Paris, only to have the war interfere with her plans for a better life. She was still spending her days hunched over her meticulous stitching, she was still freezing cold most of the time, and she was hungrier than she had ever been at home.

She was overcome by a momentary surge of self-pity and homesickness at the thought of the family she'd left behind in Port Meilhon. She pictured her brothers' cheerful grins as they came home to the cottage on the quayside: Théo ruffling her hair and Jean-Paul lifting the lid on the pot of *cotriade* she'd prepared for their supper to sneak a taste of the delicious fish stew, while Luc and Marc pulled off their boots at the front door. Did their shirts go un-mended now that she wasn't there, and their socks un-darned? She missed the sound of their laughter and their gentle teasing, as well as the quiet reassurance of her father's presence as he sat in his armchair splicing a rope or untangling a length of twine. It was funny, she thought, how instead of feeling too crowded when they were all in the tiny cottage together, the room had always felt too big and empty when they were away.

She shrugged off the feeling, telling herself that wallowing in self-pity wasn't going to help anyone. As she stuck her needle carefully back into her mother's pincushion, she reminded herself how far she'd come, despite the hardships. The city was still a place of infinite opportunity compared to the fishing village in Brittany. She just needed to make the effort, to get out a bit more so that those opportunities could find her.

Harriet

There's been another terrorist attack. The city is stunned with shock and the headlines scream their anguish around the world. Paris was already reeling from the brutal assault on staff at the *Charlie Hebdo* offices in January, and now gunmen have murdered almost a hundred concert-goers at the Bataclan Theatre, holding a group of survivors hostage for hours before the French police could end the siege. The reports flood in of lives taken, lives altered in unimaginable ways, sickening acts of brutality. They are difficult to read, but impossible not to.

Dad calls me. 'Are you sure you're safe? Why don't you come home?' he asks.

I try to reassure him that I'm surely as safe here as I would be any-where, even though I feel sick with anxiety every time I walk down the street. My heart aches for the victims as their stories come out. Most of them were young, about the same age as Simone and me. But we try to stay focused on our work; the unremitting demands of the job force us all to carry on.

From nine to five, the office is busy with the hushed hum of con-versations and the discreet chirp of telephones. I take it in turns with Simone to man the reception desk and I feel the weight of responsibil-ity of being the first point of contact for Agence Guillemet's clients. The company may be relatively small but it punches above its weight, numbering amongst its clientele several up-and-coming designers, a luxury accessories brand and a new eco-cosmetics company. Of course, the larger fashion houses have their own in-house PR teams, but Florence has carved a niche for herself in the daunting world of Parisian couture. She has a knack for spotting promising new talent and finding creative ways to promote the new kids on the fashion block. Over the years, she has earned the respect of her peers and developed an enviable network of contacts. So, as the days go by, it's not unheard of for me to find myself making small-talk with a former supermodel who is developing her own line of swimwear, or the fashion editor of a glossy magazine, or an edgy young shoe designer and his muse who wears a skin-tight jumpsuit accessorised with a pair of the most vertiginous platforms I have ever seen, which are embellished with golden pineapples.

Florence also gives me opportunities to work alongside the account managers and I am inordinately proud of the first press release I help to compile. It's for the launch of the shoe designer's latest collection, which will be showcased at Paris Fashion Week in a fortnight's time, and the account manager shows me the list of recipients and asks me to send it out. As I do so, an idea occurs to me.

'Does anyone in the UK know about this guy's designs?' I ask.

'Not yet. It's hard for us to break into that market, so we are focusing on Paris first.'

'If I were to translate the press release and send it to a couple of buyers at some of the edgier London outlets, would that be okay?'

The account manager shrugs. 'Feel free. We have nothing to lose, and perhaps it would be a good way to begin to gauge interest across the Channel.'

So I draft an introductory email and attach the translated release. After digging around a bit and making several phone calls, I come up with a few London contacts and then, with the approval of Florence and the account manager, I press send.

Simone is impressed. 'Your first press release! We must celebrate this evening. I know a great bar we can go to. There's live music on tonight and some of my friends will be there too.' I've already learned how much she loves her music; she always has it playing in the apartment, and is usually plugged in to a pair of earphones when she's out and about.

And so that night we head out, crossing the river and heading for the Marais district with its narrow streets and hidden squares. The police presence is even more evident than usual, with heavily armed officers patrolling the busier junctions. It's a reassuring sight, even if it does make my heart race with the sense of fear that lurks just beneath the veneer of city lights and traffic fumes. Simone leads me past the Picasso museum and then we duck into a bar. An acoustic duo plays on a small stage at one end of the crowded room over the buzz of chatter and laughter that spills around them.

Simone's friends wave us over to the pair of tables they've pulled together and find chairs for us so that we can squeeze in too, adding our own drinks to the clutter of glasses and bottles. The musicians are good – really good, in fact. And I begin to relax and enjoy the setting and the company. Simone's friends are a creative bunch and they include a gallery owner, a designer, an actress, a sound engineer and at least two musicians. I guess it's Simone's love of music that has cemented some of these friendships. I'm surprised at how easy it is to feel a part of this group of young Parisians. I never made any very close friends at school or at university and I realise now that I never felt I fitted in anywhere at all really. Perhaps that feeling stemmed from the sense of not belonging at home with my father and stepmother. Perhaps that undermined my confidence of my place in the world. For most of my life, I have dwelt in a sort of no man's land where loneliness has been an easier option than trying to fit in. I always felt that there was a distance between me and my peers who hadn't had to attend their own father's wedding to someone new, shortly followed by their own mother's funeral. Here, in this company of strangers, I don't feel that I have to explain that I had been all my mother had left and that I had failed to be enough to make her want to stay in this world.

The sound engineer, who introduces himself as Thierry, brings another round of drinks and nudges Simone to move up so that he can pull his chair in between us.

He asks me questions about how I'm finding my job and how I like being in Paris, and I ask him about his work, which takes him to concerts at different venues across the city. I chat away, feeling more confident about speaking French now, and find myself relaxing and enjoying his company.

At first, the conversation among the friends is light and buoyant with smiles and laughter, but then, inevitably, the talk turns to the Bataclan terror attack. The mood around the table immediately turns sombre and I can see the trauma written on the faces of Simone and her friends as the still-raw pain that the terrorist act has cast over the city engulfs us all again. The Bataclan isn't far from where we are sitting, and Thierry tells me that he knew the sound crew who were working that night. All of a sudden it feels very close to home. As I listen to his words, I watch the lines of pain that cut deep into his face, transforming his easy-going expression into a mask of grief. His friends got out and helped get the band and several members of the audience to safety, but the brutality of the act and the thought of the many young lives lost, or altered for ever through horrific wounds, both mental and physical, have changed the way people see their city. Just under the surface it seems that fear and distrust lurk everywhere.

'Do you ever worry, when you're working, that something like that might happen to you?' I ask him.

Thierry shrugs. 'Of course. But what can we do? You can't let terror win. It becomes all the more important to resist the urge to give in to fear.'

I nurse my drink, musing on his words. I hear in them the echo of Mireille's declaration of resistance and her assertion that it's up to the ordinary people to decide how life will be lived.

'Even coming to a bar on a Friday night to listen to some music takes on a new significance for us these days.' He smiles, and the sadness in his dark eyes is replaced by a flicker of rebellion. 'We're not just here to enjoy ourselves. We're here to make sure that the freedom to live our lives cannot be taken away from us. We're here for every one of those people who was killed that night.'

Thierry wants to hear what I think as he asks me about the impact the attacks had across the Channel in Britain, and how we have coped with terrorist atrocities on our own soil.

'My father was already worried about me coming to Paris,' I admit. 'Not that London is without its dangers.' After the *Charlie Hebdo* attacks, Dad had tried hard to talk me out of taking the job, right up until the last minute. At the time, I'd resented his interference and put it down as another example of the distance between us – couldn't he *see* how important this opportunity was to me? Didn't he understand how strong the longing to leave was within me? But now I realise how anxious he must have been. From this perspective, I can see that the fact that he didn't want me to go was perhaps more to do with love than with a lack of understanding. For a moment, I miss him. I make a mental note to try to call him again tomorrow, although he'll probably be too busy to talk, as usual, out shopping with my stepmother or driving the girls to their weekend dance classes and sleepovers.

Thierry and I talk on, late into the evening, long after the musicians have finished their set and joined us at the table, and by the end of it I feel a closeness to Simone and her friends that is a new sensation for me. Slowly I find myself dropping my guard, my usual reticence thawing, as – tentatively – I begin to allow my thoughts and feelings to show themselves.

It seems that, in a new language and in a city where I am naturally an outsider, I find it easier to be myself. Perhaps, here in Paris, I can begin to become the person I want to be, enjoying the liberation that a new start brings.

Then another thought occurs to me: perhaps that is exactly what Claire felt too, all those years ago.

1940

The *atelier* closed early on Christmas Eve once the final few clients had been received in the salon, coming to collect last-minute commissions which were needed for the *soirées* and events of the festive season.

Mademoiselle Vannier even managed a tight-lipped smile as she handed out the wage packets to the seamstresses. 'Monsieur Delavigne has asked me to tell you that he is pleased with your work. It has been one of our most successful seasons yet, so he has, most generously, asked me to give each of you a small additional consideration in recognition of your efforts and your loyalty.'

The girls exchanged sidelong glances. It was common knowledge that one of the *vendeuses* had left the salon only a week ago, taking with her her team of assistants and her little black book with the measurements and contact details of all of her clients. Rumour had it that she had been poached by one of the other couture houses, and one of the seamstresses had even dared to murmur that a certain 'Coco', who had cultivated particular links with the German occupiers, was known to be on the lookout for staff now that her business was doing so especially well.

The seamstresses chattered excitedly as they hung up their white coats and pulled on scarves and gloves. Claire glanced at them enviously as she thrust her pay packet into the pocket of her skirt; most of them had homes to go to and families to share tonight's *Réveillon de Noël* dinner with, no matter how frugal a feast it might prove to be this year, staying up to see in Christmas Day together. She, on the other hand, had only her three companions in the upstairs apartment and an unappetising menu of vegetable soup – which tasted mostly of turnips – and some dry bread to look forward to.

In her chilly room upstairs, she took the money from her pay packet, carefully counting out what she would need for the coming week and stowing the rest away safely in the tin that she kept under her mattress. The pile of banknotes – her life savings and her passport to the life she longed for – was growing slowly but steadily.

Then, from the drawer next to her bed, she took a small package wrapped in brown paper, and went down the corridor to tap on the door of Mireille's bedroom. There was no answer, though, and when she knocked again a little harder the door swung open to reveal only the neatly made bed where Mireille's sewing things lay in a small pile, hastily discarded.

Claire glanced around. Mireille's outdoor coat, which usually hung on the back of the door, was missing. She must have gone straight out again to meet whoever it was she usually met and to do whatever it was she usually did. Even on Christmas Eve. So it was clearly far more important to her than spending time with her friends. Claire sighed and hesitated, then placed the brown paper package on Mireille's pillow and turned to go, carefully pulling the door closed behind her.

Her two other flatmates arrived then, laughing and gossiping. When they caught sight of Claire they stopped. 'Why so despondent? Has Mireille deserted you? Don't tell us you're all alone for *le Réveillon*?' They glanced at one another and nodded. 'Come on, Claire, we can't leave you here. Join us! We're going out to find some fun. Put your dancing shoes on and come along! You'll never meet anyone, sitting mouldering up here in the attic.'

And so it was that Claire, after just a moment's hesitation, pulled the tin out from beneath her mattress again, prised open the lid, drew out some of her carefully saved wages and found herself being swept along the pavement of the Rue de Rivoli in a tide of merrymakers, who scarcely noticed the red, white and black flags that stirred against the starlit sky in the bitter wind that blustered and eddied down the broad boulevard.

❧

Mireille hurried through the narrow streets of the Marais and paused in front of a shop window, as she'd been trained to do, making sure no one was following her. The white sign attached to the door stood out starkly against the lowered blackout blinds: Under New Management, it declared, By Order Of The Administration. These notices were appearing more and more frequently in shop doors and windows, especially in this *quartier* of the city. They were businesses which had formerly been owned by Jewish shopkeepers. But now their owners had gone – whole families turned out from their homes and sent to deportation camps elsewhere in the city's suburbs before being transported onwards to God-only-knew-where. The businesses had been appropriated by the authorities and 'reallocated', usually to collaborators or to those who had earned the approval of the administration by denouncing their neighbours, or betraying their former employers who used to be the owners of shops like this one.

Ducking her head to lean into the northerly wind, Mireille turned down a small side street and tapped on the door of the safe house. Three quick, quiet taps. Then a pause and two more. The door opened a few inches and she slipped inside.

Monsieur and Madame Arnaud – she had no idea whether that was their real name – had been some of the original members of the network that she'd been put in touch with by the dyer, and this wasn't the first time she'd been sent to their house to drop off or pick up a 'friend' who needed a safe place for a night or two, or to be accompanied across the city and delivered safely into the hands of the next *passeur* in the network. She was aware that there were other groups operating in the city, helping those in need to pass beneath the noses of the occupying army and be spirited away to safety. Once, in a last-minute change of plans, she'd been asked to accompany a young man to catch a train from the Gare Saint-Lazare, so she knew some people must be getting out via Brittany. But more often her rendezvous point would be at Issy or Billancourt, or out towards Versailles, and the distinctive twang of a south-west accent on the lips of the next link in the chain would reassure her that her latest 'friend' was being passed into good hands in order to make the long and arduous journey to freedom across the Pyrenees. She often wondered whether their route would take them anywhere near her home.

Tonight, especially, she felt a pang of longing for her family, picturing them in the mill house on the river beneath this same star-frosted sky. Her mother would be in the kitchen, preparing a special Christmas Eve supper from whatever supplies she had managed to gather together. Perhaps her sister, Eliane, would be sitting there too, in the warmth of the old iron range, bouncing baby Blanche on her knee. Her father and brother would step through the door, back from delivering the last few sacks of flour to the local shops and bakeries, and her father would scoop up Blanche and swing her round, making her chortle and clap her chubby hands together.

Mireille swallowed the lump of homesickness that had hardened in her throat at this image. How she missed them all. She would have given anything to be there in the kitchen, sharing a frugal meal richly seasoned with love. And afterwards, lying in her bed in the room that she and Eliane shared, they would exchange whispered secrets. How she longed to have someone to confide in.

But that was a luxury that she couldn't afford. She forced herself to set aside her thoughts of home and focus instead on her instructions for tonight's task.

Under cover of the Christmas Eve revelries, which would hopefully be providing a welcome distraction to those soldiers unfortunate enough to have been assigned guard duties over the festive period, Madame Arnaud explained that Mireille was to accompany a man to the Pont de Sèvres, where they would be met by Christiane, a *passeuse* with whom Mireille had worked before, and she would take him to the next safe house along the route.

'But you will need to work fast tonight, Mireille,' Madame Arnaud cautioned. 'The Métro will be crowded, with few trains running, and you must rendezvous with Christiane in time to get yourself back home before the curfew. Even at Christmas, it would not be wise to be picked up by the Germans.'

Mireille nodded. She understood the risks all too well. She had been warned that if she was picked up and questioned, she should try not to divulge any information for the first twenty-four hours to give the others in the network time to cover their tracks and disperse. But she was also aware of some of the torture methods that the Nazis employed to try to get that information out of any suspected members of the Resistance and an unspoken fear was lodged deep within her. If it came to it, would she have the strength to endure such treatment?

None of that bore thinking about right now, though; she needed to concentrate fully on the task in hand. Even the slightest fear or distraction might give them away or mean that she forgot to keep up her guard at some crucial moment. One never knew what would be encountered en route to get her 'friend' safely to his destination.

'Level of French?' she asked Madame Arnaud, referring to the stranger for whom she was about to risk her life.

Madame Arnaud shook her head. 'Almost none, and an accent so terrible it would give him away in an instant. One further complication – he's injured his foot. So you'll need to give him some support if you have to walk any distance.'

A bad landing during a parachute jump, perhaps, Mireille thought. This wouldn't be the first foreign airman she had helped to escape. Or maybe this man had just had a long, terrifying journey fleeing in fear of his life because of his religion. Or his politics. Or simply because of some petty feud with a neighbour which had led to a bitter denunciation. Who knew? She didn't ask, because if she happened to be caught then the less she knew, the better.

The man appeared from a room towards the back of the house, dressed in a thick overcoat. He was limping and Monsieur Arnaud, who followed him, reached out a helping hand to support the man's elbow as he came down the two steps from the hallway to the entrance where Mireille stood waiting. The man's skin had a greyish tinge and, although he tried to hide it, she saw that he winced in pain as he stepped down on to his injured foot. Monsieur Arnaud handed him a homburg hat. And Mireille couldn't help noticing that the hat was grey and that it had a green band, just like the one worn by the man who had dropped off the newspaper on what had felt like her first proper assignment, that day when she'd first met Monsieur Leroux.

'Come,' she whispered in English. 'We must be going.'

The man nodded and then turned to Madame Arnaud, clasping both her hands in his. '*Merci*, madam, a thousand thanks, you are so very *gentille* . . .' He stumbled over the words, and the flattened vowels of his English accent made both women wince.

One thing was certain: she would have to do the talking if they were stopped and asked for their papers. She'd been briefed on his false identity and she knew he'd have an ID card tucked into the pocket of his coat, procured from who-knows-where, to match her story.

As they walked arm in arm through the Marais, looking like a young couple out for a few drinks to celebrate *le Réveillon*, she tried to make it look natural, as if he were supporting her rather than the other way around. She planned her route. She would need to try to use the Métro as far as possible to minimise his walking. At the same time, she knew she would need to avoid the busier stations like the one at the Place de la Bastille, which would be mobbed and would be more likely to have guards on duty checking papers.

She guided the man through the streets, making the occasional encouraging remark to him although she had no idea how much of what she said he could understand. But as they approached the Saint-Paul Métro station, she was horrified to see two German guards standing outside the entrance. They had stopped a man and were shouting at him to hand over his papers as he fumbled in his attaché case trying to find them.

Thinking fast, Mireille steered her 'friend' on to the Rue de Rivoli. It would be better to mingle with the pleasure-seeking crowds and move on to another stop on the Métro. They were jostled and pushed by a sea of merrymakers and the man gasped as someone stumbled into him, the pain making his leg almost give way.

'Hold on to me tightly,' Mireille muttered in his ear, wrapping an arm around his waist. With any luck he would just look like another party-goer who had drunk too much Ricard, whose girlfriend was trying to get him home to bed. They staggered along like that for some way, past the Hôtel de Ville where yet more Nazis were checking papers. By now the man was sweating with the pain from his injured foot and Mireille was struggling to help him stay upright. They would just have to risk it at Châtelet, even though it was one of the busiest stations on the line. Les Halles, the wholesale market which ran close to the Métro station, was known as a hotspot for black market activity, although this usually meant that the Germans were more likely to be shopping there than checking papers. She sent up a silent prayer to anyone who might be listening that, on Christmas Eve, the soldiers would be more interested in laying their hands on a little extra steak or a few oysters than on stopping an exhausted couple who were wending their weary way home, so obviously the worse for wear.

They slipped, unnoticed, past a group of noisy soldiers who were too busy whistling and cat-calling at a group of girls dressed up for a night out on the town to pay attention to anything else. When shouting broke out and a whistle blew shrilly, Mireille almost froze in panic, but she forced herself to keep on moving, leading the man towards the staircase which led down to the platforms. Allowing herself one quick backward glance she saw that, thankfully, the target of the police's attention was a pickpocket. In the confusion, she imagined that she heard someone calling her name, but in that crowd it could have been aimed at anyone and so she kept going, conscious of the man's gasps of pain at each downward step.

In the dim light on the platform, his face looked greyer than ever and she was worried that he might be about to pass out. If he did, it would make them the centre of everyone's attention and that was the last thing they wanted. She glanced up at him anxiously and he smiled at her. She smiled back, reassured. They would make it. She could see he was a fighter, this man, determined to keep going. He would do whatever it took to escape. The worst was over now. She calculated the journey . . . They just had to get on to the next train to come along, and then change to line nine, as long as the station at Rond-Point was open tonight, which would take them all the way to the Pont de Sèvres . . .

At last, a train rattled into the station and a flood of passengers got off. With grim determination, Mireille elbowed her way on, pulling the man behind her and then pushing him on to one of the double banquettes. As the doors closed and the train pulled away from the platform, the man next to her closed his eyes and rested against her, breathing a quiet sigh of relief.

~❦~

Above ground, in the crowds that milled around the bars and restaurants of Les Halles, Claire stood stock still for a moment. Was that really Mireille she had just seen, entwined in that man's arms as the stairway to the Métro swallowed them up? So intent on her secret lover that she hadn't even noticed when Claire called to her as they'd lurched past just a few feet in front of her. So that was her game, was it? Some friend, who couldn't even be bothered to confide in her. Let alone include her in their outings and maybe ask him to introduce her to a friend of his . . . *Well, you certainly learn who your real friends are*, she thought.

And with that she turned away and followed the two other girls into the bar, where soldiers in grey uniforms lounged at small tables, on the lookout for pretty French girls to spend their money on and help them forget how far away from home they were on Christmas Eve.

Harriet

One of the things on the top of my to-do list since my arrival in Paris has been to visit the Palais Galliera, the city's very own museum dedicated to fashion. I've seen pictures of it, but nothing has prepared me for the jaw-dropping beauty of the place. It's a gem of a palace, a perfect wedding-cake building conjuring Italian style with its white stone columns and balustrades. I enter through the ornately carved gatehouse leading off a leafy street in one of Paris's most elegant districts, and feel as if I've stepped out of the city and into a rural idyll. Trees fringe the neatly manicured parkland and, just beyond their autumnal branches, the Eiffel Tower points towards the blue of the sky. Statues dot the grounds, and the verdigris figure of a girl, the centrepiece of a fountain in front of the palace, is surrounded by ribbon-like beds of flowers, carefully planted in a mosaic of yellow and gold.

My heart beats with anticipation as I climb the broad white steps to the colonnaded entrance.

To my even greater delight, they are running an exhibition of styles from the Fifties. So I feel as if I've been transported back so close to the war years that I can almost reach out and touch the work of Claire and Mireille, reminding myself that the dresses, suits and coats they sewed were the immediate precursors to the garments I'm looking at now. I wander through the main gallery, drinking in the elegance of that golden age of haute couture. Christian Dior's 'New Look' dominates – the nipped-in waists and flowing skirts that were fashion's response to the restrictions of the war years – but as well there are classic Chanel suits and stunning, deceptively simple-looking, Balenciaga gowns encrusted with rock crystal embroidery. These are pieces that represent both the start and end of an era – the last, short-lived blooming of French couture when the war ended, which was rapidly overtaken by the fashion houses' new trend for 'ready-to-wear' fashion.

I linger in the museum's galleries, entranced by the displays. As well as the exhibition of Fifties couture, there are rooms filled with fashion history, from garments worn by Marie Antoinette and the Empress Josephine, to the black gown which Audrey Hepburn wore in *Breakfast at Tiffany's*. It is all, quite simply, breathtaking.

When, at last, I emerge into the crisp autumnal day, I decide to walk back along the river rather than ducking underground into the Métro. The leaves are turning to gold along the riverside *quais* and the waters of the Seine glint with the same golden light until they are churned to pewter, in a kind of reverse alchemy, by the passing tourist boats.

As I walk, transported back in time by the sight of those beautiful clothes in the Palais Galliera, I mull over what I've learned so far about my grandmother's life during the war here in Paris.

My feelings are mixed. Now that I know a little more, I'm impatient to know everything else that happened. But, at the same time, from what Simone's told me, I'm wondering increasingly whether I would have liked my grandmother Claire if I'd met her. Compared with Mireille, she seems to have been a bit weak and overly preoccupied with the superficial world of Parisian glamour.

She was young, of course, but then so was Mireille so that's really no excuse. She'd clearly had a hard childhood, growing up motherless and in poverty in a household full of men where she was expected to be the housekeeper from an early age.

So I can understand her longing for a life of luxury and elegance. I suppose that, in that way, she and I are not so different.

And then it occurs to me that maybe it's been passed down to me in the genes, this fascination with the world of fashion. Is that something I have inherited from Claire? Or is it simply a longing to escape from the reality of our situations in life into a world of fantasy and glamour? Either way, that thought brings with it a very strange mixture of emotions. Because I always thought I was forging my own path, that my 'passion for fashion' as my father sometimes disparagingly referred to it, was mine and mine alone. In fact, it became an important part of my identity, a part of my individuality that I clung to in a household where I felt I was scarcely noticed. But to realise, now, that perhaps it's not unique to me, that maybe it's one of those threads which run back through generations, makes me feel strangely unsettled.

It's a realisation that leads me, inevitably, to two further streams of thought and they tangle and knot themselves in the pit of my stomach. The first is reassuring, a sense of connection and continuity, a feeling that I am linked to my forebears in unknown ways; and the second is unsettling, a sense that I am trapped in a family history that I'm not sure I want to be a part of. Is this link to my ancestors a good thing or a bad thing? Who really were these people? And what other legacies have I inherited from them? From my grandmother? From my mother?

My mother. Was that same legacy something that blighted her life with the depression that ultimately destroyed her? Was there some instability built into the foundations of her being that made her crumble and collapse? In my memories, she always had a fragility about her. I remember how she would play me tunes on her beloved piano, amusing me for hours on end with nursery rhymes and teaching me the words of carols at Christmas time; those were happy times, lit by the daylight which streamed in through the French doors leading to the garden. But then sometimes I would wake up in the middle of the night and hear the strains of something else, the sad notes of a nocturne or the haunting melody of a sonata in a minor key, as she played in the darkness to while away the hours, getting herself through another lonely night.

Thinking of the home where she and I lived, an image flits, unbidden, into my mind of flashing blue lights and hands holding me back as I try to run forward through a door that is slightly ajar. In my mind, I slam that door shut, not wanting to go there again. I'm too frightened. Not yet ready. I need the distraction of focusing on finding out Claire's story first, before I can begin to revisit the more immediate past . . .

Until now, my family's history has been an enigma, a tattered tapestry filled with holes. My mother always seemed reluctant to talk about it. Was there some sense of shame that stopped her from doing so?

Suddenly, it seems vital that I find out. Simone's retelling of her grandmother's recollections is helping me slowly piece some of my own story together. But lately I've been getting the impression that she's a little reticent to continue the story – often too busy, or out with other friends. Maybe I'm imagining it, but I sense that there's been a slight coolness between her and me since the evening in the bar when I spent those hours chatting with Thierry. I try to shrug it off – after all, she introduced him as just one of a group of her friends and hadn't said that there was any particular closeness between the two of them. I tell myself that she probably doesn't want to feel obliged to invite me along every time she goes out, and of course we are always under pressure in the office. And yet it niggles away at me, the distance that seems to have grown between us and the slight feeling of awkwardness when we are in the apartment together.

But I want to hear more of the story which is mine as well as hers. I feel the need to know more about who my mother and my grandmother really were. What history has been passed through them to me? I need to know who I really am, too.

There's that programme on TV isn't there, which I never really paid much attention to, but which my stepmother used to watch sometimes, about people finding out about their ancestors. I vaguely recall that they looked up the census and marriage records and death certificates online to trace the lines of family through the generations.

Back in the apartment, after a moment's hesitation, I open my laptop and I begin my own search . . .

And I find it's easy enough. I just have to register with the General Records Office website, fill in the details of the person I am looking for and they will send me the certificates in a couple of weeks' time. I hesitate for a few moments, trying to recall my mother's maiden name, and then I type 'Claire Redman' into the search form and 'Meynardier' into the field marked 'Previous Name'. Then I check the boxes marked 'Marriage Certificate' and 'Death Certificate', before pressing 'Submit Request'.

1940

'You look nice.' Mireille watched from her bedroom doorway as Claire smoothed her hair, looking in the mirror in the hallway before pulling a coat over her dark blue dress. 'Are you going somewhere special?'

It was New Year's Eve and Paris was in a party mood, in spite of the war. Claire shrugged and reached for her key to the apartment.

'Wait!' Mireille laid a hand on the sleeve of Claire's coat, where the woollen twill was worn and fraying slightly at the cuff. 'I'm sorry. I forgot to give you your present at Christmas. I've had a lot on my mind lately. But I have something for you now. Here, take it.' She thrust a small package into Claire's hand. 'It will look good against your dress.'

'It's alright, Mireille, you don't have to give me anything,' Claire replied.

Her friend smiled at her. 'I know I don't *have* to give you anything, Claire, but I *want* to give you this. I love the necklet that you made for me – see, I'm wearing it tonight.' Mireille stroked the narrow velvet ribbon around her neck which had a scattering of jet beads sewn on to it with invisible stitches and which fastened at the front with a silver filigree button.

Claire unwrapped the paper from Mireille's gift and stared in disbelief at the silver locket that lay in her hand.

'Don't you like it?' asked Mireille.

'It's not that.' Claire shook her head. 'But I can't take it. Not your locket, Mireille. It's too precious.'

She tried to hand it back, but Mireille closed her fingers around Claire's. 'It's yours. A present for a good friend. I want you to have it. And I'm sorry that I haven't been better company of late. Here, let me fasten it for you.'

Reluctantly, Claire lifted the hair from the back of her neck to allow Mireille to settle the locket in place and secure the clasp. Then, relenting, she hugged Mireille and said, 'Well, thank you. It's the most beautiful present I've ever had. And let us settle it that we will share it. As a token of our friendship. It can belong to us both.'

'Alright then, if that means you will accept at least a half share in it.' Mireille smiled broadly and, for a moment, she almost looked like her old, vivacious self again.

Impulsively, Claire seized her hand. 'Come with me! Let's go out dancing together. I know somewhere where the music and the company are good. There's even a rumour that there'll be champagne tonight, since it's New Year's Eve. Put on your red dress and come along. It'll be fun!'

Mireille withdrew her hand and shook her head. 'I'm sorry, Claire, I can't. There's someone I have to meet.'

'Alright then, have it your own way.' She shrugged. 'Although I bet the people I'll be meeting are a lot better company than whoever it is you're hooking up with. Thanks for the locket. See you tomorrow.'

Mireille watched sadly as her friend swept out of the apartment and off down the stairs. And then, after a few minutes, she pulled on her own coat and slipped out, silent as a shadow, to be swallowed up by the crowds in the busy streets below.

~❧~

At the entrance to the nightclub, Claire left her coat at the hat-check desk even though it meant she would have to put a few *sous* in the plate on the counter for the sour-faced woman who had given the threadbare garment a disdainful shake as she'd taken it away to hang it on the rail.

My coat may be shabby, mademoiselle, Claire thought as she turned towards the powder room, *but at least I'm not stuck behind the counter on New Year's Eve with a scowl on my face.* She took a cheap gilt compact from her evening bag and leaned towards the mirror as she blotted the shine from her nose and cheeks. The women alongside her glanced enviously at the drape of the midnight blue dress, which Claire had painstakingly made from remnants of crêpe de Chine left over from one of Monsieur Delavigne's designs. It had taken her ages to piece the lengths together and she'd spent long evenings trying to get the seams to lie absolutely flat where she'd had to sew the offcuts side by side, so that the joins would be virtually invisible. She'd stitched a scattering of silver beads along the neckline to distract the eye from the patchwork nature of the gown, and draped the fabric on the bias so that it flowed over her slim hips. Her evening bag was made from the lining of an old skirt, and she'd borrowed a pair of shoes from one of her flatmates for the evening.

In the mirror, she adjusted the locket on its fine silver chain so that it lay flat against the beaded neckline, just below the delicate wings of her collarbones.

She rested a hand on her stomach for a moment, trying to calm the butterflies that seemed to flutter there. Would he be here? Would he have remembered the promise they'd made on Christmas Eve to meet up here again on 31 December? Had he really meant it?

That evening, in the bar on the Rue de Rivoli, he'd sent drinks to their table, the waiter setting the glasses in front of her and her two friends and then pointing out the blonde German officer at the bar who had ordered them. The other girls had giggled and nodded, and the man had taken this as invitation enough to weave his way through the crowds of Christmas Eve revellers and pull up a chair. He had introduced two of his fellow officers and then turned to pay particular attention to Claire, fixing her with his ice blue eyes and complimenting her on her dress. He was fluent in French, although every now and then, as an aside, he would joke with his friends in German which she couldn't understand. He was the senior officer in the group and seemed to be popular and convivial, ordering more drinks and insisting on paying for them all. At the end of the evening as he'd helped her on with her coat, he'd asked her to meet him here, tonight, to celebrate the end of the old year.

'Have you ever tasted champagne?' he'd asked. 'No? A French sophisticate like yourself? I'm amazed. Well, we shall have to see if we can remedy that.'

She had felt flattered that, of the three seamstresses, he had singled her out, and the other girls had teased her about it as they hurried back to the apartment before the curfew fell. She'd whispered his parting words to herself before she fell asleep on Christmas Eve: a French sophisticate. He was handsome and rich but the most seductive thing of all was the way he saw her and reflected that image back to herself as someone new, as someone grown-up and sophisticated, as the woman she longed to be.

Nervously adjusting the locket at her throat one more time, she smoothed the gown over her hips. Then she pushed her way through the throng of revellers clustered at the top of the staircase, laughing and exclaiming as they met up with friends, and began to make her way down into the ballroom. She scanned the crowd, and then her face lit up with a shy smile as she caught sight of him, waving at her from beside the bar. She continued down the stairs, the skirt of her dress gathered in one hand, oblivious to the admiring glances that a number of men shot her way.

'You came!' he exclaimed, pulling her to him. 'And may I say how proud I am to be keeping company tonight with the most beautiful girl in the room?'

'Thank you, Ernst.' Claire blushed, unused to receiving compliments. 'You look very nice yourself. It took me a moment to recognise you without your uniform on.' She ran her fingertips down the sleeve of his dinner jacket.

He gave a little bow from the waist, bending over to kiss her hand in a mock-formal manner, his blue eyes gleaming with amusement. 'Yes, a rare night off duty. It's good to get the glad-rags out for once.'

He turned to the barman with a wink and a nod and the man summoned a passing waiter, saying, 'Take good care of this gentleman. Champagne. And a table near the band.'

'*Oui*, m'sieur. Please, follow me.'

Ernst and Claire picked their way between the crowded tables that skirted the dance floor, and the waiter pulled out chairs for them at one which sat in a section that had been cordoned off with a red velvet rope. They sat, and a few moments later the waiter returned, smoothing the linen cloth as he set down an ice bucket and glasses. With a flourish of a white damask napkin, he opened the bottle of Krug and poured, pausing expertly to allow the foam to settle before topping the glasses up and then settling the bottle into its silver bucket and draping the damask cloth around its neck.

Light as a bubble in a golden glass, Claire floated through that evening on a wave of euphoria. At last! This was the life she'd always dreamed of, and for a few hours she could forget the chill of the draughty *atelier*, the headaches and the hunger, as she danced beneath a gilded ceiling, held in the arms of a handsome young man, breathing air which was heady with the smell of perfume and cigarette smoke. They drank more champagne and ordered oysters and Ernst talked and joked with the other Germans who joined them at the nearby tables behind the red velvet rope while she sat and smiled and watched the other women watching her with envy.

'Come,' said Ernst at last, consulting his watch. 'One last dance and then I must escort you home before the curfew.'

On the way out, he retrieved her coat for her from the hat-check woman and casually tossed a couple of francs into the plate, causing the woman to crack a smile of thanks and wish them both a Happy New Year.

They walked back across the river, and she felt as if her feet hardly touched the ground in her borrowed shoes as they joined the flow of revellers hurrying homewards now, even though midnight and the new year were still a few hours off. He held her hand as they walked beneath the soaring buttresses of Notre-Dame and then drew her to one side, down the steps to the riverside *quai* just before they crossed the Pont au Double to the *rive gauche*. There, where the dark waters of the river lapped at the stones by their feet, he took her in his arms and kissed her.

Her eyes shone as she smiled at him, seeming to reflect the starlight above them, and he stroked back her fair hair, tucking a strand of it behind her ear and kissing her again.

In that moment, on a dark night beside the Seine, she imagined what it would be like to fall in love with him. And suddenly she realised that all the things she'd thought she wanted before – the beautiful clothes, the champagne, the envy of others – didn't matter after all. All that mattered was to be loved and to be able to love in return. That was what she desired, more than anything else.

On the Rue Cardinale he took his leave, kissing her again and whispering, 'Happy New Year, Claire. I think it will be a good one for us both, don't you?'

Holding tight to that promise of a future involving 'us both', she ran up the stairs to the apartment.

Humming a dance tune under her breath, she fished her key out of her evening bag and unlocked the door. Closing it quietly behind her, she slipped off her shoes – suddenly aware of the blisters where they had bitten into her heels – and tiptoed to her room, not wanting to dispel the sense of joy by having to share the details of her evening with any of her flatmates just yet.

As she lay in her narrow bed under the eaves that night, Claire dreamed she was dancing on in Ernst's arms beneath a gilded ceiling, borne on a tide of desire – a feeling to which she had been completely unaccustomed up until now – as the clocks of Paris struck twelve and the old year died.

Harriet

I look up from the newsletter I'm translating as Simone comes back into reception, having delivered coffees to one of the office's meeting rooms.

'Your phone rang,' I say, nodding to where it sits at the end of the desk.

She picks it up and listens to a message. Her expression is inscrutable. 'That was Thierry,' she says flatly. 'He wants to know if I can let him have your number. Says he's working at a concert next Saturday night and he thought you might enjoy it.'

I shrug and nod. 'That's fine. Sounds good.'

As she taps a text message into her phone by way of reply she says, without looking up, 'He likes you, you know.'

'I liked him too,' I say, leafing through the large Larousse dictionary that I use whenever I need to look up a particular word. 'Seemed like a nice guy.'

'Yeah, he is,' she agrees.

'Simone,' I begin. And then I stop, not sure how to phrase what I want to ask her.

She glances at me, unsmiling.

'Look,' I say. 'I don't know if there's something between you and Thierry. But if there is, I don't want to do anything that might upset you.'

She shrugs. 'No. There's nothing. He's just a friend.'

She turns to her computer screen, apparently checking her emails, but the silence between us is pregnant with something more. I let it sit, giving her time.

Reluctantly, she raises her eyes to meet mine at last. 'I've known him for years,' she says. 'Too many years, maybe. We've been friends ever since I came to Paris. You're right, though. I did hope we could be more than just friends. But I'm like a sister to him, he says. So it's just not going to happen. I suppose seeing him with you – how he lights up when he's talking to you – has forced me to admit that to myself.'

'I'm sorry,' I say, meaning it.

She shrugs. 'Why should you be sorry? It's not your fault he likes you.'

Then she smiles, thawing a little. 'And he *really* likes you, by the way. I could see it that evening. There's definitely a connection between the two of you.'

I shake my head and laugh, taking my cue from her, trying to keep it light. I'm not great at relationships. At university I tended to find them a bit overwhelming and I came to the conclusion that it was easier to be on my own. It always felt like there might be too much to lose if I let myself fall in love. And I knew that I couldn't bear to lose more than I already had done.

I admit that I'd enjoyed talking to Thierry that night though. I'd felt liberated by the novel sensation of being able to be myself, in French. And a concert would be a good way to spend an evening, especially if he was busy working at it. It wouldn't be a big deal then. So, when my own phone buzzes a minute later, encouraged by Simone's smile and nod of approval, I reply '*oui, avec plaisir*' to his suggestion that he puts a ticket on the door for me next Saturday and that we might go for something to eat afterwards. Then I firmly put my phone aside and get on with my work.

One of my duties as an intern involves sorting the mail when it arrives at the agency each morning. I am stopped in my tracks today by the sight of an official-looking envelope with a UK postcode, addressed to me. I never usually get any post, so I know that this must be the certificates I requested from the records office and that they will tell me more about Claire's life. And her death, too. I set the sealed envelope aside, underneath my phone, so that I can stay focused on my work for now. I'll open it this evening, when I can have a proper look at the contents in the privacy of my own room in the flat upstairs.

I sort the rest of the mail quickly and then take it through to the office to hand it out. One of the account managers is in with Florence when I tap on her door. She beckons me in and both women smile at me. 'Good news, Harriet,' Florence says. 'That press release you sent out? We've had a response from London. The buyer at Harvey Nichols is interested in seeing more of the range. It's quite a coup.'

The account manager asks me to help draft the reply and I am kept busy for the rest of the day translating the technicalities of shoe design and construction from French into English.

At last the office closes and I run up the stairs to my attic room, clutching the white envelope. On my mother's side of the family, both my grandfather and grandmother had died before I was born. My hands are trembling a little. Because apart from the photo of Claire with Mireille and Vivienne, this is the first tangible link I have had to that generation of my family.

I'm not at all sure I'm going to like what I find when I open the envelope. I've come to think that Claire's relationship with Ernst was pretty shameful. And might there even be a chance that I am of Nazi descent? Is that legacy of shame and guilt part of my genetic make-up? My hands tremble with impatience – and just a frisson of anxiety – as I tear open the envelope.

The first certificate I read is dated, in a flowing copperplate hand, the 1st of September 1946, and is for the marriage of Claire Meynardier, born in Port Meilhon, Brittany on the 18th of May 1920 to Laurence Ernest Redman, born in Hertfordshire, England on the 24th of June,

1916. The name Ernest stops me in my tracks for a moment. Could this be 'Ernst'? Did they move to England to make a new start after the war? But the fact that he was born in the Home Counties makes that extremely unlikely. So maybe I can assume that I'm not descended from a Nazi soldier after all. The thought allows a weight to slip from my shoulders, one less burden to have to carry through life.

I put the sheet of paper to one side and read the next one, the certificate of death for Claire Redman. It is dated 6 November 1989 and the cause of death is given as heart failure. So Claire was sixty-nine years old when she died, leaving her daughter, Felicity, alone in the world at the age of twenty-nine. How I wish she'd lived longer. She might have been able to change the course that my mother's life took. She might have been less of an enigma. And if she'd still been around she might have been able to help me, giving me a sense of who I really am.

How I wish I'd known my grandmother Claire.

March 1941

'Mireille, you are wanted in the salon.' Mademoiselle Vannier's lips were so pursed with disapproval that the creases around them were drawn into pleats as tight as smocking. It was virtually unheard of for seamstresses to be summoned downstairs into the territory of the *vendeuses* and their clients.

Mireille was conscious of the glances of the other girls seated around the table who looked up from their work and watched in silence as she carefully tucked her needle into the fabric of the lining she was tacking together to mark her place, then stood up and pushed in her chair.

A feeling of dread dragged at the pit of her stomach as she descended the stairs. Was she in trouble over some slip-up in her sewing? She was often distracted nowadays, thinking about her next assignment for the network, and constantly exhausted by the strain of keeping her activities a secret from the other girls. Perhaps she was being summoned for a scolding.

She tried not to imagine the even worse possibility, that she had been denounced by someone and that the salon might be full of Nazis come to take her for questioning.

She hesitated at the door to the salon, then tugged her white coat straight and held her head high as she knocked and entered.

To her surprise, the sales woman who was renowned for dealing with Monsieur Delavigne's wealthiest clients came towards her, smiling broadly. Behind her, an assistant hovered with her tape measure along-side one of the models who was wearing a coat that Mireille recognised. She had finished sewing the lining for it just the other day.

'Here she is, our star seamstress,' gushed the *vendeuse*. 'This gentle-man wanted to meet you, Mireille, to thank you in person for the work you have done on his orders.'

Thankfully, the others in the room were too intent on fluttering about their client like moths around a flame to notice the startled look that shot across Mireille's features before she could prevent it. Because next to the fire, which blazed brightly in the hearth to keep the damp March chill at bay, Monsieur Leroux sat in one of the gilt chairs that were reserved for visitors to the salon, his long legs crossed and his hands in his pockets, in a pose that spoke of the self-assured ease of the very wealthy.

She composed herself quickly, forcing herself to keep her eyes cast down to the pattern of the Aubusson carpet on the floor of the salon so that no look of recognition could give away the fact that she had already met this man. Neither did she want to betray the fact that, this very evening, she would be running an errand for the underground network that he controlled. She had received her latest instructions from the dyer only yesterday.

'Mademoiselle,' he said, 'I apologise for interrupting your work. But I wanted to thank you for the attention to detail that you put into the garments that I commissioned. It is important, occasionally, to pass that on personally, *n'est-ce pas?*'

Did she imagine it, or had he placed a slight emphasis on the word 'important'?

He smiled at the assembled company, who all beamed back at him, having already been on the receiving end of his largesse.

He beckoned her closer and then slipped a folded five franc note into the pocket of her white coat. 'A small token of my gratitude, made-moiselle. And my thanks to you all once again.'

'Thank you, monsieur. You are too kind,' Mireille replied, her eyes meeting his for the briefest of moments to let him know that she understood.

He stood then, and one of the assistants hurried forwards with his coat. Turning to the *vendeuse*, he said, 'So you have all the measurements you require for that suit?' He gestured towards one of the new season's designs that were displayed on mannequins against one wall.

'*Oui*, monsieur. We will make it just as you wish. It's an excellent choice – I happen to know that this particular style is one of Monsieur Delavigne's favourites.'

'*Merci*. And have the coat sent to my usual address.' He nodded towards the model. 'But I will settle my account now, if I may?'

'Of course, monsieur.'

The saleswoman flapped a hand at Mireille, indicating that she was dismissed and should return to the *atelier*, while one of the assistants hurried to fetch the ledger in which the details of clients' orders were kept.

Before going back into the sewing room, Mireille slipped into the lavatory on the first floor. She pulled the five franc note out of her pocket and unfolded it. As she'd guessed, a slip of paper was hidden inside the money. And on it was written just one word, heavily underlined: 'CANCELLED'.

She realised that something terrible must have happened for Monsieur Leroux to have risked coming to see her to deliver this warning. Her hands shook as she tore the note into tiny pieces and flushed them away, making sure they'd gone, before washing her hands. They shook still as she dried them on the towel which hung on the back of the door, imagining what – or who – might have been waiting for her if she'd gone to the rendezvous point that evening. The Germans were trying to tighten the net around all Resistance activity and it was well known on the streets of Paris that those who were taken to the SS headquarters in the Avenue Foch for questioning did not usually reappear.

She had seen, too, with her own eyes, the lines of people being marched under armed guard into the city's stations and forced to board the trains heading eastwards. And, it seemed to her, they far outnumbered the people returning.

When she slipped back into her seat at the sewing table, Claire nudged her and asked her what she'd been sent downstairs for. She pulled the five franc note out of her pocket and showed it to the other girls, who exclaimed in envy.

'We'll have some sausages or a jar of *rillettes* this weekend, if the butcher has any in,' Mireille whispered to Claire under cover of the chatter.

'Don't worry about me, I'll be out to dinner on Saturday evening,' Claire replied, turning away from Mireille towards the light, the better to concentrate on stitching some intricate beadwork on to a chiffon bodice.

'But we never seem to see each other, apart from at work these days,' Mireille said sadly.

Claire shrugged. 'I know. You always seem to be out on the evenings when I am not.'

'Well, one of these days we'll have an evening in together and you can tell me all about this new man of yours.' It had recently become public knowledge in the *atelier* that Claire was 'seeing someone', after one of the girls in the flat had seen her slipping out one evening wearing a pair of silk stockings, which must have cost far more than any of them could afford on their wages. Under close questioning, Claire had admitted that they were a gift from an admirer. The same admirer she had been seeing since New Year's Eve.

Mademoiselle Vannier clapped her hands to quell the murmuring of the girls. 'That's enough now, everyone. The excitement is over. Don't expect you are all going to be invited downstairs so that clients can give you tips. That sort of thing only happens once in a blue moon.

Quiet, please! Pay attention to your work and save your gossiping for your breaks.'

Mireille reached for the lining that she'd left on the table and began, once again, to tack it together with careful, quick stitches. As she sewed, she reflected that she'd had no idea that some of the clothes she was making were commissions for Monsieur Leroux. That had been a woman's coat that the model was wearing, and it was a woman's suit that he had pointed to on the mannequin. Did he have a wife? Or a mistress? Or both perhaps? How strange it was to be linked to so many people through the network and yet to know nothing about them, even though they each held one another's lives in their hands.

It was only the following day, when she went to fetch some more silk from the dyer, that Mireille heard why last night's operation had had to be cancelled. Madame Arnaud, from the safe house, had been picked up outside the baker's shop and was found to have more than her ration of bread in her basket. That sort of black market activity was, fortunately, not enough to have her deported and she had been lucky to be released with just a severe reprimand. But then she had realised that their house was being watched, and had managed to get a message through to Monsieur Leroux to cancel the previous evening's assignment. The Arnauds would need to lie low until they were no longer under suspicion. So activities would be suspended for a while, the dyer explained, until they worked out which other houses could be used to hide the network's cargo. He would let her know when it was safe to begin again.

꩜

Claire had spent her Saturday morning in the usual way, standing in queues outside shops in the hope of picking up that week's food rations. Two women, who'd been gossiping just ahead of her when she'd joined the line, had turned and given her a scornful glance, taking in her silk scarf and fine stockings. She'd met their look with defiance, holding her head high: so what if she had a German boyfriend who loved to pamper her? Just because she wasn't a scrawny old bird with varicose veins like them was no reason for her to deserve the filthy looks that they shot at her as the queue shuffled forwards, inch by inch.

Walking home, as she turned into the Rue Cardinale, she swung her shopping bag, planning the bean stew that she would make for lunch, flavoured with a precious morsel of pork belly that she'd managed to find at the butcher's.

And then she noticed the young man sitting in the doorway of Delavigne Couture who scrambled to his feet when he caught sight of her. She didn't recognise her brother at first. When she'd last seen him, his hair had been long and unkempt and he'd been wearing his thick fisherman's jersey, the wool heavy with a mixture of engine grime and fish oil. He looked different – older, somehow, but ill-at-ease and surprisingly vulnerable in a workman's cotton jacket, with his normally tousled hair trimmed short and neatly combed, exposing a tender strip of pale skin where it had been cut away from the back of his neck.

'Jean-Paul! What are you doing here?' she exclaimed.

He took a step towards her, then hesitated as if unsure how to greet the elegant young woman his little sister had become. But she reached across the space that separated them and put her arms around him, breathing in his scent of woodsmoke and sea salt and feeling an unexpected pang of homesickness as he hugged her back.

'You look good, Claire.' He stood back to appraise her, his grey eyes crinkling as his weather-tanned face creased into a smile. 'Quite the Parisian lady. The city life obviously suits you. I don't know how you can stand living here, though; too many people and not enough fishing boats for my liking.' He gestured towards the scuffed canvas duffel bag that leant against Delavigne Couture's plate glass *vitrine*. 'I'm on my way to Germany. Been ordered to report for work in a factory there.

I've got an hour or so before I have to be at the station, though, so I thought I'd look you up on my way through Paris.'

She took him by the hand. 'Come up to the apartment, then.' Taking the key from her bag, she pushed the door open and led the way upstairs. 'Oh, Jean-Paul, I can't tell you how good it is to see you. How is Papa? And the others?'

'Papa is well. Told me to make sure you're looking after yourself in the big city and getting enough to eat. He sent you these.'

With a grin, from the top of his bag Jean-Paul drew a newspaper-wrapped parcel tied with twine and set it on the table. She opened it to find three mackerel, their skins gleaming, as silver as the sea off the Brittany coastline from which they'd been pulled.

'And the others? Marc and Théo and Luc?'

Her brother's face grew serious then and his eyes clouded with sadness. 'Théo and Luc went to fight when the war was declared. I'm sorry to have to tell you like this, but Luc was killed, Claire, when the Germans broke through the Maginot Line.'

Claire gasped and abruptly sat down on a chair, the colour draining from her face. Her eldest brother, dead for nearly two years and she hadn't known. 'And Théo?' she whispered.

'We received word that he was captured and kept in a camp for prisoners of war for a while. But when France surrendered he was released, on condition that he work in a German factory. That was the last we heard. I'm hoping that I might be able to find out where he is and request a placement in the same factory so that we can be together. Though I'm not sure whether the Germans will allow that.'

Claire buried her face in her hands and sobbed. 'Thank God Théo is okay. But Luc . . . gone . . . I can scarcely believe it. Why didn't you let me know?'

'Papa did write. He sent a letter, but it was just after the Germans had taken over so it probably got lost in the chaos. And he tried to send you one of those official postcards but it was returned to us marked "*inadmis*" because he'd written more than the permitted thirteen lines. He's been knocked sideways by the loss, Claire. You wouldn't believe how it has aged him. He spends every waking minute out on the boat these days, hardly says a word. Marc and I have been trying to support him. But some days he goes out on his own, in all weathers. Doesn't even wait for us. It's like he doesn't care that he's taking such risks, almost like he couldn't care less if he lives or dies.'

He put an arm around Claire and she could feel the definition of his muscles, like twisted strands of rope, beneath the rough cotton of his jacket as she sobbed into his shoulder.

'Don't worry,' he said at last, drawing away to fish a crumpled handkerchief out of his pocket so that she could blow her nose and dry her eyes. 'Marc has stayed behind to take care of Papa for us all. And I will be closer to Théo very soon. It will make them all happy to know that you are doing so well here in Paris. Maybe send Papa and Marc a postcard now and then if you have the time though? It would do them good even to receive a line or two from you. Papa treasures the postcards you send us at Christmas – keeps them on the shelf in the kitchen so he can see them every day.'

She nodded, hanging her head with shame that she'd been too wrapped up in her own life to spare anything other than the occasional thought for her family back in Brittany. Because she'd never received her father's attempts to write to her, she'd assumed they didn't care, that they were all there, busy with the routine of fishing all day and mending the creels in the evenings. But now she realised how very wrong she'd been. It was the war that had separated them, not a lack of concern on their part. The chaos of France's surrender and then the iron-clad strictures of the new administration had cut her off from her family. Another wave of grief and homesickness enveloped her as she wiped her eyes on her brother's handkerchief again.

Pulling herself together, she put a hand over Jean-Paul's. 'You will be alright, though, in Germany. I have a friend here, a man called Ernst.

He is from a city called Hamburg. He says that the French workers who go over there to help the war effort are well looked-after.'

Jean-Paul withdrew his hand from hers and studied her in silence for a long moment. Then he nodded slowly. 'This German "friend" of yours, Claire . . . Is he the one who buys you your fine clothes? Did he give you that jewellery?' He pointed at the locket that she wore around her neck.

A pang of guilt pinched at her heart at the tone of his words which, although he kept his voice level, sounded accusatory to her ears.

She met his eyes with a look of defiance. 'No, Jean-Paul, this locket was a gift from my friend Mireille. Ernst does like to buy me pretty things sometimes, though. Why shouldn't he spend his money on me if he wishes?'

'But he's the enemy, Claire,' her brother replied, struggling to keep his voice level, suppressing his anger. 'He is one of the ones who killed Luc. Who put Théo in a prison. Who has torn apart not just our family but our country too.' He shook his head in sorrow. 'Do you never think of us? Have you forgotten your family so completely, Claire?'

That noose of guilt around her heart drew even tighter and for a moment she felt dizzy as a wave of overwhelmingly conflicting emotions washed through her. She shook her head. 'It's not like that. You don't understand. Ernst and I – we're in love. He cares for me, Jean-Paul, in a world where I have no one else who cares.'

'You're wrong, Claire. You have us. Your family. You have always had your family.'

'But you're not here, are you?' A spark of defiant anger flashed in her eyes. 'I have had to make it on my own, ever since we lost Maman. And, in case you hadn't noticed, the world has changed now.'

The sorrow in his eyes hurt her far more than his spoken accusations. 'Maybe your world has changed. But some of us refuse to give in so easily. I don't have a choice about going to work in Germany – it was either me or Marc who had to go, so I volunteered to spare him.

But you can bet that fancy silk scarf of yours that I will be trying to find Théo and that, the first opportunity we get, we will be out of there. This war isn't over yet, you know.'

He stood up and swung the duffel bag over his shoulder. 'I should get going. Don't want to risk being late at the station.'

'I'll come down with you,' she said, but he shook his head again.

'No need, Claire, I'll see myself out.'

She tried to give him back the crumpled handkerchief but he gently pushed her hand away. 'Keep it. From a brother who cares.'

'Jean-Paul, I'm sorry . . .' She began to cry again and the words choked her.

He hugged her again, briefly, and then turned to go. As she heard his footsteps fading away down the staircase, she pushed aside the silver fish whose glassy, expressionless eyes watched her from their bed of damp newspaper, and laid her head on her arms, sobbing uncontrollably as she breathed in the smoke and salt scent of home on the handkerchief that was clutched tightly between her fingers.

Harriet

Hearing the story of Claire and Mireille in those years of war, I struggle to reconcile the contrast between the glamour and extravagance of the couture industry with the hardship and deprivation that the seamstresses had to endure, like the vast majority of French citizens at the time. It's a strangely grotesque juxtaposition.

Simone tells me she has asked her grandmother to write down more of what she remembers, but of course Mireille is a very old woman now and progress is slow. So I try to curb my impatience.

By way of a distraction, while I wait for Mireille's letters to arrive, I find myself reading a lot of books and articles about that period of history on the Internet to fill in the background to the two friends' lives in the attic apartment. As I piece it together, I've continued to write down the story of Claire and Mireille, padding it out with the historical background where I can. Somehow it seems important that I do so, even if only to record it for myself so that I can go back and reread this part of my family history, taking time to digest it as each new chapter comes to light. I become so immersed that sometimes it feels strange to look up from my writing, my feet tucked beneath me as I sit curled up on the sofa in the sitting room of the little flat, and realise that Claire and Mireille aren't just through the wall in the next room. I can almost hear their voices, picturing them sitting at their sewing: mending their own clothes, perhaps, or remaking a hat or a skirt for themselves.

As soon as I can, I go back to the Fashion Museum at the Palais Galliera and wander once again through the rooms. On my first visit here, I was dazzled by the finery, the bling and the glitz of fashion from centuries ago to the present day. But this time I look more carefully. Amongst the rooms filled with stunning exhibits that clamour for attention, there is a much more modest display. A gardener's canvas apron; a hairdresser's white coat; a pair of denim trousers and a shirt once worn by an unknown worker. The denim is patched and faded, but it speaks a simple truth. These clothes tell their own stories of the lives of the people who wore them, once again bringing history to life in the present day. And how ironic it is, I muse, as I stand in front of these clothes, that today distressed and torn denim is the height of fashion. It turns out that these simple, worn and aged garments have been the inspiration for modern-day designers.

From my museum visits I've also learned that, even in the darkest times, women managed to find a sense of pride in their appearance. Parisiennes found ways of making-do, and the styles of the war years reflect that: elegant turbans hid dirty hair or greying roots; cork wedges were glued on to shoes when high heels wore down; legs were daubed with ersatz coffee grounds, and charcoal lines drawn up the back to create the illusion of stockings. In the face of ubiquitous Nazi propaganda, the women of Paris found their own ways of sending back a message to their occupiers: dressed in their home-made fashions, they held their heads high; they were not defeated.

The luxury and excess of the modern-day fashion industry seem a world away from those war years. I'd arrived at the agency too late and too wet behind the ears to be allowed to help out in any sort of hands-on capacity at Paris Fashion Week back in September. I'd had to watch from the sidelines (or rather from behind the desk in reception) as the pace of work in the office grew more and more frenetic and then suddenly I was left alone, to man the phones that didn't ring, as everyone was out at the week's events, morning, noon and night. Simone had appeared at irregular intervals to fill me in on the latest collection or on who she had seen at that evening's reception.

With a few more years' experience than I have, Simone is a good deal more laid-back about the opportunity to sit in the audience, among the fashion editors and the celebrities, and watch as the latest couture collections, which will set the trends for a season that is still months away, are paraded down the catwalks.

Now that things have quietened down in the office after the flurry of activity that followed in the wake of Fashion Week, which has kept everyone at Agence Guillemet busy through the autumn months, I decide to treat myself to lunch at the Café de Flore. I know it's one of the stops on the tourist trail and, inevitably, the prices are beyond my normal budget which doesn't usually stretch to much more than a coffee and a croissant for a Saturday morning treat from a patisserie in one of the quieter side streets off the Boulevard Saint-Germain. But ever since Simone described how Mireille met Monsieur Leroux there, I've promised myself I would make a point of going one day. I ask Simone if she'd like to come with me, but she shakes her head, curls dancing, and says she's been asked to help one of the account managers prepare a tender for a new client.

I shrug on my coat and leave the office, walking up the street towards the Boulevard Saint-Germain. After a moment's hesitation, I send Thierry a text, asking him if he'd like to join me for lunch.

I enjoyed the concert he'd invited me to the other night and was impressed watching him at work, seeing him in a new light. He was calm and capable, seated behind a bewildering array of technology, his fingertips carefully balancing the sound levels over the course of the performance. A gaggle of his friends came along for burgers afterwards and it was a relaxed evening, although we still talked a lot about the Bataclan victims, whose memory will be ever-present. We've met up a few times since, with the same crowd. I've noticed that Simone hasn't joined the group, though, always making an excuse to be elsewhere. The slight coolness that crept into our relationship since Thierry and I first met is still there, I think, but it's obvious that she's making an effort not to let it get in the way of her friendship with either of us. I'm relieved that, with a bit of encouragement, she's agreed to join the group at the bar next Friday night.

When we've been out together, Thierry always pulls his chair up beside mine and we talk for hours, mostly about work but sometimes about the latest news of police raids and arrests as the threat of terrorism bubbles away just beneath the surface of city life. I've told him, too, about the photograph that brought me to Paris, and have recounted some of Claire's and Mireille's stories. So I think he might enjoy accompanying me to the Café de Flore, just around the corner from the Rue Cardinale, where Mireille's meeting with Monsieur Leroux took place. But my phone buzzes with his reply – sorry, but he's loading in kit for a gig on the other side of town and can't make it. Another time, he promises.

At the café on a corner of the busy Boulevard Saint-Germain, I find a seat at a table for two, squeezed between two larger tables, and place my order. As the waiter bustles away to fetch bread and a carafe of water, I take a good look around. The café can't have changed much since the war years. The dark wood panelling and white columns are still in place and the bar's brass fittings gleam amongst the bottles of Aperol and Saint-Raphaël. I can imagine Mireille coming here for the first time, and how her heart would have been thumping as she wove her way between tables filled with German officers to meet her contact at the back of the noisy room. I suppose sometimes the best camouflage is to hide in plain sight. But what guts that must have taken.

My disappointment at Claire's less active role has been tempered a little by the facts about her home life that I've started to glean. I relate strongly to her desire to leave home, where she felt there was nothing for her, and to try to find another place for herself in the world. Like her, I'm drawn to the excitement and creativity of the fashion world.

And, like her, I know how it feels to lose your mother. She must have loathed her life in the little Breton fishing village, the same life that had worn her mother – my great-grandmother – to a shadow before overwhelming her completely.

As I'm thinking about Claire's loss – of how she must have felt following her mother's simple coffin through a churchyard to a freshly dug grave – a police car speeds past outside, its siren screaming. Through the café windows, I catch a glimpse of flashing blue lights and then they're gone.

It's just a momentary vision, but the wake of the noise and the lights swamps me with a sudden wave of panic so powerful that it knocks the breath out of me. I reach for the carafe of water and pour a little into my glass, my hand shaking, as I try to calm myself.

There are times that I do not think about. Moments I have put away in a compartment of my mind which has stayed sealed for years. But now, here in the Café de Flore, amongst the tourists and the chic Parisienne ladies-who-lunch, an image flashes before my eyes, as though someone's hand has reached inside my head and turned a key, opening that compartment in a split second while I am distracted by thoughts of Mireille and Claire.

In my mind's eye, I see the flashing blue lights of another police car. This one isn't speeding past, though. Instead, it's parked at the gate outside my house. I feel hands reaching out to restrain me, holding me back as I try to run towards a door which stands ajar. I hear the neighbours talking in low voices and I hear the sinister sibilance of the word they use: *suicide*. It's a nightmare I've had many, many times, ambushed at night by dreams of those flickering blue lights and of running from them, running and running and getting nowhere, from which I wake gasping for breath, with tears running down my cheeks and my heart pounding in my throat.

And every time I wake up and discover that it's just been a dream. But it is still not okay. It is never okay.

The waiter sets my salad down in front of me and I pull myself together, trying to summon a smile, shaking my head as he asks whether there is anything more I need. I go through the motions of picking at my lunch. Ordinarily I would devour it, but I have no appetite today. I'm too busy pondering that flash of awareness triggered, no doubt, by the thoughts of my great-grandmother's death and the passing police car.

And then I realise that alongside the shock of that all-too-vivid image that I've suppressed for so many years, there sits another niggling feeling which forms itself into a question in my mind: whose hand was it that reached into my head and opened that locked compartment? I have a feeling that it doesn't belong to anyone I know. It doesn't belong to my grandmother Claire, nor to my mother.

As my racing heartbeat slows and I glance around the crowded, noisy café, picturing Mireille and Claire here, half a century before me, I realise that I'm searching for someone else, someone who is missing. The third girl in the photograph.

Where is Vivienne?

1941

Every head in the sewing room turned when Mademoiselle Vannier entered with the new girl. In the momentary silence, as the whirr of the sewing machines paused and the low murmur of snatched conversations stopped, one of the steel pins that Mireille was using to piece together a blouse fell to the floor with a faint patter. She bent, quickly, to pick it up before it could roll into one of the cracks between the boards and be lost: replacements were expensive now that supplies of metal were being channelled into the munitions factories in Germany.

As she straightened up, Mademoiselle Vannier was introducing the new seamstress. 'Girls, this is Vivienne Giscard. She joins us from an *atelier* in Lille, where she has gained valuable experience working with chiffon. She will also be helping you, Claire, with trimmings and bead-work. And she'll be staying upstairs in the apartment. Please help her to feel at home.'

Mireille shifted her work along, making space at the table, and a chair was found for Vivienne, who smiled at her new neighbours as she set her sewing kit down and pulled on a neatly pressed white coat.

Mireille immediately liked the look of this latest addition to their team. She had wide hazel eyes and long, copper-coloured hair which she wore braided into a thick plait to keep it out of the way of her work. It would be good to have a new flatmate, especially now that the other girls had moved on and it was just Mireille and Claire in the apartment.

Their paths seemed to take them in very different directions and the distance between them felt wider than ever. So maybe the presence of this new girl would help to lighten the atmosphere a bit.

That evening, the three girls shared their evening meal together, and Vivienne produced a bar of chocolate to round off their supper of bread and soup. 'One of the few advantages of Lille being part of Belgium these days!' she said, as she peeled back the wrapper emblazoned with the Côte d'Or palm tree and elephant. 'They really do make very good chocolate, when they can get the ingredients.'

Mireille's mouth watered in anticipation and she gave a small sigh of contentment as she took one of the squares and let it melt on her tongue. 'I can't remember when I last tasted anything so delicious. How did you manage to get your hands on it?'

Vivienne smiled, and her wide eyes seemed to illuminate her whole face when she did so. 'It was a going-away present from my family. I think they were worried that there wouldn't be anything to eat in the big, bad city.'

'Well, they were pretty much right on that front,' laughed Mireille, gesturing towards the empty soup bowls and the scattering of crumbs on the breadboard which were all that remained of their scant supper. 'Are your family still in Lille?'

'My parents live north of there.' Vivienne waved a hand vaguely and passed the chocolate again.

'Do you have brothers and sisters?' asked Claire as she popped another square into her mouth.

'Just one brother. How about you?'

As the girls chatted, savouring every last delicious morsel of the chocolate, it seemed to Mireille that a new friendship was being shared around the table as well that evening – and that tasted even better than anything a Belgian chocolatier could have concocted. Claire, too, seemed happier and more relaxed with a new flatmate to fill the silences, as intangible and as chilly as a river mist, that had permeated the apartment in recent weeks.

As well as bridging the distance between Mireille and Claire, Vivienne brought with her news of a very different France beyond the city limits.

'When Hitler's armies advanced, Lille was besieged. It was a terrifying few days. The French garrison fought desperately and managed to hold the city long enough to allow allied troops to be evacuated from Dunkirk. But in the end, the power of the Nazis was overwhelming. They drove their tanks into the centre of town and our troops were forced to surrender. Thousands of soldiers were marched through the Grand'Place as prisoners of war. It took hours for them to pass by.' Vivienne shook her head, recalling the sight. 'And then all those thousands of men were taken away. And suddenly our city wasn't French any more. The Germans drew new lines on their maps and decreed that Lille was now part of the Belgian administration. It's been a bewildering couple of years.'

Vivienne described how she had been forced to work in the spinning mills, producing thread for the Nazi war effort. 'But I managed to continue to make some money on the side with my dressmaking. Having no new clothes, it turned out that my skills were needed more than ever by our friends and neighbours. I have perfected the art of remaking coats into dresses and dresses into skirts. I even made a suit for the Comtesse de Rivault, out of a pair of curtains that she'd salvaged from her home before it was appropriated as a billet for German officers. She was the one who helped me get the job here at Delavigne Couture. She was a good client, before the war.'

As Mireille lay in her bed that night, waiting for sleep to come, she pondered her new friend. Vivi, as they had quickly taken to calling her, seemed a true kindred spirit and Mireille was glad to have her in the flat. And yet, as the hunger pangs – which those few squares of chocolate had been unable to assuage – griped in her belly, she realised that Vivi had disclosed very little information about herself. She had shared lots of details about her work in a local dressmaking *atelier* before the war had overwhelmed Lille, where she had specialised in the tricky job of sewing chiffon evening gowns for society ladies; she had told them how hard the work had been in the factory, running the machinery that spun thousands of yards of yarn every hour under the watchful eye of a German foreman; and she had described the sleepless nights spent listening to the bombing raids by the British air force on the nearby metalworks and railway yards. But, Mireille realised, as her eyelids began to grow heavy, what she had described had seemed impersonal, somehow, a little like a cinema newsreel. She had shared very little about her family – the parents and the brother that she'd mentioned in passing.

Never mind, she thought, there would be more such evenings together when they would share their rations and their stories. And her lips curved in a smile of contentment as sleep finally came, as it always did in the end in spite of the hunger and the cold and the ever-present, nagging anxiety that she would be caught or denounced as a Résistante. At last she set aside the burdens which she endured in silence through her waking hours, and slept.

～❦～

Claire enjoyed Vivi's company too. She was a breath of fresh air in the apartment and it was nice having someone she could confide in about Ernst. Vivi asked questions and seemed to understand the relationship in a way that Mireille could – or would – not. Although Claire had to admit that even Mireille was a bit less uptight with Vivi around. There was an ease and a lightness about Vivi that was infectious, and her friendship had greatly improved the atmosphere in the sewing room as well as the apartment, as far as Claire was concerned.

One evening Ernst took Claire out to dinner at Brasserie Lipp, a lively restaurant on the Boulevard Saint-Germain which was renowned for its hearty German-style menu. Claire couldn't remember the last time she'd eaten so well as she picked up her cutlery and made inroads into her plate of great slabs of pork, dripping with Calvados and cream. Ernst ate his with gusto, but she soon set down her knife and fork as she discovered that the rich food was more than her stomach was used to or could cope with. She glanced around the room, admiring the tiled panels on the walls depicting flowers and foliage, and the grand, tall mirrors. And then she did a double-take as a familiar face caught her eye. Reflected in one of the mirrors was the profile of a young woman whose hair fell in a thick russet braid down her back. It was Vivi! Claire craned her neck slightly to see who she was with. There were two others sitting at the same table. One was a sandy-haired man, wearing a crisp white shirt and a paisley necktie; he had a distinguished air about him and looked relaxed, clearly at ease in this expensive ambience. As she watched, he lifted a bottle of white wine from an ice-bucket beside the table and reached across to fill the glass of the third person seated at the table, a slightly dumpy woman in a grey uniform. *Well*, thought Claire, *so I'm not the only one who enjoys the company of our German neighbours.* She wondered whether she should go across and say hello to Vivi, perhaps introduce her to Ernst. They could make a party of it, maybe, and all go on to dance in a nightclub somewhere.

But when she suggested it to Ernst, he glanced across and seemed to recognise the woman in uniform. 'No,' he said, mopping grease from his lips with a linen napkin, 'let's not. I know her from the office – she's very dull. I'd much rather enjoy your company without having to share you with anyone else. Maybe you can introduce me to your friend another time, though. She looks very pleasant.'

'She is,' said Claire. 'She's great fun. And a good seamstress as well.'

The next day, as the other girls chatted away in the sewing room, Claire quietly asked Vivi whether she'd enjoyed her meal the night before. Was it her imagination, or did Vivi look a little startled?

'I didn't realise you were there too,' she said. 'You should have come over and said hello.'

'Don't worry.' Claire had smiled. 'You can introduce me to your friends another time. And I won't tell Mireille. I think we both know how stuffy she can be!'

Vivi had nodded, lowering her eyes to her work, as the sound of Mademoiselle Vannier's heels clicking across the floorboards had put an end to any more talk.

❧

There was just one thing that niggled a little in Claire's blossoming friendship with Vivi. That glimpse of a social life was rare and her subsequent invitations to restaurants and nightclubs were all politely rejected. If anything, Vivi seemed to Claire to be far too conscientious about her work. Often, when everyone else had packed up for the evening, Vivi would stay on alone in the sewing room, bent over some particularly intricate beadwork, or painstakingly stitching the hand-rolled hem of a chiffon gown, her needle flashing beneath the light of an angled lamp as it picked single threads, one by one, from the delicate fabric that pooled in her lap.

'You're working too hard!' Claire told her when she appeared in the apartment long after the city had been plunged into darkness for the curfew.

Vivi smiled, but her face looked drawn with tiredness. 'The work on that tea-dress is taking longer than I'd expected. But tomorrow is Saturday, so I won't have to get up too early.'

'Let's have an outing then. You've scarcely had a chance to see anything of Paris. Ernst and I were supposed to be going to the Louvre tomorrow but now he has to work. So let's you and I go instead. Mireille too, if she wants to come.'

And so it was that the three girls put on their best skirts and jackets and stepped out into the street together. Vivi pulled a camera from her bag, saying, 'If we're going to go sightseeing then I need to take some pictures.' She motioned to Claire and Mireille to stand in front of the Delavigne vitrine.

'Wait!' cried Claire. She ran over to where a man had just dismounted from his bicycle. 'Monsieur, would you be so kind as to take a picture of the three of us?' she asked.

'*Bien sûr.*' The man grinned at the sight of the girls dressed up for an outing, and snapped the photograph. '*Bonne continuation, mesdames.*' He smiled as he handed the camera back to Vivi and went on his way, wheeling his bike along the boulevard and whistling cheerfully to himself.

Laughing and chattering, Claire, Mireille and Vivi walked to the river and crossed to the right bank, with Vivi pausing to take photos of Notre-Dame and the Île de la Cité.

The lime trees in the gardens beside the Seine were clad in their fresh, green finery and waved and nodded at the girls as they passed along the *quai* on that bright and breezy Saturday in May.

Despite feeling the disappointment of having been let down by Ernst, Claire's heart lifted as they walked. There would be other opportunities to come here with him, on the summer days that lay ahead. He and she would wander through these same streets, hand in hand, making plans for their future together. She even dared to imagine other summers to come when she might stroll here, with a wedding ring on her finger, pushing a pram containing a chubby, blonde baby who would chuckle and wave back at the sun-dappled linden branches overhead. But, for today, the company of her friends more than made up for Ernst's absence, she realised.

She felt more light-hearted than she had done for months. She'd been so isolated since coming to Paris, and Jean-Paul's visit had made her see just how cut off she had become from her family and her roots in Brittany. She'd written to her father and Marc back in Port Meilhon and, although the officially permitted postcards only allowed space for a few bland lines, she had told him that she was well and happy in Paris, that she missed them and that she sent them her love. She'd felt a sense of relief as she'd handed the card in at the post office and felt the thread of connection to her family re-establish itself, only then realising just how heartfelt the sentiments that she'd written really were. And she treasured the card that she'd received back from her Papa with its few lines which told her how much he cared.

None of the three had visited the Louvre before, so it was with a sense of awe that they entered the museum's cavernous entrance hall, passing between a pair of guards who stood, like sentries, at the door.

They wandered through rooms where some of the walls and plinths were bare since so many works of art had been mysteriously spirited away, and several galleries were closed completely. But there remained enough paintings and sculptures to hold their interest. The girls drifted apart a little as they moved slowly through the open galleries, losing themselves in the timeless landscapes and the faces of the portraits that gazed out at them across the years.

Turning a corner, Claire found herself in a room containing vast alabaster sculptures from the Italian Renaissance. She was dimly aware of Mireille and Vivi entering the gallery behind her as she stepped up to a reclining woman, cordoned off behind a red velvet rope, and admired the way her draperies, carved from something as solid as stone, could appear as fluid and fragile as the silks with which the seamstresses worked every day.

All at once, her eye was caught by the profile of a young man who was circling a vast statue of a Roman emperor up ahead. It took a moment for her to recognise him in his civilian clothes, but then her heart leapt with gladness. He'd come after all.

'Ernst!' she called, and she started towards him, her face radiant at the unexpected joy of seeing him here.

Hearing his name, he turned towards her. But instead of sharing her pleasure, his face fell and he took a step backwards, away from her, raising one hand as if to fend her off if she came any closer.

Confused, Claire hesitated, her smile faltering. And then she froze as, from behind the statue's plinth, appeared a woman dressed in a smart tweed suit. She held the hand of a little boy whose hair was almost the same white-blonde as his mother's. As Claire watched, horrified, the woman reached out her free hand to caress Ernst's back, saying something in German. And the little boy reached out his arms to be lifted up by the man he called '*Vati*'.

As the trio turned away and walked out of the gallery, Claire felt her knees give way and she clutched at the red velvet rope – just like the one that had separated the tables in the nightclub on New Year's Eve – as she tried to steady herself.

And then Mireille and Vivi were at her side, holding her up, preventing her from crumpling to the floor. Leading her away, as her heart shattered into a thousand pieces.

Harriet

Having heard this latest chapter of Claire's story, I plan a visit to the Louvre. It's been hard to find the time to do much sightseeing because the rhythm of the year at Agence Guillemet is dictated by the Shows – with a capital 'S'. Right now, even though it's January and the damp, grey lid of the winter sky sits over the city, we're preparing for the Haute Couture Spring/Summer Shows which will take place later in the month. I'm already excited about them, and am determined to do a good job so that when it comes to the preparations for the next Paris Fashion Week I'll be able to be more involved. I know it'll be exhausting, but exhilarating too and I can't wait to experience it.

At last there's a brief lull. It's a bleak Sunday and the apartment feels chilly and a little claustrophobic – the perfect day for a visit to the Louvre. Thierry agrees to accompany me and we meet beside the glass pyramid that marks the museum's sleek, modern entrance in the Place du Carrousel. He's waiting for me when I get there, his hands pushed deep into the pockets of his parka, hair buffeted by the wind that swirls around the open square. We hug, briefly and a little awkwardly, realising that this is the first time we've been out together, just the two of us, without a crowd of friends and concert-goers thronging around to cover any silences.

But it turns out there aren't any silences, other than very comfortable-feeling ones, as we spend the afternoon wandering through the galleries. The museum is a good deal fuller these days than it would have been in the war years when the French hid some of their greatest treasures and the Germans appropriated many others. The collections have been gathered back now and the Louvre is a changed place, of course, with its sleekly modern glass pyramids outside and new additions to the layout.

In one room, Thierry wanders on ahead as I stop in front of an alabaster statue, a reclining woman draped in fluid robes which belie the solidity of the stone from which they are carved. Could this have been the sculpture that my grandmother was looking at when she came upon Ernst and his family here all those years ago?

Ever since I've heard about Claire's humiliation and heartbreak in the Louvre, I've longed more than ever for a more tangible sense of connection to her. I've pored over the photograph and my heart has bled as I've imagined the day it was taken: a day which started so well, full of joy and optimism as she'd got dressed in her best clothes and set out with her friends. A day which had ended so badly.

I realise that, increasingly, my feelings of shame at my grandmother's naivety and terrible choice of partner have been replaced by sympathy for her – and a cold fury at Ernst. How dare he have treated her so shabbily, toying with her emotions, using her youth and her innocence to facilitate his deception? Was the damage done by that devastating encounter in the Louvre one of the things that contributed to the fragility of her heart? Was she strong enough to be able to recover from it, or did something break in her that day? Did the impact of that fleeting encounter knock her so hard that she was irreparably damaged? Can a broken heart be real?

And, if so, was that one of the moments that sealed my own mother's fate, too, the moment that wounded my grandmother?

A sadness overwhelms me as I feel more keenly than ever the loss of my grandmother and my mother. And I feel afraid, too. Because I wonder whether it is my inescapable fate to feel that they have abandoned me . . . And to know that my connection to life could be so fragile and so tenuous as well.

I try to shake off these morbid thoughts, hurrying away from the sculpture gallery, feeling the need to catch up with Thierry and have his comforting presence beside me. And how I wish I had Mireille and Vivienne beside me too, at times like this, so that I could absorb some of their strength and their *joie de vivre* as well.

1942

Mireille and Vivi had been so kind to her when they'd got back to the apartment after that awful encounter with Ernst and his family in the Louvre, but Claire had shut herself in her room, not wanting to see the pity written on their faces, knowing what an idiot she'd been.

Mireille had tapped on the door in the evening, bringing Claire a bowl of stew. 'Come on,' she'd urged, with a kindness that brought tears to Claire's eyes. 'You need to eat. Keep your strength up.'

Claire had shaken her head, feeling sick with humiliation, but Mireille had insisted, perching on the bed beside her.

And then the floodgates had opened and Claire began to sob. 'How could I have been so stupid? Did he single me out because he could see I was a foolish girl who would fall for his charms?'

Mireille shook her head. 'You're not stupid. Just young and inexperienced in the ways of the world. Perhaps he sensed your innocence. He fed you the words you'd wanted to hear.'

'Yes, but I swallowed them without stopping to wonder whether there was any truth in them.' Claire's cheeks blazed as she recalled the asides he used to make to his fellow-officers when they went out, how they'd all laugh. At the time, she told Mireille, she'd assumed they were just harmless jokes, part of the role as the life and soul of the party he enjoyed playing when in company. But now she wondered how many of those asides had been at her expense.

Overcome with humiliation and shame, she sobbed on Mireille's shoulder as she spoke of her family. When she'd been with Ernst, she'd pushed the memories of Jean-Paul's words to the back of her mind, justifying her actions by telling herself that he didn't understand how hard it was to live in the city. Women were powerless at the best of times, and the war heightened that feeling, but being with Ernst had given her a sense of security as well as the luxury of being pampered and envied. Now she saw that that sense of safety had been built on the fantasy that she'd spun for herself out of silk stockings and glasses of champagne. 'How could I have betrayed my own brothers in that way? Oh Mireille, I can't bear to think what they must think of me. Jean-Paul went off to the work camps knowing that I was . . .' she hesitated, choosing her words carefully, '. . . Enjoying the attentions of the enemy. How I wish I could tell him now that I know how wrong I've been!'

Mireille stroked her arm, comforting her. With a sigh, she said, 'Well you're certainly not the first girl to have had her head turned by the promise of a little luxury and indulgence. But the important thing is that you've learnt your lesson now. The next time a dashing German officer crosses your path, you won't take the bait quite so easily, I reckon.'

'I won't take the bait at all,' Claire retorted, with a vehemence that made Mireille smile. 'I hate the Nazis. For everything they have done. To me. To my family. And to my country.'

⁘

As she nursed her broken heart and tried to focus on her work in the months that followed, Claire sensed that change was in the air. When the Germans first invaded, there had been a sense of numb incomprehension amongst the citizens of Paris. And perhaps it had been tempting to believe the propaganda posters that had appeared, showing kindly-looking Nazi soldiers protecting France's people and providing food for France's starving children. But as the calendar rolled over to another new year, the mood had shifted.

There was a sense of volatility sweeping through the city. Stories of protests and acts of defiance were rife and some Résistants even dared to attack their German occupiers. Of course, the retaliation against such acts was swift and brutal: executions took place in the streets, and everyone had heard talk of the trains that pulled cattle trucks filled with human cargo, which departed more and more frequently from the Gare d'Austerlitz and the Gare de l'Est. There were rumours, too, of an internment camp in the Drancy suburb to the north-east of the city centre, to which the Jewish residents who had been rounded up were sent. The fact that this camp was patrolled by the French police rather than by German guards only added to the sense of angry unease that more and more of Paris's inhabitants were beginning to feel.

And now this unease was beginning to work its way into Claire's consciousness. She worried for her brothers, Jean-Paul and Théo. There had been no news of them. Had they managed to meet up in Germany? She hoped they had and that they worked alongside one another in some factory somewhere, keeping each other's spirits up until the day they could return to their home in France. She grieved for Luc, and nausea rose in her throat when she thought of his body lying in a war grave in the east, all that time that she had so foolishly spent with Ernst – an agent of the very regime which had killed her brother. It was as if she'd been sleepwalking through those months, seduced by the illusion that money and glamour would change her life, distracting her from the reality of what was happening in the world around her.

As time went by, though, and the mood in the city around her changed, Claire felt a change happening within herself as well. Her heart had begun to mend – as hearts will do if they are given enough exposure to time and the kindness of good friends – and as it mended, it transformed into something new. The hard lesson that she'd learned had forced her to reflect on the person she really was, and on the person she wanted to be, and she discovered a new core of resolve within herself.

And so it was, one evening when Vivi had stayed on at her work in the sewing room again, that Claire knocked on the door of Mireille's room.

'Come in!' called Mireille from within.

Claire stepped over the threshold, into the tiny bedroom under the eaves, and stood in silence for a moment, her hands clenched into fists at her sides. Then she said, 'I want to help. Tell me what I can do, Mireille. I am ready to fight back now.'

Mireille rose from where she sat on her bed and pushed the door closed, quietly but firmly. Then she patted the quilted cover, motioning Claire to sit down.

'It's not that easy, Claire. Are you certain that this is a step you want to take?' she asked in a low voice.

Claire nodded. 'I hate them. I hate what they have done to me, personally – to my family – and what they continue to do to our country. I'm sorry it's taken me so long to get here, but I'm ready now.'

Mireille gave her a long, appraising look, as if seeing her friend for the first time. 'Very well then,' she said at last. 'I'll speak to someone. I'll let you know.'

Claire slept more deeply that night than she had done in many years, as if her newfound resolve provided an extra blanket to warm the bitter chill that had kept her frozen for so long. And as it melted, it bonded the final pieces of her shattered heart back together, into something altogether stronger.

❧

Mireille and Claire crossed the Pont Neuf one bright morning in February. It was the Sunday before Lent and the bells of Notre-Dame were ringing, summoning the faithful to Mass, but the girls pressed on, crossing to the right bank of the Seine and continuing along the quayside, following the silver ribbon of the river downstream until they reached the Tuileries garden. There were no special pastries in the windows of the bakeries that they passed, nor would there be any chocolates to be enjoyed when Easter finally arrived that year. The privations of the war were biting harder than ever now, making themselves felt in the constant hunger that gnawed at the girls' stomachs. They had grown so used to the pangs now, though, that they hardly noticed any more.

At the entrance to the park, Mireille put a hand on Claire's arm, stopping her for a moment. 'Are you still sure that you want to do this, Claire? You haven't had second thoughts?'

'No. More than ever, I am sure.'

Mireille smiled, taking in the look of determination on her friend's face. It was a new expression, one that she hadn't seen in Claire's gentle demeanour until recently, and it revealed a side to her character that had lain dormant. But now it had been awakened and Mireille recognised a flame of resolute defiance in her friend, the same flame that burned in her own breast.

It had taken several weeks for Mireille to convince the other members of the network that Claire could be relied upon. She'd been upfront with them about Claire's liaison with a German officer, but had also told them that she had grown certain of her friend's commitment to work against the invaders during their heart-to-hearts over the past few months. Eventually the dyer had told her that Monsieur Leroux was prepared to meet her friend, as there might be a role for her. 'Bring her to the Tuileries on Sunday morning. He will be walking past the Jeu de Paume at eleven o'clock. He wants to talk to her, to see if she really is suitable.'

She recognised his tall figure from a distance as they approached. He was strolling past the entrance to the gallery which housed Monet's beautiful waterlily paintings. Now, though, the artworks were kept behind locked doors and a German soldier stood guard outside.

Monsieur Leroux appeared completely unconcerned by the soldier's presence and even nodded pleasantly in the guard's direction as he passed by. When the girls approached, a little more slowly now given the presence of the Nazi soldier in the background, he made a show of stopping, as if surprised and pleased to recognise the two girls who also happened to be out for a stroll, enjoying the sunshine on that bright, early spring morning. He raised his hat to them and Mireille introduced Claire, who looked at him quizzically for a moment, as if she recognised him from somewhere, but couldn't quite place him. He smiled at the two girls and then, as if politely suggesting that they continue their walk together, he gestured towards a distant avenue of pleached hornbeams, and they fell into step beside him.

He looked, for all the world, like the playboy he was reputed to be. Mireille had heard the models speculating about him as she'd been pinning up the hem of a woman's coat that he had commissioned. 'Apparently he has several mistresses. He always keeps his accounts separate and pays them in cash, so they won't find out about each other I suppose. He must be absolutely loaded! He seems to favour our Nazi visitors, too. I saw him at the Brasserie Lipp the other evening and he was wining and dining a "grey mouse". I reckon she wanted to eat the sauerkraut there to remind her of home. Anyway, I hope this coat isn't for her – she was a real dumpling. One of the other girls says he hosts Nazi officers and their wives there sometimes, too.'

'He's very handsome, that sandy hair makes him look so distinguished,' the other model had remarked, languorously rearranging her silk dressing gown where it had slipped open to reveal the black lace of the camisole she wore underneath. She took another drag on her cigarette and blew the smoke towards the ceiling of the room behind the salon, where the models waited in between clients' visits.

The first model had sniffed. 'He's alright, if you like that sort of thing, I suppose. His looks are a little too Germanic for my liking, along with the company he keeps. Ouch!' She remonstrated, pulling away from Mireille, who knelt at the model's feet with her pincushion. 'Watch what you're doing with those pins, clumsy! If you catch these stockings with one, it'll cost you a whole week's wages to replace them.'

And Mireille had ducked her head and smiled to herself as she'd put the last pin in place on the hem of the coat.

If only they could see him now, she thought to herself, as they wandered down the broad, central pathway towards the pond in the middle of the gardens. As if reading her thoughts, he shot her a quick smile before turning his attention to questioning Claire about her family and her home back in Brittany. His tone was casually conversational, but Mireille could sense that he was testing Claire, still making up his mind whether or not she could be relied upon as a member of the network.

They reached the hornbeam avenue and sauntered beneath the straight-cut walls of the trees' branches. At first glance, the twigs were dead-looking. But Mireille knew that if you looked a little more closely, you could make out the tightly furled buds, waiting to clothe the trees in their summer finery. As the three of them walked down the avenue, they nodded greetings to the few others that they passed who had also decided to skip Mass and enjoy the brightness of a clear spring day instead. After half an hour, they had doubled back towards the Jeu de Paume and Monsieur Leroux prepared to take his leave before they came back in sight of the guard. He smiled and nodded at Mireille, signalling that he was convinced that Claire would be an asset to the network.

Turning to Claire, he said, 'Well, Mademoiselle Meynardier, thank you for volunteering to help us. You will make a very useful messenger, I believe. Mireille will advise you, and pass you your instructions from time to time.'

He turned to go, but then stopped. 'Oh, I almost forgot!' He reached into the inner pocket of his jacket and pulled out a package, containing three bars of chocolate with the distinctive palm tree and elephant design on the wrappers. 'You'd better make sure you eat these before Lent begins on Wednesday, mesdemoiselles.'

The girls gasped in delight.

'*Merci*, monsieur. Look, Mireille,' Claire exclaimed, 'we can give one to Vivi too!' She turned to Monsieur Leroux. 'She's our friend – another of the seamstresses, who lives above the shop with us. She loves chocolate as much as we do.'

'Indeed?' he replied. He cast an appraising glance over Claire. Did Mireille imagine it, or was there a flash of amusement in his hazel eyes? 'Well in that case it's extremely fortuitous that I managed to lay my hands on three bars for you.'

Then his expression grew serious again and he said, 'Go well, girls. And be careful.'

꙳

Claire's pulse had fluttered with nerves when Mireille had given her her first assignment – a message to be passed to Monsieur and Madame Arnaud with instructions for moving on a Jewish businessman they'd been harbouring for a few days while an escape plan could be put in place. That first job had gone smoothly and Claire had made it to the safe house and back, encountering just one impromptu road block on the way. She'd managed to smile at the guards as they checked her identity papers and she hadn't wavered when they asked her to open the attaché case she carried. She had shown them the sheet music inside and explained that she was on her way to a singing lesson, as she'd been briefed to do by Mireille. That time, she'd memorised the addresses and instructions, so there was no risk of the Nazis finding anything as they'd leafed through the papers. They had nodded her through the barriers and one had even wished her a good evening as she continued on her way into the Marais.

So she felt a little more confident the next time, when Mireille handed her the note with a rough map sketched on the back and instructed her to deliver it to Christiane, the *passeuse* who lived out to the south-west of the city at Billancourt.

'Are you sure you're up for this?' Mireille asked her, anxiously. 'It's a long way to go and you'll need to keep the note concealed. Take the attaché case again and the sheets of music, and use the same excuse of a singing lesson if you're stopped. I'd take the note myself, but I have to be at the station this evening . . .'

Claire smiled. 'I'll be fine, Mireille. I can unpick the facing underneath my coat collar and hide the note there. A few stitches will hold it in place and no one will be any the wiser. And I've memorised the directions for where to meet Christiane. Don't worry, I'll see you back here in time for the curfew.'

Dusk was falling as the two girls crossed the river. Army trucks filled with soldiers, whose uniforms were emblazoned with stark black and red insignia, rumbled past them, and on the northern horizon the beams of distant searchlights created a false sunrise, sweeping the skies for allied planes. On the right bank, Claire and Mireille embraced quickly and then went their separate ways.

❦

On her return to the Rue Cardinale, as Mireille opened the door of the apartment she was met by Vivi.

'Oh, Mireille! I'm so glad you're back. I wasn't sure where you'd gone . . .' She looked past her into the stairwell. 'But where is Claire? I thought she'd be with you?'

Mireille shook her head. 'No. She remembered she had an errand to run. She'll be back very soon, I expect.'

'Where did she go?' Vivi's face was pale in the light of the hallway. Mireille was taken aback by the urgency of her tone. Vivi never usually asked any questions about the comings and goings of her two flatmates and, until now, she had shown no interest in where they went and what they did in their free time.

'I . . . I can't say. I mean, I'm not sure . . .' Mireille faltered.

Vivienne grasped her by the arms then, more insistent now. 'Mireille, you have to tell me. This is crucial. I know about your missions. But tonight . . .' She took a deep breath, stopping herself, choosing her words a little more carefully. 'Okay, you don't have to say exactly where she is, but just tell me which direction she's gone in.'

Mireille's mind churned, trying to take in what Vivi had just revealed, realising – as the penny dropped – that this must be truly urgent for Vivi to have disclosed the fact that she was in the know about the network.

'She . . . she went south-west.'

Vivi's eyes widened and seemed to darken in the whiteness of her face. 'Where south-west?'

Again, Mireille hesitated, and was shocked when Vivi shook her with a strength that belied her apparent fragility. 'You have to tell me, Mireille,' she insisted.

Mireille shook her head. She couldn't give away that information, it had been drummed into her not to. Even sharing details with those on her own side put everyone at even greater risk. And then, out of the blue, she remembered Monsieur Leroux and the look in his eyes when she and Claire had been taking leave of him in the Tuileries that day – Claire had told him that they'd give the third bar of chocolate to their friend Vivi and his eyes had betrayed a glint of amusement. He knew Vivi. She was something to do with him. Mireille remembered, too, how he had questioned her at the Café de Flore, about her work in the *atelier*, about the seamstresses that lived above the shop, and it dawned on her that he had placed Vivi there in the apartment, with them.

Vivi shook her again, more urgently. 'Trust me, Mireille. You have to trust me.'

Mireille looked deep into her friend's eyes and saw a light of plead-ing in their clear hazel depths. And then she said, 'Billancourt.'

Vivi released her grip on Mireille's arms and her hands flew to her own face in horror. 'No! Not there! They're bombing there tonight. I've only just heard . . . The Renault factory . . . we have to go, now, and get her back.'

Terror gripped Mireille as Vivi's words sunk in. 'But it's late – the curfew . . . Oh, Vivi!'

Vivienne was already pulling on her coat. 'I'm going. We have to at least try to warn her. You don't have to come. Just give me the address.'

Mireille shook her head and now it was her turn to lay a restrain-ing hand on her friend's arm. 'I'll go, Vivi. I know the route she'd have taken. There's no point us both risking it. You know that – probably better than I do.' She hugged Vivienne tightly for a moment. 'Thank you. For telling me. Now stay here and wait. Claire is my responsibility. The network couldn't afford to lose all three of us.'

Reluctantly, Vivi slumped against the door frame. Mireille knew that this was the right thing to do, although she was also aware that the other members of the network would have disagreed and told her to stay put too. Better to minimise the risk, they would say. Better only to lose one of you. But this was Claire. She couldn't sit there in the apartment and do nothing, knowing that she'd sent her friend into the danger zone. She had to go and find her and bring her back safely.

❧

Claire had to wait ages for a connecting train. The Métro only ran spo-radically these days and there were frequent cancellations and station closures. But, in the end, one rattled into the station and she boarded it, praying that the Billancourt stop would be operational this evening. Otherwise she'd have to walk back from the last station on the line at the Pont de Sèvres and that would make her even more late for her rendezvous with Christiane. The train jolted and swayed and the dim carriage lights flickered repeatedly. At least she felt safe underground, even if it was a false sense of security. Everyone knew the Paris Métro tunnels weren't deep enough to offer protection if there were a bombing raid. She glanced at her watch and sighed. It was taking longer than she'd hoped. She'd have a long walk back to Saint-Germain if she missed the last homeward-bound train, and would run the risk of being caught out after the curfew.

Frustrated by delays along the line, it was already late as Claire climbed the steps out of the Métro station at Billancourt. An official began to lock the gates behind her.

'Was that the last train tonight?' she called to him.

'Yes, miss.' He glanced at his watch. 'And you'd better be getting home now – it'll be the curfew in ten minutes.'

Now that she'd come this far, Claire knew she had no choice but to go on. It wasn't far to the rendezvous point. She should have been there an hour ago, so perhaps Christiane would have given up and left, but she had to try at least. There was nothing to lose, in any case – she was already in trouble for being out late if she was stopped by the police or a road block.

The café on the corner, opposite the new apartment blocks that had been built to house the local factory workers, was closing when she reached it. There was no sign of Christiane, only a couple of waiters wiping down tables and stacking chairs. She stood outside, uncertain what to do next. Should she risk waiting in case Christiane came back, or should she cut her losses and start to make the long journey back to Saint-Germain? It was miles, and she'd need to navigate her way through back streets to try to avoid being caught.

As she hesitated, the lights were switched off in the café and the street was plunged into total darkness. The windows of the surrounding homes and businesses were blacked out and many had tightly closed shutters to seal their inhabitants inside – and shut her out.

Nothing moved on the suburban street. There were no passing cars and no latecomers hurrying home. She was too late.

Just as she turned to go, a tiny movement in one of the windows of the apartment block opposite caught her eye. It was almost nothing. Perhaps she'd imagined the glint of light, as if a corner of the blackout had been lifted and then hastily dropped again. She felt uneasy at the thought that someone might have seen her, but decided to wait another minute to see if anyone came.

In the shadows on the silent street, there was an almost imperceptibly soft click as a door was opened. Then a young woman, who fitted the description of Christiane that Claire had been given, slipped silently across the road. Claire removed her hat and her pale hair made her appear other-worldly in the darkness.

Christiane whispered the code word and Claire gave her reply.

'It's so late,' Christiane said in a low voice, her eyes dark pools in a white face. 'Come, we'll be safer in the doorway, in case anyone's watching.'

They moved to stand inside the door of the building opposite and Claire quickly slipped the tightly folded map from beneath her collar, passing it over without a word.

Christiane glanced at the piece of paper and then pushed it into her pocket. 'You should come in and stay the night with me here,' she said.

Claire shook her head. 'No. We mustn't risk being caught together. Your neighbours might have seen me. I'll make my way home. Don't worry, I'll stay away from the main roads. If anyone stops me, I'll explain that the trains had already stopped running by the time my music lesson finished.' She raised the battered attaché case.

Christiane nodded. 'Very well. Go, quickly now. Stay safe. And thank you for this.' She patted the pocket of her cardigan, where the paper rustled faintly.

Claire slipped back out into the street and heard the door shut softly behind her as she walked away, trying to make her footsteps as quiet as possible on the hard pavement. The darkness seemed to press in on her more closely as she slipped down a narrow side street. By this circuitous route, it was going to take even longer for her to navigate her way back to Saint-Germain, but it would be safer.

And then she felt the strangest sensation. It was as if the darkness had begun to vibrate around her. She pressed a hand to her ear to try to clear the feeling from her head. But then the vibration grew, transforming itself into the low, droning hum of an aeroplane. She glanced up nervously, but the darkness revealed nothing. She began to walk faster and then broke into a run as the noise was amplified, filling her head with its dull roar.

All of a sudden, as though all the street lights had been switched back on at once, there was a bright light overhead and she glanced skywards again to see the blazing white streak of a flare falling languidly towards the roofs ahead of her.

As if in a dream, the last thing she thought she saw was the outline of her friend Mireille, silhouetted in the sudden blinding flash that followed, before the roaring darkness engulfed her.

⁂

As Mireille had hurried down the winding staircase from the apartment and out into the Rue Cardinale, she'd almost collided with a man she vaguely recognised as a neighbour, who was wheeling his bicycle and whistling softly to himself as he headed home for the night. The yellow star pinned to his overcoat shone like a small sun in the light that spilled from the open doorway.

'Woah! What's the hurry, mademoiselle?' he laughed and reached out a steadying hand as she swerved, nearly falling as she tried to avoid him.

'Please, monsieur, can I borrow your bike? It's a grave emergency. I'll bring it back safely, I promise. You can collect it here, from Delavigne Couture, tomorrow.' She crossed her fingers and sent up a prayer that this last part was true. But if the bike didn't make it back then she probably wouldn't either, so she wouldn't have to face the consequences, she reasoned.

Reluctantly, the man agreed to let her borrow it because he recognised her – she was one of the three girls who had stopped him on the street corner and asked him to take their photograph. And he could see from the terrible look on her face that it really must be important. 'But take good care of it, I beg you, mademoiselle. I'll need it to get to work in the morning.'

She called her thanks over her shoulder as she pushed down hard on the pedal and swung herself on to the saddle, already heading for the bridge.

As she went, pedalling furiously to try to reach Claire in time, swerving past pedestrians and around other cyclists, she thought hard. If Claire had managed to make it there and back without any delays, she would have been able to catch the last Métro home. But if that had been the case she should have been back by now. The stations Mireille passed were all being locked for the night. Her lungs were burning as she raced for miles along the boulevards. She prayed that the truckloads of soldiers returning to their barracks would leave her be. Hopefully they'd just think that she was in a tearing hurry to get home before the curfew began. Her dark curls flew as she cycled along the quayside, following the curve of the Seine as the river swept southwards to create the deep bend in which the suburb of Billancourt nestled.

She knew where Claire was supposed to be meeting Christiane – it was a spot that she'd used as a rendezvous point a few times herself. She turned into the road where the café sat on the corner but it was deserted. Even through the pounding of the blood in her ears and the noise of the wind rushing past her face, she could hear the roar of the planes as they approached, preparing to unleash the biggest allied air bombardment of the war so far on the factory that was used to produce so many trucks for Hitler's army.

Suddenly the sky lit up with falling flares, illuminating a slight figure in the side street she was passing. She leapt from the bike and called to Claire, running towards her. And then the first plane dropped its bombs on Billancourt and the streets exploded.

The rush of wind and debris engulfed the spot where Claire had been. It hit Mireille a split second later, but it was enough time for her to spin round and tumble into the recess of an adjacent doorway, shielding herself from the worst of the blast and from the shockwaves from the next explosions that sucked the air from her lungs. She picked herself up, ignoring her bleeding hands and knees, and ran into the cloud of thick dust that choked the narrow street. Another flare lit the scene, allowing Mireille to make out the huddled bundle on the pavement just in front of her. She grabbed Claire beneath her arms and dragged her inert body back into the doorway, shielding her with her own body as another blast rocked the earth beneath them.

The white light of the flares became tinged with a warmer orange glow as the factory buildings erupted in flames and the next explosion ripped through the air. She could hear the planes' engines screaming as they sped up and banked away from their target having dropped their payloads.

Her eardrums rang with the force of the blasts after the first wave of planes left. The fires that raged through the nearby buildings added their crackling roar to the din. She carefully assessed Claire's injuries by the light of the flames. She had suffered a blow to the back of her head and her hair was drenched with dark blood. But otherwise her body seemed to be intact. To Mireille's relief, Claire's eyes fluttered open then, her dilated pupils dark as deep black pools. Her gaze was glazed, but with a struggle she seemed to focus on Mireille's face. After a few moments, while Mireille tried to blot the blood from her wound with her scarf, all the while speaking reassuring words, Claire tried to sit up. Her body swayed and then she leant forward and vomited trying, not entirely successfully, to avoid her coat.

'Does anything else hurt?' Mireille asked her.

Dizzily Claire shook her head and then winced, putting a hand up to her hair and looking in numb disbelief at the dark stickiness that stained her fingers.

'You're concussed,' Mireille said. 'And in shock too. But Claire, we need to move you. There may be more planes coming and we need to get out of here. Do you think you can try to stand, if I help you?'

Claire didn't speak, but she reached out a hand and Mireille heaved her on to her feet. Claire retched again, acrid bile spilling from her mouth on to the front of her coat.

'Sorry,' she muttered.

Mireille slung Claire's arm around her shoulders and wrapped her own arm around Claire's back, taking a few tentative steps out from the doorway into the street. Everything was covered in a thick layer of grey dust, as if it had snowed, and they managed to totter along a little way. With a flood of relief, Mireille made out the shape of the discarded bicycle beneath the shroud of dust and debris. She propped Claire against the side of a shop and bent to retrieve it.

And then she felt the air begin to resonate once again as the next wave of bombers approached. 'Quick,' she said, her voice pitched high with alarm as she grabbed Claire again. 'Can we get you on to the saddle? You can keep an arm around my shoulders and I'll wheel the bike along – we'll be able to move faster that way.'

Somewhat precariously, she managed to manoeuvre both Claire and the bicycle into the main road. The wheels crunched over a scattering of broken glass where the café windows had been blown out by the shock wave. She prayed that there were no very sharp shards which would puncture the tyres. Hurrying as fast as she could along the deserted road, Mireille heard the roar of the aeroplane engines as they came in low, and the next flares illuminated the night. Keeping her head down, she gasped for breath and the sinews of her back burned with the effort of pushing the bicycle, weaving round chunks of shattered concrete and splintered shards of wood. The motion made the bike wobble dangerously as dizziness made Claire's body sway, threatening to unbalance them both.

She turned a corner, just as the next wave of bombs began to drop. Thankfully, the buildings here sheltered the girls from the shock of the explosions that rocked the ground beneath Mireille's feet. At the end of the street, she risked a backwards glance and saw that the apartment blocks that had been built for the factory workers had disappeared in an inferno of flame and smoke.

Claire muttered something, and Mireille had to lean close to her to make out what she said.

'Christiane . . . We need to go back for Christiane.'

Swallowing the surge of nausea that rose up, burning her throat, Mireille pushed onwards.

Claire tapped her on the shoulder, stronger and more insistent this time. 'Turn back, Mireille . . . Get Christiane!' she croaked.

'No!' Mireille screamed, her voice a shriek above the storm of noise. 'It's too late for Christiane, Claire.' And hot tears mingled with the dust that coated her face as she trudged onwards, away from the burning buildings that had nestled within the loop of the River Seine.

⁓❧⁓

Waves of nausea made Claire dream she was out on the sea in her father's fishing boat as she drifted in and out of consciousness while the two girls made the long trek back to Saint-Germain. The wail of sirens racing past jerked her back to an awareness of her surroundings. Her head throbbed and the occasional jolting of the bike against a kerbstone made a stabbing pain pierce the backs of her eyes as she leant heavily on Mireille. Her friend was tiring, she realised, and she struggled to balance herself to try to lessen the strain as Mireille trudged doggedly onwards.

Nobody stopped them. When the drone of the bombers' engines and the accompanying distant thuds of bombs finding their targets again and again finally faded away, the trucks that screeched past them were far too intent on getting to the scene of the devastation to bother with the two tattered, ghostly figures that limped by in the opposite direction with a battered-looking bicycle.

In the early hours of the morning, they reached the Rue Cardinale and Claire leant wearily against the wall while Mireille fumbled in her pocket for her key. She watched as Mireille dusted off the bicycle as best she could – it was definitely sporting a few new battle scars after its eventful outing, but at least it was still intact – and left it propped in the stairwell. Then, with Mireille's help, Claire climbed the stairs to the top floor.

At the sound of the apartment door opening, Vivi came running to help them. 'Oh, thank God!' she cried. 'You're safe. I thought you'd both been lost . . .' She hurried to fetch a bowl of warm water and a towel so that she could tend to the wound on the back of Claire's head. The blood had dried, encrusting her hair, and Vivienne very gently began swabbing it away, turning the water in the bowl as dark as wine as she repeatedly wrung out the cloth.

Her gentleness and kindness made Claire weep, as her senses – which had been frozen with shock – began to thaw.

'Let's get you out of this coat,' Vivi murmured, removing the vomit-drenched garment which was beyond saving. She bundled it away, into a corner. Then she turned to Mireille. 'You too, Mireille. Go and get yourself cleaned up. Don't worry, I'll look after Claire.'

An hour later, Claire was tucked up in her bed, wearing a fresh nightgown and a clean dressing around her head. Mireille and Vivi came to sit beside her.

Claire reached out a hand and Mireille held it tight. 'I can't believe you risked your life to save mine, Mireille. I will never forget what you did tonight,' she whispered. And then she began to sob as she thought of Christiane, and of the other civilian lives lost in the bombing raid.

'Ssshhh,' Mireille hushed her, stroking her fine hair, restored to its white-gold sheen, away from her face. 'Try to sleep now, Claire. Tomorrow we will continue our work. For Christiane. And for all the others who are suffering. We will continue our fight.'

As Claire's eyelids grew heavy, safe now, and lulled by the soothing presence of her two friends, a thought occurred to her. 'But Mireille . . . how did you know? That the bombers were coming?'

Mireille glanced across at Vivi and smiled. 'Let's just say we are lucky to have friends in high places.'

And then Claire smiled too as she watched them creep out of her room, ducking beneath the sloping eaves of the roof and leaving her to sleep.

❧

Mademoiselle Vannier gave a frown of disapproval the next morning when Mireille reported that Claire had had an accident and would need a few days off work to recover. When Mireille took her up to see Claire in the apartment, the supervisor tutted, saying, 'What were you doing, you foolish girl? Out cavorting and merry-making with some young man or other, I suppose. Don't you know how dangerous it is these days? Apparently there was terrible bombing over in the west of the city last night. You might have been killed if one of those bombs had gone astray.' But she also took in the pallor of Claire's face, which was almost as white as the bandages around her head, and she gave her a kindly pat on the hand, saying, 'Stay where you are. Vivienne can finish off the beading on that evening gown for you. I'll have some broth sent up. Have a good rest and we'll soon have you back on your feet.'

That evening, having checked that Claire was sleeping peacefully, Mireille slipped back downstairs to the *atelier* where, as usual, Vivi had stayed behind. She watched for a second from the doorway. In the empty, darkened room, Vivi bent low over something she was working on, her russet braid glowing in the pool of light from the single angled lamp on the table beside her.

Suddenly realising that she wasn't alone, Vivi jumped and quickly pulled over the froth of a bright pink chiffon skirt that she was supposed to be hemming, to cover what looked like a square of plain white silk. Mireille pretended she hadn't noticed, letting Vivi preserve the illusion that she simply continued to work on the unfinished garment from earlier.

To cover her friend's slight confusion, Mireille said, 'I love that colour. They're calling it Schiaparelli pink. Mademoiselle Vannier thinks it's common though.' She smiled. 'Sorry to have disturbed you. I just thought I'd come and see if you needed a hand. I know you've been given extra work to cover for Claire. I'm not as good as you two at beadwork, but I could hem that for you, if you like?'

Vivi smiled, but shook her head. 'That's so kind of you, Mireille, but I'm very nearly finished.' She held up a corner of the fabric – although Mireille noticed that she kept the white silk square carefully concealed beneath it – and said, 'See, just one more panel to go. I'll be up soon.'

'Okay,' said Mireille. 'There's a little bit of rabbit stew left from the other night. I'll warm it up for you if you like?'

Despite the lines of tiredness that pinched Vivi's features, her face glowed as brightly as her hair when she smiled her thanks. 'I'd love that.'

Mireille turned to go, but stopped as Vivi spoke again, resting her hand on the fabrics which covered the table in front of her. 'And Mireille? Thanks.'

The look that passed between the two girls said far more than those few, terse words. It was a look of understanding: a mutual recognition of so much that needed to remain unsaid.

Harriet

If Mireille hadn't had the courage and the determination to pedal so furiously towards the bombing raid over Billancourt that night in 1942, I wouldn't be here now. Claire would have been one of the many thousands of people who perished in the bombardment – mostly civilians like Christiane, who lived in the accommodation that had been built to house the workers close to the Renault factory. Claire would never have married Laurence Ernest Redman and they would never have had the daughter that they named Felicity. As I trace those fine, fragile threads of fate back across the years, I am more and more astounded that I am here at all.

Life can seem so very tenuous sometimes. But perhaps that fragility is why we treasure it so. And perhaps it is our profound love of life that makes us so terrified of losing it. Mireille didn't hesitate to go back and find Claire. Vivienne would have gone in an instant as well, if she hadn't had to stay behind. And I can only imagine the dogged determination that kept Mireille going as she gritted her teeth and practically dragged Claire, dazed and bleeding, from the other side of the city back to the safety of the apartment in Saint-Germain.

So, if we cling on to life so hard and value it so much, how deep do depression and despair have to drag someone before they reach a place where they can't bear to go on? It must have been a slow descent into hell that my mother endured before she could bear it no longer and ended the pain with a couple of handfuls of sleeping pills. She washed them down with the remnants of a bottle of brandy that had sat on a shelf in the kitchen for several years, bought by my father in happier times and used to set light to the pudding on the Christmas table.

When I'd managed to break free of the hands that held me at the front gate, that day when the blue lights of the police car illuminated the dusk in front of my home, I ran inside and saw the empty bottle on its side on the floor, next to the sofa where a paramedic in a hi-vis jacket bent over my mother's body. As more hands grabbed me and pulled me away, all I could think of, at the sight of that bottle, was having been entranced by the will-o'-the-wisp blue flames that danced around the dark mass of sticky fruit, transforming it into something magical. Blue flames that flickered like the blue lights of the police car which someone gently lifted me in to, while I waited for my father to come and get me. I knew that he would take me to a house where I wasn't really wanted, a house where I certainly didn't want to be. My mother had abandoned me to that fate. All of a sudden, I felt those flickering blue lights burning me, engulfing me in flames of shock and anger and pain which felt as if they would consume me completely. A police woman crouched in front of me, beside the open car door, holding my hand, trying to soothe me. I leant forward and threw up into the gutter, narrowly missing her neatly pressed trousers and shiny black shoes.

I see now that it's one of the paradoxes of life that if we love it so much that we are frightened of losing it, it can make us live a half-life, too scared to get out there and live whole-heartedly because we have too much to lose. In the same way, I think I protect myself in relationships, too scared to love whole-heartedly because then there would be too much to lose there too. I think of Thierry, of how drawn I feel to his calm, quiet presence and yet I feel myself drawing back, not letting myself fall in love because I'm afraid that there'd be too much to lose. I wish I had the courage of Claire, Vivi and Mireille. Then maybe I'd be able to live – and love – wholeheartedly.

To shake off these morbid thoughts, I head to my usual refuge in the elegant sixteenth *arrondissement*. The trees are bare now, in the park that surrounds the Palais Galliera, and the ribbon-like flower beds that surround the fountain are planted in shades of deep purple and dark green. There's an exhibition about one of France's oldest fashion houses, Lanvin. I immerse myself in the world of its founder, Jeanne Lanvin, drinking in her beautiful creations. I stand for a long time in front of an evening gown in the iconic deep blue that was one of Lanvin's trademarks. It has a heavy embellishment of silver beadwork on the sleeves. I wonder whether Claire ever saw a dress like this and whether it could have been the inspiration for the midnight blue gown she created from offcuts. It's the off season and the museum is almost deserted, so I am startled out of my reverie by the sound of footsteps on the mosaic-tiled floor behind me. A silver-haired woman in a tailored black jacket comes to stand beside me in front of the exhibit.

'It is beautiful, is it not?' she says.

I nod. 'The whole thing is stunning,' I say, sweeping a hand at the rest of the exhibition.

'Do you have a particular interest in Lanvin?' she asks.

I tell her that my grandmother worked in another couture house in the war years and so I am drawn to designs from that era. But this dress, especially, reminds me of what I've heard about her.

She smiles. 'I'm glad. Fashion lives on to tell the story of those who created it and wore it. It is one of the reasons I am drawn to it too. Imagine how pleased Jeanne Lanvin would be to know that seventy years after her death we still remember her. Her designs live on, inspiring today's designers. That is a sort of immortality, I think.'

We both gaze at the dress in silence for a few more moments and then she says, 'Well, I must be getting on. Good day, mademoiselle.'

Her footsteps fade and I am alone in the gallery once more. I stoop to read one of the information sheets displayed alongside the dresses and my eye is drawn to a simple black and white image. It's the Lanvin logo, a line drawing of two figures. A mother and child hold hands, as if they are about to begin to dance or to play a game. They are dressed in flowing robes and wear crown-like headdresses.

The image is distinctive and, I realise, curiously familiar. It must be my imagination, but the scent of flowers seems to fill the air around me. And then I remember where I've seen this mother-and-child image before. It was on the black flagon of perfume that sat on my mother's dressing table.

I read on, and learn that Jeanne Lanvin created the logo to represent her close relationship with her only child, a daughter named Marguerite. And it was Marguerite who chose the name for the famous floral perfume with woody undertones that her mother created: Arpège. She named it for the arpeggio of scents – each note following the next – that brings harmony to the perfume.

The room around me seems filled, suddenly, with the sound of a piano playing and I am transported back to my childhood.

It must be the memory of the scent and of my mother's fingers moving gracefully over the keys of her piano that makes me remember that other photograph that I found in the box of my mother's things, the one with the light shining on her face as she gazed into mine, like a Madonna and child.

Standing there alone, in the exhibition hall surrounded by Jeanne Lanvin's creations, I experience a moment of complete happiness, a memory of what it feels like to be filled with joy that bubbles up from somewhere deep within me. As it fades, it leaves in its wake the knowledge that I don't feel so alone after all. It's as if the logo depicts not just Jeanne and Marguerite but all mothers and children: my own mother and me, holding hands, full of love, preparing to dance together through our lives.

The woman's words echo in my mind: 'That is a sort of immortality, I think.' And it dawns on me that perhaps there are very many different ways to keep someone alive in your heart.

1942

Since the bombing of the Renault factory in Billancourt, the war had made its presence much more keenly felt in Paris. The city streets echoed with the sounds of marching troops and the rumble of military vehicles, as the rumours continued daily of Jewish citizens being rounded up in increasing numbers and held in segregated camps at Drancy and Compiègne.

One evening, Mireille arrived back in the Rue Cardinale to find the bicycle that she'd borrowed from her neighbour on the night of the bombing raid propped against her door. There was a note tied to the handlebars, and a sob caught in her throat as she read it.

For the mademoiselle with the dark eyes. I have to leave, so I want you to have my bicycle. It will be of use to you – and none to me, where I am going. Best wishes, your neighbour Henri Taubman.

Recalling the yellow star pinned to his coat, she fervently hoped that he was making his escape, rather than being sent to one of those camps in the suburbs.

A sense of profound unease spread through the city from one quarter to the next and spilled over into a demonstration one day when the Communist women of the Rue Daguerre took to the streets to protest against the now severe shortage of food outside warehouses that were filled with food for soldiers on the German front. Shots were fired, arrests were made and, Mireille heard on the grapevine, the instigators were sent to those same camps. They did not return. Against this back-drop the girls often lay in their beds listening to the thuds and cracks of explosions as the Allied bombing raids continued sporadically. And the Germans clamped down harder than ever with road blocks, barriers at the Métro stations that remained open, arrests and shootings to keep the local population in check.

Mireille's missions for the underground network felt even more dangerous but, at the same time, even more vital. Visiting the dyer one day to collect some bolts of silk, he handed her a small packet for Vivienne, wrapped in brown paper, and then gave her a set of instructions of her own for that evening. She was to meet a man on the north side of the city and accompany him safely to the Arnauds' house in the Marais, avoiding using the main Métro stations where the Germans were doing frequent spot-checks.

And so it was that she sat at a table at a café on a sloping, cobbled Montmartre street and sipped on her cup of ersatz coffee as she waited for her next 'visitor' to turn up. She was expecting a shabbily dressed refugee, perhaps, or another foreigner whose grasp of French was tenuous at best, so she was surprised when a young Frenchman slipped into the chair across from hers. He pulled a blue and white spotted handkerchief out of his pocket – the sign that she'd been told to watch for – and blew his nose; then he asked whether 'Cousin Cosette' was well, using the code word she'd been told to listen for.

'Her leg is much better these days, thanks for asking,' she replied, repeating the confirmation code that the dyer had given her. She downed the dregs of her coffee, making a face at the bitter tincture of roasted chicory and dandelion roots, then got to her feet and the young man followed her out into the street.

As they walked down the hill, she slipped him the false papers she'd been given for him and he tucked them into his pocket without looking at them. She took him to the Métro station at Abbesses and they stood on the semi-deserted platform waiting for a train. Cocooned underground and under cover of the noises of the railway, she felt able to talk to her charge a little more freely than usual, as long as they kept their voices low. The clatter of distant trains, the dripping of water and the sound of other passengers' footsteps echoing off the tunnel walls, muffled their conversation.

His eyes, which were almost as dark as her own, held a gleam of determination in their depths, and the day's growth of stubble etched on his chin helped to define its strength. His black hair sprung back from his forehead with a vitality which was mirrored in the confident spring of his step and the interest with which he watched her face as she talked. They didn't exchange names – they both knew the dangers involved – but she recognised his accent as being from the far south of the country with the twang of a native of Provence or the Languedoc. He told her that he'd grown up near Montpellier, the eldest in a sprawling family of sisters and brothers, and that he'd signed up in 1939. He was one of the lucky ones in the French army who had been evacuated from Dunkirk, and he'd joined the Free French in England, continuing the fight under the command of General De Gaulle.

Mireille nodded. She'd heard from the dyer that sometimes messages were broadcast from England by the exiled General, rallying the troops that were left to him and trying to raise the morale of the people he'd had to leave behind.

'I was parachuted in last week. Dropping off a few gifts for the folks in the homeland.' He grinned as he said this and Mireille guessed that the 'gifts' were probably wireless sets or weapons or orders for covert operations, although she didn't ask him to elaborate.

'Got held up on the way, though. Turned out there was a Boche unit camped out in the town so we couldn't risk getting the plane back in. It's easy enough parachuting in to France but getting back out is another story. So they fixed me up with your lot. Told me I'll be enjoying a holiday in the Pyrenees in a few days' time. But they said I'd need a specialist to get me across Paris. I can't say I was expecting one as beautiful as you, though.'

Mireille shook her head and laughed. 'Flattery will get you nowhere! But yes, I'll try and get you through the city safely. I don't know exactly which way they'll be taking you after that, though – the routes change all the time to try to keep one step ahead of the Germans and the police.'

She kept her eyes on the tracks, watching the mice that scurried among the rubble between the sleepers when the station was quiet, aware that he was watching her closely and that it was making her cheeks flush. Shaking back her curls, she met his gaze boldly and said, 'I know we're not supposed to ask questions. But I do have just one: what happened to your parachute?'

He laughed, surprised. 'I buried it in a turnip field, as instructed. Why do you ask?'

'It just would have made a nice blouse and a few pairs of camiknickers too, for me and my friends.'

'I see,' he said, gravely. 'Well next time, mademoiselle, I will be sure to keep it with me and bring it to you here in Paris. I'm sure General De Gaulle and the rest of the Allied Command would be delighted to know army equipment was being put to such very good use!'

All at once, the mice on the tracks scattered and a few seconds later they heard the sound of an approaching train, silencing them both.

They sat side by side, and Mireille was acutely conscious of the man's arm touching hers through their jacket sleeves as the carriage swayed and jerked. They didn't speak, as there were other passengers sitting within earshot, but she couldn't help feeling the powerful undercurrent of attraction that passed between them.

She was jolted out of this pleasant reverie when the train drew to a stop at a station well before their own and a guard shouted that the train would terminate here. They followed their fellow passengers, some grumbling, some silently resigned, up the stairs to the exit.

As they reached the top of the stairs, Mireille's heart beat against her ribs like a trapped bird. At the barrier, half a dozen soldiers were pulling people out from the crowd of passengers who'd been turned off the train. A few yards ahead of them, one man hesitated, looking around for another exit. His momentary delay caught the attention of two of the soldiers and they unceremoniously pushed the other passengers out of the way and seized the man by his upper arms, marching him off. Mireille noticed that they were stopping anyone who wore a yellow star pinned to their clothing. She drew the young man's arm through hers, pulling him close so that she could mutter in his ear, 'Don't hesitate. Don't look left or right. Just walk with me.'

When it was their turn at the barrier, Mireille forced herself to look relaxed, although her shoulders were stiff with tension. Through the sleeve of her coat she could feel the muscles of the young man's forearm harden as he clenched his fist.

One of the soldiers looked them up and down and seemed about to stop them. But then he waved them through and turned his attention to the couple behind them, demanding to see their papers. Mireille breathed again, allowing her shoulders to relax just a little.

Outside in the street, a truck was parked on the pavement. A pair of guards leaned their rifles against the tailgate as they smoked cigarettes. Mireille glimpsed the pale, anxious faces of the people who'd been made to board it, as she and the young man walked on in sickened silence until they were out of earshot. Then Mireille withdrew her arm from his and tucked her hair behind her ears, her hands shaking with equal measures of fear and anger. She noticed that the young man's fists were still tightly clenched and his jaw was set in a hard line.

'So this is what they do,' he said, looking as sick as she felt. 'Herd people into trucks like cattle and send them to those so-called work camps where they treat them like slaves. We've heard the reports, back in England, but seeing it happening right in front of me . . .' He tailed off, swallowing his frustration.

'I know,' she replied, leading him towards the river. 'It's grotesque. What's even more horrible is that half the time it's the French police who man those barriers, not the Germans. It's getting worse all the time.'

They walked on, subdued, alongside the mud-brown waters of the Seine. Mireille stumbled as her shoe caught on an uneven paving stone and he put out a hand to steady her. Wordlessly, he took her arm again and she gleaned a small degree of comfort in his proximity.

She didn't want to risk going back into the Métro, so they continued on foot. He told her more of his life in the south as they followed the river upstream. He'd worked as a stonemason and had done his apprenticeship with his uncle who had been overseeing some maintenance work on the Cathédrale Saint-Pierre in Montpellier. He continued to hold her arm but his free hand described the complex, soaring lines of the Gothic arches he'd helped repair, painstakingly carving each piece of honeyed sandstone to fit perfectly where worn or damaged sections needed to be removed. She noticed the strength in his hands, and yet there was a grace in them too. As he talked, she could picture the delicate, lace-like detailing that he was capable of creating from such unyielding materials.

She told him a little about her life in the south-west too, about the mill house on the riverbank where she'd grown up, about the way the mill wheel was driven, harnessing the power of the water to turn the heavy millstones to grind the grist into flour as fine as freshly fallen snow. She described the kitchen, where her family would gather for meals cooked by her mother using the produce they grew in their garden, and the clear, golden honey that her sister produced from the beehives she tended, to sweeten their days.

It felt like such an indulgence to be able to talk about such things, sharing their memories with each other, and Mireille found herself wishing that she had more time to spend with this young man. They were approaching the Marais now, though, and in a few more minutes she would hand him over to Monsieur and Madame Arnaud. Then he would be spirited away on the unseen routes of the secret network, passed from one safe house to the next until a guide could lead him on the difficult and dangerous journey over the Pyrenees. She longed to be able to tell him her name, and to give him her address so that this comfortable feeling of connection between them could be continued one day. But she knew that to do so would place the pair of them – and a whole network of other people besides – in a perilous position if he was caught.

As they neared the narrow entrance at the end of the street where the Arnauds lived, she gently extracted her arm from his, feeling a strong pang of reluctance as she did so, longing to stay close to him for a little longer.

She heard the shouting just as she was about to turn the corner. There was a harsh cry of 'HALT!' followed by a woman's scream.

In that split second, Mireille saw, with horror, the scene that was unfolding outside the safe house. A black car was parked at the door and an officer in the dark uniform of the Gestapo was pushing Madame Arnaud into the back of it. At the same time, another soldier had pushed Monsieur Arnaud to the ground and was aiming a couple of vicious kicks at his belly.

The young man's fists clenched tight at his sides and his whole body tensed, as if he were about to spring forward and try to intervene.

Mireille realised with horrible clarity that their presence would surely seal the Arnauds' fate once and for all, and their own as well. There was nothing they could do to help. She grabbed the young man's arm and pulled him onwards, passing the end of the narrow street where the safe house, which had provided refuge to so many escapees over the past year, had suddenly become safe no longer.

❦

In the dusk of the clear Paris evening, Claire had pushed open the tiny square window in her bedroom to allow the evening air to flood in. Soon darkness would fall and she would have to close the window and pull down the blackout blind, shutting out the stars. But now she breathed in the faint smells of coffee and cigarette smoke and listened to the sounds of clinking china which wafted up on the night-time air from the café opposite the end of the road. The streets were far quieter these days since there was very little traffic. Most of Paris's inhabitants either walked or cycled everywhere. With increasing frequency, clients were sending skirts in to be remade as culottes, which were more practical for wearing on a bicycle whilst still retaining a degree of elegance.

From this height, she couldn't see the street immediately below, but she heard the key turn in the lock and the front door open and close. She was always anxious when Mireille was out on her own, watching for her safe return, so it was with relief that she heard the footsteps climbing the metal stairs up to the apartment.

She pulled her window shut and drew the blind then skipped into the hallway to open the door for her friend. To her surprise, a tall young man wearing a gaberdine raincoat stood behind Mireille. Claire knew better than to ask questions, so she simply stepped aside and let them in.

The room that had been Esther's – the room where she had given birth to her baby – hadn't been used by any of the seamstresses who'd lived in the attic rooms since. Claire and Mireille had always kept the door shut, as opening it would have brought back too many memories, especially for Mireille, who had witnessed Esther's death when the German plane had dived low to machine-gun the river of refugees fleeing Paris at the time of the invasion. But now they needed somewhere to hide the young Free French soldier for a few days until a new escape plan could be put in place for him.

Claire could see the fear that flickered in Mireille's eyes – although she tried to hide it and remain her usual calm and practical self – as they discussed their options. They both knew that the capture of the

Arnauds by the Gestapo meant that one of the network's escape routes had effectively been shut down. Claire shivered when she thought of them being taken to the Avenue Foch for questioning. How long would they be able to hold out if they were tortured? Would they be able to avoid divulging any useful information for the first twenty-four hours of their internment, giving the other *passeurs* time to cover their tracks and allowing the safe houses to be shut down? Would Mireille be the next member of the network to be arrested if the Arnauds gave the Gestapo what little information they knew about her? And if Mireille were arrested, then would Claire be as well? There would be no arguing their way out of things if they were discovered harbouring a fugitive. But it seemed there was no other option: the apartment beneath the eaves was needed as a safe house now.

She and Mireille moved aside the row of mannequins which were being stored in Esther's old room. Each one had been made to the exact measurements of a particular client, although more and more were having to be put into storage these days as clients disappeared or were unable to afford the soaring prices of couture. As the rooms on the floors below had filled up with dressmaking forms, some of the overflow had found its way to the spare rooms on the fifth floor.

They made up the bed, each donating one of their own blankets, while the young man perched on a chair in the sitting room and wolfed down the heel of bread which Mireille had given him, spreading it with the last scrapings from a jar of rillettes which were more fat than meat.

Although they tried to work quietly, Vivi heard the to-ings and fro-ings and came out of her room to investigate. When Mireille briefly explained what had happened, Vivi winced with shock.

Keeping her voice low, although her tone was urgent, Vivi said, 'You know this is putting everything at a terrible risk, Mireille. We can't allow the strands of the network to become entangled with one another. His presence here threatens all of us, right to the very top.'

Claire wondered what she meant by this, but noticed that Mireille seemed to understand the significance as she didn't ask Vivi to explain further.

'We have no option,' Mireille whispered back. 'What else can we do? Turn him out on to the streets with nowhere to go? He'll be sure to be arrested sooner or later, and he knows where we live now. Even though he's tough, he's only human. You know what methods they use to get information out of people. Hiding him here is the safest option. The Arnauds don't know my real name and they don't know anything about my background so there's very little they can give away.'

'And the dyer? What if they divulge his role? If he's arrested, we all go down.'

Mireille's chin lifted and her dark curls trembled. Claire recognised the signs: this was her friend's look of determination, not fear, and they all knew how stubborn she could be when she'd made her mind up about something.

'I know, Vivi,' Mireille replied. 'But we all understood what we were getting in to. I still believe this is our safest option.'

A sad smile played over Vivi's face as she seemed to accept that Mireille was right. 'Very well,' she said reluctantly, 'we'll hide him then. But none of the others downstairs must suspect a thing.' She turned towards Claire. 'Do you understand?'

'Of course!' Claire retorted, indignantly. 'I'm just as involved as Mireille is. As involved as you, too, I expect,' she couldn't help adding.

Vivienne shot her a wary glance, but then let it go. 'Come on then, we need to get him sorted out for the night. And this bedroom door needs to be kept locked from the inside. He won't be able to risk moving around in the daytime. You know how these floorboards creak. Mademoiselle Vannier will be up here like a shot if she hears anyone up here when we're all supposed to be in the *atelier* – especially if she suspects one of us might be hiding a man!'

Claire found it hard to sleep that night. She tossed and turned in the darkness and thought, at one point, that she heard the almost imperceptible pad of bare feet passing her door. Perhaps she'd imagined it, or maybe it was just one of the others going to use the bathroom, she told herself. When she did fall into a restless sleep, it was filled with troubled dreams of men in black uniforms chasing her through the streets, their boots loud on the pavement. As they caught up with her, she woke with a cry to find Vivi crouching by her bed, shaking her awake.

'Hush,' she whispered. 'I'm here. Everything will be alright.'

'I was having a nightmare,' Claire gasped, still shaken.

'Shh, I know. You were talking in your sleep, I heard you through the wall. But it's okay. You're alright. We're all okay. Try to get back to sleep.'

Claire shook her head. 'I don't want to sleep any more, in case the dreams come back.'

'Come on then.' Vivi held out a hand. 'We'll go and make a tisane. We need to be up in half an hour, in any case.'

They tiptoed past Mireille's door and crept into the kitchen to put the water on to heat, then sat in a companionable silence, cupping their hands around their bowls and inhaling the sweet-sharp smell of lemon balm tea.

'How long do you think he'll have to stay here?'

Vivienne drew her red-gold braid over one shoulder. 'Not long. Don't worry, they'll get him out. And Mireille was right last night – hiding him here is the safest option all round. Now then, you and I and Mireille need to keep to our usual routines at work. It's absolutely imperative that no one has any reason to suspect there's anything out of the ordinary going on in the apartment on the fifth floor.'

Claire nodded and took a sip of her tea. Vivi's calm presence was reassuring. The three girls were in this together now, bound not only by their friendship but by the secrets that they kept for one another.

❧

Mireille was wondering how she might find an excuse to visit the dyer the next day, when, fortuitously, Mademoiselle Vannier asked her to go and collect some lengths of fabric that would be needed for making up some of the samples for the autumn collection.

Her first question when she reached the shop, was whether there was any word about Monsieur and Madame Arnaud. The dyer pressed his lips together grimly and shook his head. 'We've suspended all activity along the network for the time being. There haven't been any further arrests so far, so it looks like they've managed not to divulge any information that could be of use to the Gestapo. God only knows whether the two of them will be able to hold out, though.'

From the shelves behind him, he gathered up the orders he'd completed for Delavigne Couture and laid the paper-wrapped packages on the counter. Then, reaching into a cupboard he drew out a smaller parcel from behind a pile of colour swatches. 'Make sure Vivienne gets this. And tell her to keep it hidden for the time being. She won't be able to use it until we've worked out a new route . . .' He stopped, realising that he'd already said too much. 'I'll get word to Monsieur Leroux. Don't worry, there are other networks that we may be able to tap into until we can get things up and running again. In the meantime, can you keep your visitor hidden, do you think? Come and let me know if it becomes a problem. We must be careful . . . although I know I don't need to tell you that. Just sit tight for a few days. We'll work something out.'

'*Merci*, monsieur.' Mireille slipped the parcel for Vivi into the inside pocket of her coat and then gathered up the larger packages.

The dyer held the shop door open for her. 'Try not to worry,' he told her. But his reassuring tone couldn't disguise the tension that was etched into the creases on his forehead.

During the working day the girls stayed out of the apartment, leaving the young man there alone. He'd promised not to move around, for fear of someone hearing a soft footfall or the creak of a floorboard when visiting the storerooms immediately beneath the fifth floor. Mademoiselle Vannier and the other seamstresses often had to retrieve a client's mannequin, or go in search of a particular pattern or a bolt of cloth. But in the evening, after everyone else had gone, Mireille, Claire and Vivi could relax a little and their 'guest' could be allowed out of his room to share their supper with them.

His face lit up when he saw Mireille that evening. 'I have a name!' he said, brandishing the false identity papers that she'd given him. 'Allow me to introduce myself: Frédéric Fournier at your service, mademoiselle.' He made an elaborate bow, taking her hand and kissing it theatrically.

'Hmm,' said Mireille, pretending to look at him appraisingly, although she made no move to withdraw her hand from his, 'it suits you. But we will call you Fréd. It looks like you'll be spending a few days here with us, Fréd, so I hope you won't get too bored, stuck up here with nothing to do.'

'On the contrary,' he said with a smile that mirrored hers, 'I have plenty to do. Tonight I am planning on doing my laundry, if I may make use of the facilities in this excellent establishment, and then I hope to spend a most enjoyable evening in the company of my very kind hosts.' He looked down at her hand which he was still holding and then gave it a gentle squeeze. 'One of my very kind hosts in particular,' he said, quietly. And then he raised her hand to his lips again and kissed it with a tenderness, this time, that melted her heart.

While he was in the bathroom, washing himself and his socks, Mireille went to find Vivi in the kitchen where she was attempting to make a meal that was scarcely adequate for three stretch to feed four. Mireille hadn't had a chance to tell her what the dyer had said earlier, but she did so now. She also handed over Vivi's package and passed on the message about keeping it hidden for the time being. Vivi frowned, but said nothing and took the parcel to her room.

That evening, Mireille and the newly named Frédéric sat up late into the night, long after Claire and Vivi had gone to their beds, continuing to talk about their families and their lives before the war turned the whole world upside down. She was careful to avoid telling him anything that might put her family in danger if he were caught, but it still felt good to share a part of herself with this man and to hear his stories in return.

In a time and place where they had so little, the hours they spent in each other's company felt like one of the best gifts she'd ever received.

ം

After work the next evening, Claire went out to try and find some extra food. The three girls had each chipped in from their savings, so she had a few francs in her pocket in case the grocer might have anything beneath the counter that could be bought by slipping a little extra money into his hand. Usually the girls avoided the black market and made do with their official allocations of rations, but with an extra mouth to feed they were all hungrier than ever.

By the time she got home there was a satisfying heft to her shopping bag, where a jar of *confit de canard* was concealed beneath some dusty potatoes and a bunch of wizened carrots. They would have a feast!

On the first floor, she was surprised to hear a low murmur of voices coming from the sewing room. Vivi must be working late, yet again, she thought, but she heard a male voice too and wondered whether Fréd had risked leaving the apartment.

The door stood slightly ajar and through the narrow crack she caught a glimpse of a man's hand resting on Vivi's shoulder. It was a gesture of complete ease, of a closeness and a comfortable intimacy which stopped Claire in her tracks. Vivi had never let on that she had a boyfriend. In fact, she rarely went out at all these days and when she did it was usually at Claire and Mireille's insistence that she join them for a walk or a visit to a local café. If it was Fréd who sat so close to her then he must have made a very fast move. Anyway, Claire had seen the way Fréd's face lit up whenever Mireille appeared, so it would be all the more surprising if this were him.

The two figures were intent on whatever it was that Vivi was working on and, as Claire watched, the man's hand moved from Vivi's arm to point at something on the table.

Claire shifted slightly, trying to get a view of the man's face, but as she did so the bag of shopping swung a little, pushing the door open.

Two faces looked up at her, startled. And then the man said, 'Good evening, Claire. It's nice to see you again.'

'*Bonsoir*, Monsieur Leroux,' she replied.

He stood, and as he did so she noticed that Vivi slipped whatever it was they'd been studying so intently on to her lap.

'I'm sorry to have interrupted you,' Claire said, backing away from the doorway. 'I just wanted to tell Vivi that I've got some supper for us all.' She held up her bag. 'It'll be ready in about half an hour.'

'That's quite alright. I need to come upstairs to speak to you all, in any case. There is a plan for your surprise guest's onward journey, but I need to discuss it with you. Here' – he took the bag of shopping from her – 'allow me to carry this for you. Vivi will follow in a minute once she's tidied up here.'

He was certainly a very attractive man, she thought, but Claire noticed that he used the less formal version of Vivienne's name, and that an undercurrent of understanding seemed to run between the two of them. Maybe Vivi was one of his mistresses, she thought. It would certainly explain how she'd been recruited to work at Delavigne Couture. And then, like the pieces of a jigsaw puzzle fitting into place, an image came into her mind of the reflection in the mirror that she'd glimpsed at Brasserie Lipp all those months before. The man sitting at the table with Vivi and the Nazi woman had been Monsieur Leroux. That was why his face had looked familiar when they were subsequently introduced in the Tuileries gardens. Given his closeness to Vivi, he must have known all along that Claire was consorting with a German officer. She felt her cheeks burn at the thought, and was thankful that she was preceding him up the stairs so that he couldn't see her shame. If she was completely honest with herself, during that evening at the Brasserie Lipp, she had felt a little flicker of triumphant scorn for the party she'd glimpsed at the table across the room; now that she realised who he really was, her shame was redoubled. No wonder he'd been so reticent about taking her on in the network. Had it not been for Mireille's persuasiveness, she would surely have been ostracised completely.

On the fifth floor, there was no sign of Mireille, and the door of Fréd's room was closed. In the little kitchen, Claire busied herself preparing the supper, heating the duck legs and peeling the potatoes. She'd refused Monsieur Leroux's offer of help as there was such little space to move for just one person, let alone two. He leant in the doorway and watched as she began to fry the potatoes with a little of the fat from the *confit* jar, adding slivers from a clove of garlic, whose tantalising smell wafted through the apartment as the pan began to splutter and sizzle.

When she glanced up from the stove, he smiled at her. With a flourish, he pulled a bottle of red wine from a deep pocket in his coat which he set on the worktop beside her. Then, from another pocket, he produced three bars of Côte d'Or chocolate which he handed to Claire. 'I'd better give you these, because I know you will share them out fairly,' he said, making her blush.

Summoned by the sounds and smells of her cooking, Vivi, Mireille and Fréd soon appeared and set out plates and cutlery in the sitting room.

Monsieur Leroux joined them round the table, but refused a plate of food, saying he would be eating later. He sipped his glass of wine, though, watching them devour the food which was the best meal they'd had in some time. Fréd raised his glass, declaring the duck legs far tastier than anything he'd eaten in England, and they all toasted the chef. Did

Claire imagine it, or were Monsieur Leroux's eyes on her each time she glanced shyly in his direction?

He let them finish their supper before he got down to the real business of his visit to the Rue Cardinale.

'We have a plan to get you out, Fréd. Not by the south-west, as we usually do, but via another network which works out of Brittany. I have to warn you, it's a more dangerous route, but a faster one to get you back to England.'

Fréd shrugged. 'Suits me,' he said. 'The sooner I get back and can resume the fight against the Boche again the better.' Claire noticed the look of regret in his eyes though when he turned to Mireille, who sat beside him, and took her hand in his, adding, 'Although I will be very sorry to leave my new friends behind, in Paris.'

'We can't risk using the trains,' Monsieur Leroux continued. 'There are too many checks at the stations, especially on the route to Brittany. The Germans have been trying harder than ever to protect their Atlantic defences ever since the Allies blew up the locks at Saint-Nazaire. So it will be a cross-country route. And they don't have many *passeurs* to spare to show you the way, which means navigating for yourself in some places.'

'I'll be okay,' Fréd said stoutly. 'I've never been to Brittany before, but I'm sure I can find my way around.'

'With your southern accent you'll be conspicuous, though, if you're travelling alone. And that is why we've come up with an additional strand to the plan.' Monsieur Leroux turned to face Claire. 'Just suppose you were travelling home to see your family, to introduce them to a young man who wished to ask your father for your hand in marriage . . . You know the Bretons, who can be a tricky bunch at the best of times, and you know your way around. If you can get Frédéric to Port Meilhon, the network can get him out. He'll be back in England in a couple of days, and we have some critical intelligence that we need to get back to the allied command as quickly as possible so you'll be doing us an additional favour, now that the south-west route has been shut down for the time being.'

Claire's blood chilled in her veins at the thought of such a dangerous journey. She had managed to conquer her nerves so far and carry out her assignments in the city, but this mission was in a different league entirely. Then she met his frank gaze and swallowed her fear. 'I can do it. I'm sure Mademoiselle Vannier would give me some leave since I haven't taken any for ages. Besides, ever since my "accident" I still get dizzy sometimes and she's been urging me to try to get a travel pass and go and see my father for a bit of sea air. But I'll need to see if the Germans will give me a permit to travel. And what about Fréd, he'll need one too? I don't know how long it will take to apply for them . . .'

'It's already sorted,' said Monsieur Leroux. 'I have the papers here for you both.' He set down the official-looking documents from the Préfecture de Police, headed '*Ausweis*' and stamped with the two-headed eagle and swastika of the German administration. 'You can leave tomorrow afternoon. Get yourselves to the Pont de Neuilly by four o'clock, where there will be transport to take you as far as Chartres. You'll each have a room there for the night and then they'll take you on to Nantes. It's not exactly the most direct route, but it's the only one we've been able to organise at short notice. From Nantes you're on your own, though. You'll need to use public transport, if you can find any, or ask for a lift. You have to make it to Port Meilhon by Friday night. It's crucial that the boat makes it out on the tide when it's too low for the larger German vessels to patrol close in.'

Claire glanced around the table at the faces that were watching her intently. Mireille's dark eyes were filled with fear; Vivi's clear hazel gaze was as calm as usual, but a flicker of concern betrayed her anxiety. Fréd smiled at her, encouragingly. And then she turned to Monsieur Leroux. His eyes were kind, but an added warmth shone from them that she hadn't noticed before. It was a warmth that made her heart beat faster and brought a flush of colour to her cheeks.

'Okay,' she said, pushing back her chair to cover her confusion. 'I'd better go and pack my bag then.'

As she was folding a couple of things she'd need on the journey, Monsieur Leroux appeared in the door of her bedroom. 'I have one more item for you to take, Claire.' He held out a small, flat package which was wrapped in oilskin, the edges of which had been sewn together tightly. 'It is vital that this goes with Fréd when he leaves, but it will be safer if he doesn't know about it until the last minute. Carry it with you at all times. They'll be less likely to search you than him if you are stopped. Do everything you can to keep it safe, but make sure you give it to Fréd as he leaves the French shore. Do not trust anyone else with it. Do you understand?'

She nodded, and as she took the package from him, he folded his other hand over hers and held it tightly for a moment before letting go. Claire met his gaze and thought she read a question in his eyes, but it was one that she couldn't answer now.

She looked at the package he'd handed her, taking in the neatness of the stitches that sealed it shut. Suddenly some things made sense. She couldn't help asking, 'Is this what Vivi was working on earlier?'

He put a finger to his lips and then laid his hand over hers again, squeezing her fingers, and she took comfort from the touch. He always seemed to have this air of quiet assurance, she told herself, trying to ignore the other things she'd begun to notice about him, like the way he looked at her and the way his chiselled features made her want to spend more time with him than she had. It was just his calmness and confidence that she found so attractive, she thought, as if – whatever came along – he knew he could take it in his stride.

She only wished she felt that same confidence herself.

Harriet

Just when I was starting to feel a bit more admiration for Claire, being brave enough to agree to become a *passeuse* and take the Free French airman on the dangerous journey to escape through Brittany, she seems to be falling in love with another womaniser. I can only hope Monsieur Leroux isn't going to break her heart all over again. He sounds almost as unsuitable as Ernst, this good-looking Lothario. He sounds as if he used women, even if it was for the sake of the underground network that he ran.

I have a horrible feeling that history is going to repeat itself and Claire is never going to learn any lessons from her mistakes.

But then, do any of us, ever?

Some of the rooms in the Palais Galliera are closed today, as they are changing the exhibitions. Jeanne Lanvin's creations – and that Lanvin-blue dress with the silver beads – are being returned to the archives in the basement of the museum where they will be carefully preserved until the next time they are brought out. I sit outside, on one of the benches that circle the building, among the statues that are dotted through the palace grounds, writing down the latest instalment of Claire's story.

My phone buzzes and I smile when I see Thierry's name on the screen. And then I smile even more broadly when he asks if I'd like to meet up for dinner tonight, at a little bistro he knows of that serves the best *moules-frites* in Paris.

1942

They'd been travelling for almost two days now and Claire hadn't been able to relax her guard for a moment, despite everything having gone smoothly so far. They'd got out of Paris safely and spent the night in the hotel in Chartres exactly as planned, travelling on to Nantes the following day. Now on the final leg of the journey, Claire was shocked to see the devastation the war had inflicted on Saint-Nazaire. She remembered the city from her youth as a place filled with hope and promise, the gateway to a new life away from Port Meilhon. But now it resembled a town that had forgotten what hope looked like. Buildings were pitted and pock-marked with machine-gun fire, and the once-proud shipyards were sealed off and deserted. The dry dock, which had been capable of accommodating the German navy's biggest warships, had been blown up in a recent raid by British commandos.

She glimpsed these fragmented scenes as she and Fréd rattled along the pot-holed roads in the back of a van which had been taking a delivery of fish to a food depot on the outskirts of the city. Although empty, the van still smelt strongly of its previous cargo. Again and again, she swallowed the acid bile that rose in her throat as a result of the overpowering smell, combined with the stomach-churning jouncing of the van along the pocked and broken roads. The sight of the bombed-out buildings along the way brought back vivid memories of the night in Billancourt when she'd so narrowly escaped death. An image of

Christiane's face seemed to float against the backdrop of the ruined landscape, and the scent of dust and smoke mingled with the odour of fish oil in her nostrils. She hoped the persistent twitch at the corner of one of her eyes didn't give away how panicked she was beginning to feel.

As if physically holding herself together, she kept her arms folded, letting her fingertips surreptitiously trace the reassuring outline of the package Monsieur Leroux had given her, which she'd sewn into the lining of her coat for safekeeping.

Fréd was a largely silent travelling companion, lost in his own thoughts, although his solid presence was a reassuring one. He'd let her do the talking when they'd come upon the fish van that morning. When Claire had mentioned her father's name, the driver's weather-beaten face had creased into a grin of recognition and he'd readily agreed to give them a lift all the way to Port Meilhon, even though it would take him a little way past his own home in Concarneau.

At last he dropped them off, with another grin and a wave, at the top of the narrow, cobbled lane that led down to the tiny harbour. Claire stood for a moment, thankful to be still again after the hours of lurching in the back of the van. She took deep breaths of the sea air, relieved that the horrible feeling of nausea was passing. It was reassuring to be in familiar surroundings. The fishing village smelt as it always had done, of salt and seaweed and the damp lengths of rope which tethered the little fleet of boats to their moorings along the quayside. Seabirds shrieked at one another overhead, keeping a beady eye out for easy pickings whenever a boat came in.

Claire had never thought she'd be so glad to be home, but now she felt an overwhelming longing to see her father and her brother Marc, and to be enveloped in their strong arms again.

Fréd smiled at her. 'Nearly there now,' he said as he picked up her bag and his own. 'Lead the way.'

She spotted them down by the boat, her father's tall figure lifting empty creels from the stack on the quayside and passing them down to

Marc on the deck. She was about to run to them when Fréd put out a hand to stop her. 'Wait,' he said quietly.

Out towards the end of the harbour wall, a crude concrete block-house had been built and a German sentry stood on top of its flat roof. Fortunately, his back was to them as he scanned the iron-grey sea for ships through a pair of binoculars. From the dark slits that were the eyes of the blockhouse, protruded the barrels of two machine guns. One pointed seawards, but the other was trained on the little harbour and on the men who worked on their boats there. Beyond the blockhouse, just before the little lighthouse at the end of the seawall that marked the entrance to the harbour for the fishing fleet as they returned home on dark nights, an anti-aircraft gun pointed to the sky, taunted by the jeering seabirds that wheeled above it.

The sight of her father and brother working beneath the threaten-ing presence of the machine gun, which was trained upon them from the blockhouse, shocked Claire to the core. A gasp escaped her as Fréd pulled her back around the corner into the shelter of the lane. He put a finger to his lips, cautioning her to keep quiet.

'We can't go to them now, Claire, not with that German sentry on duty. We'd only draw attention to ourselves and that's the last thing we want to do. Even with your excuse of coming home to see your family, they'll be on the lookout for any new arrivals, for anything out of the ordinary. We'll have to hide until darkness falls.'

Claire nodded, realising that he was right, even though the urge to run to her father and put herself between him and the sights of that gun turret was strong. She glanced around, then seized his hand. 'Come on,' she said. 'We can get into the alleyway behind the house. The back door is never locked. We'll be able to wait for them inside.' She led him to a tiny gap in the wall on one side of the lane which opened on to a narrow, sandy path running between the back-to-back gardens of the fishermen's cottages, each with its own outhouse. She pushed open the gate in a peeling picket fence and picked her way past the little patch of vegetables – neat rows of plaited leek leaves and feathery carrot tops – that had been cultivated in the sandy soil of the garden. She turned the handle of the back door and, with a smile of triumph at Fréd, pushed her way inside.

Her heart thumped at the sight of her family home. The rooms seemed smaller, somehow, and yet they were filled with artefacts that reminded her of her mother – the yellowing lace cloth on the sideboard where a few pieces of china were displayed, painted with a bright Breton design of leaves and flowers – and of her father, too. His chair by the fireplace sagged with the weight of his tired body, returned from the sea. She picked up an unravelling ball of twine which sat on the shelf alongside the chair and absent-mindedly rewound it, tucking the end in neatly and replacing it next to his seat.

In the kitchen, the stove had been damped down for the day while the men were out on the boat. Taking comfort from the feeling of being home again after so long, and from the familiarity of actions which had been a part of her daily life from as far back as she could recall, she riddled the embers and coaxed the fire back into life, then set a pan of water on the top to heat. 'We could probably both do with a wash after that journey.' She smiled. 'And then we'll see what there is for supper. Papa and Marc will be hungry when they get in. I doubt they'll be long.'

Even though dusk was falling now, Claire didn't light a lamp, nor did she draw the blackout curtains across the low, salt-scoured windows. The wind from the sea made the boats in the harbour jostle and nudge one another with the promise of a fresh breeze at dawn, when they would head out beyond the harbour walls once again to plough their way through the waves.

At last she heard them coming up the path and then stamping their boots on the rough seagrass matting at the front door to remove the sand. She waited for the door to open and then close behind them, making sure they were safely inside and hidden from view before going to meet them. In the darkening cottage, it took a few moments for her father to register that the figure standing before him in the hallway was Claire. Without a word, she held out her arms to him. And then he stepped up to her and buried his face in her hair as he wept.

She hugged him tightly, pressing her face into his chest, overwhelmed by the simultaneous strength and the fragility of this man – her father – who had lost his wife and one of his sons and had seen the remainder of his family torn apart by the war. Beneath the rough wool of his fisherman's sweater, she felt his body heave with silent sobs, and her tears mingled with his as she kissed his cheek.

While their supper simmered on the stove, Claire asked for news of Jean-Paul and Théo. But her father just shook his head sorrowfully. 'There's been no word for months now. We just have to hope that they are together and that they are keeping their spirits up. They'd be proud to know that their little sister is playing her part in getting this war finished so that they can come home to us.' Despite the warmth of his words, offering hope, it seemed to Claire that a darkness shadowed his eyes, betraying his anxiety.

Later, over hearty bowls of fish stew, Marc, Claire and Fréd talked about the war and about their experiences, while Claire's father, who had always been a man of few words, watched his daughter's face with an expression of bewildered wonder at having her back in the family home so unexpectedly.

Marc checked his watch. 'It's time for the broadcast, Papa.' He got up from the table and crossed to where a wireless set sat in the corner of the room. It took a few seconds to warm up, but then the crackle of static cleared and the sound of a German propaganda station filled the cramped room. Very carefully, Marc adjusted the dials, turning down the volume and retuning the set. There was a snatch of dance music and then it stopped. After a brief silence a voice said, '*Ici Londres! Les Français parlent aux Français . . .*'

And then the distinctive opening bars of Beethoven's Fifth Symphony played: three short notes followed by one more, stronger and more sustained. Claire looked at Marc in surprise. He held a finger to his lips.

Fréd leaned close to her, to explain. 'It's the letter "V" in Morse code. "V" for Victory,' he whispered. 'The Free French transmit these messages every evening from the BBC in London. They always open with these notes, encouraging Europe to resist. And then they let the networks know whether or not certain operations are to go ahead. It drives the Germans crazy – they know these messages are being transmitted but they can't decode them because they sound like complete nonsense! And some of them are dummies to camouflage the real ones. Listen out for a message about "*Tante Jeanne*". That's the one for us, Monsieur Leroux said. If we hear it, we know everything is in place for tomorrow night.'

She held her breath, as the broadcaster announced, 'Before we begin, please listen to some personal messages . . .' There followed what sounded to her like a jumbled collection of meaningless phrases.

And then she heard it. '*Tante Jeanne* has won the dance contest.'

Fréd grinned broadly and Marc got up to switch off the radio set, carefully retuning the dial to the German station and turning the volume back up before he did so.

She stood up from the table to clear the dishes, but as she did her father reached out his hand to take hers. 'You've changed, Claire. Your mother would have been so proud of you. For everything. For your work in Paris and the work that has brought you here as well.'

Stooping to kiss the top of his head, she said, 'We've all changed, Papa. I know now that no one can escape the stranglehold of this war on our country. But I've come to realise that we might be able to endure it if we stand together. Mireille and Vivi have shown me that.'

'I'm glad to know you have such good friends in Paris.'

'And I'm glad I have such a good family in Brittany. I'm proud of my roots, Papa, and of the home you have always made for us here in spite of all the hardships. I don't think I realised before just how much a part of me that is. You and Maman gave me the security and the love that helped me to be brave enough to leave, and to be brave enough to return now too.'

Her father smiled, then said gruffly, 'It's time to turn in now. You must be tired after your long journey. Marc and I have an early start tomorrow to get the boat out before sandbanks in the channel become impassable on the low tide. That means we'll be back early too, though.'

'I'll be up before you leave,' she promised. 'I want to make your coffee for you just like I used to.'

Marc stood up too, stretching his lanky frame. 'Yes, time for bed. And then tomorrow evening we will get Fréd here to the cove for you.'

She gave him a questioning look, raising her eyebrows, and he laughed. 'You're not the only member of the family who moonlights, you know, Claire!'

※

The new moon, whose pull had drawn back the ocean to expose the harbour's muddy floor, was swathed in the shadows of the night when the four figures slipped silently up the hill from the house. They kept to the maze of back lanes between the clustered cottages, out of sight of the sentries in the pill-box on the harbour wall who, they hoped, would have given up scanning the dark expanse of the sea, knowing that the tide was now too low for enemy warships or submarines to get close to the Breton coast.

Claire's father held out a helping hand as she scrambled up the side of the rocky promontory, through the scrubby pines that lent an extra layer of cover to the darkness. Marc tried to make her stay behind in the cottage, but she was adamant that she needed to come too, mindful that she had to carry out Monsieur Leroux's instructions to the letter. The oilskin package crackled in her pocket.

Her scalp prickled with a mixture of sweat and fear beneath the dark woollen cap that she wore to hide her hair. She was conscious that they were at their most exposed here, climbing the slope which faced the harbour, and at every moment she expected a searchlight to sweep the hillside or a harsh voice to shout, 'Halt!' followed by the rattle of machine-gun fire cutting them down in their tracks. But they climbed on steadily and there was nothing but silence and darkness and the soft night breeze which smelt of the sea and cooled the nape of her neck.

Marc led the way, moving carefully but with a stealth and speed born of familiarity with the terrain. His feet scarcely dislodged the pebbles on the sandy path that was etched into the heathland at the top of the ridge.

And then they began the steep descent into the tiny, concealed cove on the other side of the headland. The bare rock of the cliff face was almost vertical, but Marc pointed silently to hidden handholds and footholds – barely visible in the starlight – that had been chiselled into it here and there, allowing them to make their way down.

The sea had eaten away at the base of the cliffs towards one end of the cove, hollowing out a cave. Usually it could only be reached by wading or swimming through the waves that lapped along the shoreline, but tonight the low water scarcely covered the uppers of their boots.

In the pitch blackness of the cave, all was silent apart from the soft sound of the water lapping against the stone walls. The darkness and the shifting of the sea around her feet almost overwhelmed Claire for a moment, her head spinning with a wave of dizziness, and she might have fallen were it not for her father's steadying hand beneath her elbow. She jumped, involuntarily, as a match flared, illuminating the faces of two more men, who stood in the darkness alongside a small wooden sailing dinghy, its furled sails the same colour as the ink-black sea. One of the men bent to hold the match to the wick of an oil lamp that had been set down on a rough shelf cut into the wall of the cave, casting a soft glow over the scene.

The boatmen shook hands all round and if they were surprised to see a young woman in the party, they didn't show it. Claire had no idea how the lines of communication worked within these secret networks, although she supposed messages were passed by notes slipped from hand to hand, as well as by hidden wireless transmitters and the coded messages that were broadcast over the airwaves from the BBC in London. So perhaps they had been expecting her to be there, accompanying Fréd, and he was just the latest cargo to be transported. They clearly seemed to know Marc and her father well, and Claire's heart swelled with emotion as she realised that they, too, had been playing their part in the Resistance.

As the men prepared to board the boat for departure, Claire drew Fréd aside into the shadows. 'Here,' she said quietly, 'you're to take this and deliver it to the man who will meet you on the other side.' She handed him the slim parcel which had been so well wrapped to protect its contents from the lengthy sea journey around the point of Finistère and across the Channel to England.

'Okay.' He nodded. 'I'll see it gets there. Thank you, Claire, for everything. I could never have found my way here without the help of you and your family.' He embraced her warmly and then tucked the package she'd given him into his shirt.

'*Bonne route*,' she said. He turned to leave, but then looked back at her as if he were about to say something more. They were both silent for a moment. And then she said, 'And I'll give your love to Mireille, shall I?'

He grinned as he climbed aboard the dinghy, saying, 'So you're a mind reader too, are you, as well as a fellow commando?' And he saluted her before taking his seat, as she handed over the lantern which the boatman extinguished. Then Marc and her father pushed the little sailing boat out on to the open water and it was swallowed up by the darkness.

She listened to the sound of the oars until it, too, was extinguished by the hush of the waves which washed on to the sand in the tiny, hidden cove.

Harriet

With each part of Claire's story that is revealed, I feel as if the foundations of my life are shifting like wave-sculpted sand beneath my feet.

Before I came to Paris, I had created a framework for my life which was built on the few remnants of family that were all that remained after my mother's death had swept so much away. I'd boarded up rooms within my mind where painful memories were stored, and shored up the walls with my own loneliness. But now I can see how much I shut out, while I was constructing that carapace. The stories of Mireille and Vivi have encouraged me to unlock some of those doors and take down the blackout on the windows of my own history, allowing me to discover more of Claire's story.

So now I know that a strand of the fragile threads from which my grandmother's life was woven connects me to Brittany, to a tiny fishing community clinging to the rocky, Atlantic-battered finger of land that points west. That wind scoured sliver of land produced men who were tough enough to take on the ocean and win, and women who were resilient enough to raise their families against unforgiving odds.

When I relay this chapter of Claire's story to Thierry, over a shared pan of *moules marinière* in a bistro in the Marais that evening, he laughs.

'Well that explains a lot about you,' he says, depositing an empty shell in the bowl that sits between us.

'What do you mean?' I ask, immediately on the defensive.

He reaches over and helps himself to a few more of the matchstick chips that accompany the mussels. 'Brittany is one of the most fiercely independent regions of France, and the Breton people have a reputation for stubbornness and determination.' He uses the chips for emphasis, pointing them at me before popping them into his mouth. 'And you are one of the most fiercely independent women I have ever met. It's obvious that Breton blood runs in your veins. Alongside your British *sangfroid*, of course. What a combination! Now I understand how you had the confidence to come to Paris, fresh out of university, and talk your way in to one of the most sought-after positions in one of the most competitive industries.'

I digest this for a moment, along with another handful of chips from the basket. Is that how people see me? Independent? Confident? It's the last thing I've ever felt. But maybe Thierry is right, maybe it has been there all along, a seam of Breton granite that underpins my temperament.

Claire had it too. Although she had wanted to leave her simple family home for the bright lights of Paris, her Breton roots ran deep enough to anchor her when the storms of war raged.

Now I know that she could be brave. And with that knowledge, instead of envying the courage of outsiders and feeling weak in comparison, I can begin to feel the strength of my own family running in my veins.

Shame has been replaced by self-respect, dishonour by dignity. It's words that have made this change, the words that tell my grandmother's story. And I want to know more.

On an impulse – and impulsiveness is another aspect of my character which has lain buried beneath layers of fear, anxiety and protective caution until now – I lean forwards and say to Thierry, 'How would you like to come with me on a road trip? Maybe next weekend, if you're free?'

He smiles a slow smile and I notice how it lights up his face, like a sunrise. 'To Brittany?' he asks. 'You and me together?'

I reach across, take his hand in mine, and I say, 'You and me. Together.'

❧

We check into a bed and breakfast in Concarneau, a pretty fishing port not far from Port Meilhon. The journey from Paris has taken hours so we dump our bags and hurry out to look for somewhere where we can get a late supper. The town has a distinct out-of-season air to it and several of the restaurants are closed, but the lights of a bistro on the quayside beckon us in. We find a table and order bowls of *cotriade*, the delicious local fish stew served on slices of toasted bread, and a bottle of local white wine.

Afterwards, thankfully stretching our legs after the long drive, we wander beside the marina which is full of yachts moored up for the winter, tucked safely into the elbow of the harbour's arm where they'll be protected from the fury of the Atlantic's winter storms. The boats' rigging clinks against masts stirred by the ocean's soft night-time breath.

We cross the causeway to the little island that sits within the bay and meander through the narrow streets of the Ville Close, Concarneau's medieval walled town. Hand in hand, we walk past the clock tower and out on to the harbour walls. From a cobbled jetty, we pause alongside the rusted hulk of an immense ship's anchor and look back towards the shore. The lights of the town are reflected in the dark water, sequins dancing across a bolt of black satin.

Thierry wraps me in his arms and I feel that I have found a harbour of my own, a place where there is shelter from the storms of life. I feel at peace. And the only sounds are the quiet lapping of the water against the sea wall and the beating of our two hearts as we lose ourselves in a kiss that I wish would never end.

❧

The next day, we drive in contented silence a few miles further west along the coast. The hamlet of Port Meilhon is tucked away in a forgotten corner of the craggy Finistère peninsula. It looks as if it hasn't changed much since the days when Claire's father and brothers – my great-grandfather and great-uncles – worked the waters in their Breton fishing boat. The pill-box on the harbour wall has been removed and only a few roughened remnants of concrete show that it was ever here at all. But as we stand looking back towards the row of fisherman's cottages that line the tiny harbour, I can picture in my mind's eye the guns trained on the men as they stacked their creels on the quayside.

I haven't been able to find any record of exactly which cottage belonged to Claire's family, but I imagine it to be one of the middle ones. There are no wisps of smoke rising from any of the chimneys these days, though. Most of the cottages appear to be holiday homes, their shutters securely fastened for the winter.

Hand in hand, Thierry and I climb the hill to where we've left the car. As we pass the little grey stone church that watches over the harbour, I hesitate.

'Come on,' he says. 'Let's go in.'

The thick oak boards of the salt-scoured door are silvered with age and the ironwork is rusted, but with a little encouragement the handle turns and we step inside. The interior is simple, with whitewashed walls and wooden pews, but the chapel has an air of serenity, symbolising the quiet dignity of the generations of fishermen's families who have come here to give thanks for the safe return of boats from the sea, or to grieve for those lost to the ocean's cruel force.

Outside, a tiny graveyard has been created on a terrace scratched into the hillside behind rough granite walls. And it is here that I find the stones that bear the names of my family. Thierry spots them first. 'Harriet,' he says quietly. 'Come and see this.'

First there is Aimée Meynardier, née Carlou, beloved wife and mother, and beneath her name is carved that of her husband, Corentin:

my great-grandparents. Claire's father died in 1947, it says, so he survived the war. But then I read the names on the stone that stands alongside theirs and my heart breaks. 'To the memory of Luc Meynardier (1916-1940) killed fighting for his country, beloved son and brother; to the memories of Théo Meynardier (1918-1942) and Jean-Paul Meynardier (1919-1942), killed at Dachau, Germany'; and beneath these three names has been added another – that of Marc Meynardier, Claire's fourth brother, lost at sea in 1945.

So my great-grandfather buried all four of his sons. Or rather, he didn't bury any of them. None of their bodies were ever brought home to rest alongside their parents. They lie in unmarked graves, or as ashes scattered in a German forest, or as bones picked bare on the ocean floor, and only this stone records their names.

And who was it that buried my great-grandfather, Corentin? Did Claire stand here, with her English husband beside her, and weep for the entire family that she had lost?

As I lick my lips, I taste salt and I can't tell whether it's from the Atlantic wind that blusters through the gravestones or from the tears that run down my face.

Thierry gathers me into his arms and kisses them away. He holds me close, sheltering me, and his eyes search for mine. 'Those were terrible times,' he whispers. 'But they are over now. And you are here, to visit your family and to honour their memory. How proud they would be, Harriet, if they knew you had come to find them. How proud they would be to know you. And to know that, through you, they live on.'

1942

The summer heat was oppressive. The sun blazed through the tall windows, turning the sewing room into an oven. The curtains couldn't be pulled to shut out the glare as the seamstresses needed the light to sew by. The smell of scorched starch and the steam from the ironing tables made the air even hotter and heavier, until sometimes Mireille felt she could scarcely breathe. She longed to sit beneath the willow tree on the riverbank back home, cooled by the dappled shade cast by the graceful arch of its branches overhead as she listened to the hushed song of the river.

The brutality of the war seemed to grow day by day. There was no word of what had become of Monsieur and Madame Arnaud and, when she'd gone back to look one day, their house had been locked and deserted.

Christiane's body had been recovered from the rubble of the factory workers' housing at Billancourt. Claire, Mireille and Vivi had been to visit her grave in a cemetery to the south of the city. Vivienne and Claire had wept as they placed the sprigs of lily of the valley, that they'd picked from the front garden of a boarded-up house, at the foot of the simple headstone that marked where Christiane lay. But Mireille had stood, dry-eyed, her heart frozen with too much sadness and too much pain and too much loss. The last time she'd stood beside a grave, it had been to bury Esther in a hastily dug, shallow plot alongside so many of the other refugees who'd been mown down on the road that day as they'd fled Paris.

She tried to stem the flow of her thoughts and focus on her work, but even with the windows pushed open as wide as they would go, she had to pause frequently to wipe her hands and brow so that the drops of sweat didn't stain her work. Silk was the worst for showing water marks, but the new artificial fabrics that they often worked with these days, now that silk was so scarce, were almost as bad.

As the afternoon wore on, Mireille felt the heat wrap itself around her like a heavy cloak that she couldn't shrug off. She glanced around. Many of the other girls seated at the table looked as if they were struggling to stay awake, exhausted by hunger and hard work and the ever-present fear of the enemy's iron grip on the city in which they lived. A weariness had crept into Mireille's bones, sapping her body and her mind of their characteristic energy. This was another reality of the war, she realised – the quietly toxic corrosion of the spirit. The garments that the girls worked on in the *atelier* seemed grotesque, suddenly, rather than the beautiful creations that she had taken such a pride in before. Circumstance had transformed them into tastelessly ostentatious declarations of wealth in this time of hardship and deprivation. The women who visited the salon these days were the frumpy 'grey mice' or the hard-faced wives and mistresses of Nazi officials, or the greedy, self-obsessed 'queens of the black market', as the models called them behind their backs. All of them sought to cover the ugliness of reality with a fine gown or an elegant coat. When had it happened, wondered Mireille as she let out the waistband of a satin evening skirt, the tipping point when French fashion had changed from being perceived as something the country could take pride in to something grotesque and vulgar, tainted with shame?

At last, Mademoiselle Vannier told the seamstresses to begin clearing away, signalling the end of another working day. The thought of sitting upstairs in the cramped apartment, which would be even stuffier than the sewing room up there under the roof of dark slates which had been baked by the sun all day, did nothing to lift Mireille's spirits. So instead, she headed out into the streets and made for the river. With no real sense of where she was going, she crossed the Pont Neuf on to the Île de la Cité in the middle of the stream, turning away from the busy hub around Notre-Dame and made her way towards the downstream end of the island. And then she realised what it was that had drawn her here. Unseen by the stream of homeward-bound workers and the truckloads of soldiers that sped past, intent on other prey, she slipped into the narrow stone stairway which led down to a small patch of trees and grass below. Apart from a boatman who was busy making fast his boat for the night, that end of the island was deserted. As if beckoned by the graceful arms of its branches, Mireille walked to the very end point where a willow tree trailed its green fingers in the waters of the Seine. She'd noticed it there, from afar, as part of the scenery along the river, but only now did she seek refuge beneath it. Some instinct drew her to it, an instinct which the weight of her despair couldn't crush.

Just as she would have done if she'd been at home with her family, Mireille settled herself under the canopy of willow leaves, leaning her back against the trunk. She kicked off her shoes and rested her weary head against the rough bark, letting the tree's bulk take her sadness and cast it out on to the ever-flowing river. She wished her family were there with her: her parents would reassure her and lend her some of their quiet strength; her brother, Yves, would make her laugh and help her forget her cares for a while; and her sister, Eliane, would listen and nod and understand so that Mireille wouldn't feel all alone in the world. Blanche – Esther's baby – would gurgle and busy herself making mud-pies in the earth that sustained the tree, and she would chuckle as she was hugged and loved by the family that had taken her in. Mireille's longing for them tugged at her heart, as powerful and as constant as the current of the river.

And she longed for someone else, too. The young man she'd known for just a few brief days, whom Claire and Vivi knew as 'Fréd', who had held her and kissed her, in the fleeting, precious moments she'd spent alone with him before he'd left on his dangerous journey back to England. And then he had whispered his real name in her ear so that she'd know who this man truly was: this man who loved her.

She sat beneath the sheltering arms of the willow tree as dusk fell, bringing with it a faint breeze from the river. She lifted the weight of her hair away from her neck and allowed the evening air to cool it. The images of the faces she held most dear, coupled with the reassuring solidity of the tree's trunk at her back, reminded her that there were some things that the war couldn't ever destroy.

What she had felt that afternoon in the *atelier* was what the occupying forces wanted her to feel: defeat. If she gave in to it then she would have lost and they would have won. But now she knew she could always come back here, to this place which was the nearest thing to her true home that she could find in the city, amongst the hard-paved streets and the tall buildings that shut out the sky. She could come here and be with those she loved, joined to them by the ribbons of water that met, at last, in the ocean beyond. And those vital lines of connection would give her back her sense of what really mattered. They would make her feel part of a larger whole. And she knew that they would keep her from being defeated.

⁂

Claire had been delivering a message to a tobacconist's shop just off the Place Chopin and was walking home, swinging her attaché case which felt a good deal lighter now that it merely contained the sheets of music for her 'singing lesson' which had camouflaged a sealed brown envelope. Not that the envelope had weighed anything at all, really, but she always felt a load slip from her shoulders once a delivery had been successfully completed, allowing her to return home buoyed up by a sense of relief.

It was pleasant to be out, after the oppressive heat of the day. The evening was still warm and she couldn't bear the thought of a hot, stuffy Métro ride, no doubt preceded by a long wait on a dirty platform, so she decided to cross the Pont d'Iéna, facing the imposing bulk of the Eiffel Tower, and walk back along the river. As dusk fell, it promised a faint hint of coolness and she looked forward to feeling the gentle river breeze on her hot cheeks.

As she walked along, she was surprised by the stream of buses and police trucks that overtook her. One of the buses stopped at a junction before turning on to the bridge, and as it did so she caught a glimpse of frightened-looking faces behind the windows. A child turned to look at her from the rear window as the bus drove on and his eyes were large and dark in the paleness of his face.

She came to a place where queuing vehicles formed a wall outside the winter velodrome. A road-block had been set up to prevent people from walking or cycling past. Soldiers stood at the barrier, checking the papers of passers-by and Claire felt a pang of fear grip her guts. But she knew that if she were to turn and walk away she would draw attention to herself. She had nothing to hide, she reminded herself; her papers were in order and she had a valid-sounding excuse for being out. So she resisted the impulse to run and stood in the short line at the barrier, waiting her turn. The wall of buses and trucks crept forwards in stops and starts, directed by French policemen. She couldn't see what was happening on the other side, but it seemed as if they were disgorging their passengers at the entrance of the cycling arena before driving off again.

The soldiers who were checking papers waved the couple in front of her through, but as they attempted to make their way towards the velo-drome, an officer, wearing the black uniform of the Gestapo, stepped out between the buses and shouted at them to go around the other way. As he strode over to berate the soldiers at the road block, Claire realised who he was. The uniform was new, but she recognised his blonde hair and broad shoulders. She glanced around, wondering if she could walk away unnoticed while he was giving the soldiers a dressing down, but it was too late – he'd recognised her too. She felt his eyes upon her and when she turned to face him, a look of amusement played about the thin line of his lips.

'Good evening, Ernst,' she said calmly, as she held out her papers for the sentries to check, trying to stop her hand from shaking as she did so.

'Claire!' he exclaimed. 'What an unexpected pleasure seeing you here.' He turned to the pair of soldiers and barked some commands at them in German, then drew Claire to one side. He reached out his hand, attempting to take hers, but she merely gave him her identity card, pretending not to have understood the gesture.

He glanced at the piece of paper in his hand which bore her pho-tograph, then back at her. 'It's been a while,' he said. The smile slowly faded from his face as she refused to smile back at him. 'You didn't reply to my invitations to meet for dinner, after we'd bumped into each other so unexpectedly at the museum that day.'

'No,' she replied evenly. 'After seeing you with your wife and your son, they weren't invitations I felt like accepting.'

He frowned, irritated now. 'But Claire, surely you knew what your position was? What did you expect? We had fun, you and I. You cer-tainly didn't object to the nice things I gave you – the stockings and the perfume. And you didn't seem to mind drinking champagne and having fine dinners bought for you at the best restaurants in Paris.' His eyes were cold and hard, and glinted like steel.

She met his gaze steadily. 'If I'd known you were married, I never would have accepted those things from you.'

She held out her hand for her identity document, attempting to bring the encounter to an end and be on her way, but he held it just out of her reach and smiled again, relishing his power.

'Not so fast, mademoiselle, I think I need to ask you a few questions. What brings you to this part of the city tonight?'

She held up her attaché case. 'A music lesson. I have singing classes sometimes.'

'Permit me,' he said, with exaggerated politeness, taking the leather case from her and opening it. 'Ah, you have hidden talents I see,' he observed, fanning out the sheet music. 'Hidden from me, anyway. You never mentioned that you sang, on all those evenings we spent together.'

She continued to meet his gaze levelly. 'No, it's something I've only recently taken up. I have more time to spare in the evenings these days.'

He shoved the sheets of paper back into the case and handed it back to her. Then he held out her identity card but, just as she reached to take it, he whisked it away again, amusing himself as a cat does with a mouse, she thought.

'So who are you keeping company with now then? Apart from your singing teacher who lives all the way across town from the Rue Cardinale?'

She was silent, but continued to hold out her hand for her ID document.

'Those two other seamstresses, I suppose.' He grinned. 'The ones who were with you in the museum that day? I never did think they were a very good influence on you, you know, Claire. Perhaps you should be a little more discerning in the company you keep.' His piercing blue eyes swept over her, and seemed to linger on the scuffed attaché case.

She tried to force herself to stay calm, keeping her voice level. 'I could say the same to you, Ernst.' She gave him a cool, appraising look that took in his black uniform from the silver braid on his cap to the polished toecaps of his boots. 'I suppose all this is something to do with your new role, is it?' She gestured towards the buses.

He laughed. 'No, not at all. We leave such everyday duties as rubbish disposal to the French. I have far more important people to track down.'

Her gorge rose as she realised what he was saying, and she fought to swallow her nausea. As her anger surged, overflowing, she blurted out, 'You are despicable.' She was shaking all over with rage and fear, but stood her ground, waiting for him to give her back her papers.

Just then a commotion broke out at the road block as the soldiers tried to detain a man. Ernst glanced over his shoulder towards the source of the shouting. A flicker of annoyance passed across his features as his work got in the way of the game he'd been enjoying playing with Claire. 'Go on then, take it.' He thrust her identity card at her. 'I have more important things to do than waste any more of my time on you. But you can't come through here. You'll have to go the long way round. I'm afraid the privileges you once enjoyed are no longer available to you these days, Mademoiselle Claire.' And he dismissed her with a flick of his hand before drawing the revolver from the leather holster slung from his belt and turning his back on her.

She walked away quickly, her whole body still shaking, and she replayed his words in her head as she hurried homewards. What had he meant by the things he'd said about Mireille and Vivi? Was he just testing to see how she'd react? She shouldn't have let him goad her until her anger got the better of her. And what did he mean about having more important people to track down? She told herself it was simply malice – his love of the powerful position he now held, coupled with his annoyance at being rejected by her, but something in the way he'd said those words made her skin prickle with fear. And what were those buses full of frightened-looking people doing there? There were so many of them, being herded into the sports centre. Where would they sleep? How long would they be held there? And for what purpose?

Back in the apartment, she lay awake long into the hot night, gazing unseeing into the blackness, haunted by Ernst's words and by the dark, scared eyes of the child who had looked out at her through the windows of that bus as it drove onwards towards its darkly sinister destination.

Harriet

When the pressure of work at Agence Guillemet builds to a level where tempers fray and exhaustion kicks in, I take refuge once again in the Palais Galliera. Sitting among the exhibits grounds me and always gives me that sense of reconnection with the roots of fashion, reminding me that these are more than just clothes: they are tangible relics of our history.

I wander through the main gallery, where an exhibition of 1970s fashions brightens the space with their vivid colours and flowing, hippy-ish lines.

I allow my thoughts to settle as I sort through the latest strands of family history that Simone has shared with me – both hers and mine. I've been reading up, too, about what was happening in Paris at the time. I realise that Claire witnessed the horrific Vélodrome d'Hiver roundup, when more than thirteen thousand Jews were arrested by the French police, as part of a Nazi-directed programme. They were held in unbearable conditions in the very heart of the city before being sent to the death camps. Of those thirteen thousand people, four thousand were children. And one of them was the little boy whose eyes, looking out of the bus window, haunted Claire's dreams. How terrifying it is to think that, little by little, day by day, this vast city could have become so paralysed by fear and oppression that its people could have allowed that to happen.

My train of thought is interrupted by a woman in an elegantly cut black jacket who has walked into the gallery. Her silver-grey hair is cut into a bob and she looks vaguely familiar. Then I realise she's the woman I saw here before, at the Lanvin exhibition. She stops to read the description of a psychedelic jumpsuit with widely flared sleeves, taking out a small notebook to jot down a few notes. Then she gives me a nod of recognition and a smile and continues on her way.

I check my watch. It's time to get back to the office. We're planning a product launch for the agency's eco-cosmetic client and it's going to be held on the Côte d'Azur in the summer. There are logistics to plan, models' contracts to arrange as well as their hotels and transport, press releases to write and a particularly demanding photographer's emails to reply to. Stress levels among the account managers are at an all-time high. Even Florence, who gives the impression of always being cool, calm and collected, has been seen to hurry through the office. The South of France launch is scheduled for the second week of July, immediately following the Haute Couture Autumn/Winter Shows which are always held in Paris then. Simone has told me that, with staff stretched so thin, there might be a bigger role for the two of us in one or other of these events.

And while the Haute Couture shows would be nice, we're keeping our fingers crossed for Nice!

1943

It was another bitterly cold winter. On the increasingly infrequent days when there was coal for the boiler, the seamstresses huddled over the cast-iron radiators during their breaks, attempting to warm cracked, frost-nipped fingers that were reddened and stung with angry chilblains. Mireille wore a pair of fingerless gloves that her mother had sent, knitted from an old jersey of her brother's. She'd sent pairs for Claire and Vivi too at Christmas time. Once again, the girls wore as many layers of clothing as they could fit under their white coats, padding their gaunt, bony bodies just as the snow padded the angular rooflines and gables of the buildings in the streets around the Rue Cardinale.

Whenever they could afford it, the three friends would go and sit in one of the cafés on the Boulevard Saint-Germain in the evenings after work, where it was warmer than in the apartment above Delavigne Couture. They'd order a bowl of watery cabbage broth, crumbling pieces of hard bread into it, and try to make their supper last as long as possible so that they could delay the moment when they'd have to go home and climb between bedsheets that felt damp with cold. From a corner in one of the cafés, Radio Paris declaimed reports of the latest German victories. Back in the safety of the apartment, Vivi whispered that many of these were lies. The radio station was German-controlled. In reality, their armies were suffering more defeats than successes these days, stretched across many fronts. Mireille took heart from that, and didn't ask Vivi how she knew these things. But, at the same time, she was aware that the three seamstresses were taking greater risks than ever in their Resistance work. A new French police force had been set up, known as the Milice, and they were intent on capturing as many members of the Resistance as possible. It had been announced that there would be a twenty-thousand-franc reward for denouncing a Résistant, a strongly tempting incentive for citizens who were starving and one that was already proving horribly effective.

It had taken a while to re-establish the lines of communication through the network after the losses of last year. Everything seemed a lot less stable these days. Safe houses were changed frequently and Mireille was instructed to use different routes for each 'delivery' she did, to try and avoid the possibility of detection by the Milice and the Gestapo.

She shivered as she stood beneath the clock at the Gare de l'Est, watching its hands tick slowly round to the half hour. The train she'd been instructed to meet was overdue, but there was nothing unusual in that. Timetables were less and less reliable and often trains were cancelled completely if the rolling stock or the line was needed by the German forces for other purposes. It was another bitterly cold day and her winter coat provided little protection against the easterly wind that cut through the worn fabric. She looked up as a train pulled in at one of the platforms, but it appeared to be an empty freight service as no passengers got off.

Then a shouted command made her jump. 'Out of the way! Stand aside!' She pressed herself against the brick column that supported the clock as two soldiers waved their rifles to clear a way through. Behind them, escorted by more armed soldiers, a line of female prisoners were marched across the station concourse and over to the platform where the empty train waited.

Some of the women were smartly dressed, others were dirty and dishevelled; some of them wept, while other faces were blank with shock. But Mireille could smell the fear on all of them as they passed close to where she stood – a mixture of sweat and urine and breath that was stale with dread.

One woman reached out to Mireille and thrust a folded scrap of paper into her hand as she was hurried past. 'Please, madame,' she begged, 'get this message to my husband.'

A soldier gave her a shove with the butt of his rifle. 'Back in line!' he screamed at her. Then he pushed Mireille with the flat of his hand so that she had to take a step backwards, and snarled at her, 'And you – stay out of the way. Unless you want to join them.'

The women were loaded into the freight cars while the soldiers patrolled the platform, sliding the heavy doors shut when the carriages were full. With horror, Mireille noticed that the sides of the trucks were formed from wooden planks with gaps between them. What would become of those women as the train rolled eastwards into the wind which would slice through those gaps like a cold steel blade?

She glanced at the piece of paper in her hand. It was a folded note, with an address printed on the outside. She pushed it into her coat pocket as the train she'd been waiting for pulled up at another platform. The note would have to wait: she had work to do.

Later that day, once she'd delivered the man she'd met from the train to a safe house in the sixteenth *arrondissement*, she picked up her bike where she'd left it near the station and took a detour on her way home to deliver the note to the address which had been scribbled on the folded paper. She knocked on the door, but there was no reply. The house appeared to be deserted, the door locked.

She hesitated for a moment, leaning her bike against the wall, then unfolded the note in case there was any other clue in it as to who it was intended for. Her eye scanned the hastily written scrawl.

My dearest, they have taken me. I don't know where I'm going, but I will come back to you as soon as I can. Look after our girls. I pray for their safety and yours. Kiss them from their maman who loves them – and you – forever. Nadine.

She looked around, unsure what to do, and then noticed a curtain twitch in the window of the house next door. She knocked there. After a few moments' hesitation, the neighbour opened her door a crack, peering at her suspiciously.

'I have a letter,' Mireille explained. 'For the man next door. His wife asked me to deliver it to him.'

The neighbour shook her head. 'He's gone. The Germans came and took them all, the father and the two kids. Gone – I don't know where.'

'Could you keep this for them? Give it to them when they come back?'

The neighbour looked at her doubtfully, then reluctantly extended a hand through the gap in the door to take the note. 'Alright, I'll keep it. But they won't come back. They never do, do they?'

She shut her door with a finality that seemed to underscore her words.

Shaken, Mireille cycled slowly back to the Rue Cardinale, through frozen streets that seemed eerily empty.

She propped her bike in the hallway and climbed the stairs to the apartment, feeling exhausted. It had been a long day and she was chilled to the bone, having cycled miles into the icy wind. She was back much later than she'd anticipated and was looking forward to the company of Claire and Vivi and a bowl of warm soup. She paused on the stairway to pick up a glove that had been dropped there. It looked like one of Claire's. Mireille smiled – she'd be glad to have it back.

She opened the door and stepped into a silence so profound that it made her ears ring. 'Claire?' she called. 'Vivi?'

There was no reply. She shrugged. They must have gone out – maybe to the café. Claire would be missing her glove, in that case. The door to Claire's room stood ajar and she pushed it open, meaning to leave the glove on Claire's pillow. But she stopped in the doorway, a sense of profound unease seeping into her bones. The room was untidy, drawers pulled open and clothes dropped on the floor. The cupboard door swung on its hinges and Mireille could see the silver beads of the midnight blue evening gown glinting within, although the few other clothes that used to hang there alongside the dress were gone.

She ran to Vivi's room, panic flooding her veins now. If anything, it was even worse. A chair was overturned and the contents of the wardrobe and chest of drawers were strewn across the bed. A jar of pens and pencils which had sat on the windowsill lay smashed on the floor, and sheets of crumpled paper had been scattered from the overturned wastepaper bin.

Mireille sank slowly to the floor and buried her face in her hands. 'No,' she whispered. 'Not Vivi. Not Claire. You should have taken me, not them.'

It was only later, when she reached the dyer's shop, gasping for breath having run all the way and hammering on his door, begging him to let her in, that she realised she was still clutching Claire's lost glove.

❧

Mireille must have forgotten her key, Claire had thought, as she went down to answer the door. So she was smiling when she opened it. But her smile froze into a mask of horror when she registered the black and silver insignia on the caps of the three men who stood there.

Over the past few months, the anxiety she'd felt following her encounter with Ernst that summer's day outside the Vélodrôme d'Hiver had receded into the background and over time had become just one of the facets of the ever-present tapestry of fear that formed the backdrop to daily life in a time of war. Every now and then, he would invade her troubled dreams and she'd wake to find Vivi at her bedside again, having been awoken herself by Claire's cries, hushing her, reassuring her that everything was alright.

But now she found herself in a nightmare from which no one could awaken her. The look of cold impassivity on the faces of the three men was more horrifying to her than the grotesquely leering gargoyles that had pursued her in her dreams. She felt a numbness descend in her mind and her body as the first of the men demanded that she take them upstairs to the apartment so that they could investigate a report they'd received.

'What kind of a report?' she asked, playing for time.

'Suspected subversive activities on the premises,' the Gestapo officer had barked back, holding out a hand to gesture that she should lead the way.

Her feet felt like lumps of lead as she climbed the stairs. She led them past the door to the sewing room, which was closed, as it always was at the weekends. *Please*, she prayed silently, *let Vivi be in there. Let her hear them and hide. And don't let Mireille return while they're here. Let them search my room and find nothing and leave.*

She found her voice then, forcing herself to speak so that if Vivi were in the *atelier* it would be a warning to her. 'I can't imagine what these "subversive activities" that you refer to might be,' she said, as calmly as possible. She turned to look back to where they followed, close on her heels. 'We make clothes here, nothing else.'

'Shut up and keep going!' One of the men gave her a push which made her almost lose her footing so that she had to grab the stair rail to stop herself falling forwards. She resumed the climb, treading heavily, deliberately, on each step so that if Vivi was in the apartment she might hear her coming.

'But really, messieurs, I cannot imagine why you are here. As you will see, we have nothing to hide.' Again she protested, raising her voice as much as she dared so that her words would carry, in the hope that they would alert Vivi to the additional sounds made by the three pairs of heavy boots on the staircase.

'In that case, mademoiselle, you have nothing to fear from our visit, do you?' The second man's tone was a sinister sneer.

As she opened the door to the apartment, one of the men grabbed her arm and held it in a steely grip. She could feel the fingers of his black leather gloves bruising her skin through the layers of winter clothes she wore. The other two kicked open the doors leading off the hallway and Claire caught a glimpse of Mireille's empty room. Then she saw Vivi's startled expression and the quick movement of her hands as she pulled what looked like a pair of earphones from her head. Some sort of radio set sat on the table beside her.

'Well, well, what have we here?' The Gestapo officer shot a triumphant grin at his colleague. 'We thought we'd come to trawl for sardines and instead it looks as if we've caught a shark in our net. What an unexpected pleasure!'

Claire made as if to run to Vivi, but the man gripping her arm shook her so hard that she bit her tongue, her mouth filling with the metallic taste of blood. 'Oh no you don't!' he shouted at her. 'And where's your other friend? We were told there were three of you.'

Claire shook her head. 'She's not here. She left.' Thinking fast, she said, loudly enough for Vivi to hear, 'She went out one day last week and never came back. We don't know what's happened – perhaps you can tell us, monsieur?' Defiantly, she looked him in the eye.

He raised a black-gloved hand and slapped her cheek, hard. 'We ask the questions and you give us the answers. I hope you are a quick learner, mademoiselle, otherwise you're going to make things a whole lot worse for yourself. And for your friend, here, too.'

Tears ran down Claire's face, their saltiness mingling with the blood in her mouth, but she pressed her lips together and refused to cry out. She heard a crash from Vivi's room and craned her neck to try to see what was happening, but the man pushed her into her own room and slammed the door, barking, 'Stay there until I say you can come out.' She heard his footsteps crossing the hallway as he went to join his colleagues.

Desperately, she cast around for something she could do to distract them from Vivienne. Could she create a diversion? Lead them away? Go and get help? For a second, she wondered whether she could squeeze through the tiny window and escape across the rooftops, but even if she could get out she knew that she couldn't leave Vivi, the friend who had sat by her bedside, soothing her in the aftermath of her nightmares, calming her fears.

It had become clear that Vivi held a key role in the network and that she must have been passing on crucial information to the Resistance, but she'd never suspected that Vivi had a wireless receiver hidden in her room. What other secrets was Vivi party to? Her close relationship with Monsieur Leroux could be the downfall of the whole network. Claire trembled as she thought how many lives were at stake.

All at once, Claire knew what she needed to do. She had to try to stick with Vivienne, to help her stay strong and not divulge what she knew. Together, they had to hold out for twenty-four hours, that's what they'd been told. Mireille would be able to alert the others. It was up to Claire and Vivienne to buy them the time to cover their tracks. Wherever they were going, she was determined that they would go there together.

Quickly, she started pushing as many warm clothes as she could into a bag. Then she jumped with fright as her bedroom door was kicked open again. 'Well done, mademoiselle, I see you have had the foresight to pack for a little holiday,' sneered the officer. 'Well, let us see how you like our departure lounge on the Avenue Foch.'

The other two were already marching Vivi down the stairs as the man pushed Claire out of the apartment. She hurried to try to catch up with her friend, dropping one of her gloves as she went. She tried to pick it up but he gave her another shove, sending her sprawling headlong on to the next landing. Again, she felt the vice-like grip of his fingers as he pulled her to her feet and forced her to continue onwards down the stairs and out into the Rue Cardinale.

A black car was parked there and Claire found herself bundled into the back, next to Vivi. She shot a glance at her friend's face. One eye was swelling, beginning to close, but otherwise she just looked deeply shocked. Claire felt for her hand and squeezed it. 'I'm here,' she whispered, echoing the words Vivi used to say when Claire's nightmares woke them both. 'Everything will be alright.'

Vivienne turned to look at Claire then, as if only just registering her presence for the first time. Her eyes were glazed with fear, but she focused on her friend's face and nodded once. Then she gave Claire's hand a squeeze in return and they held on to each other tightly as the car sped through the streets of Paris, heading west.

Harriet

Shocked by the knowledge that Claire was arrested and taken to the Gestapo headquarters for questioning, I've been reading some reports that I've found online about inherited trauma. There's no doubt my grandmother must have been terrified at being captured and that she must have felt horrendously guilty that Vivi was caught too, apparently operating a wireless radio set from her attic room.

I read an article that says new research in the field of genetics has shown that an increased likelihood of suffering from depression can be inherited. Trauma can cause changes in some areas of a person's DNA, it says, and these changes can be passed on to the next generations, one after the other.

I'm beginning to see how high the odds were stacked against my mother. Was there a genetic fragility in her make up – changes to her DNA that she inherited from the trauma Claire suffered – that caused her to snap when life's knocks came? In her case, they came one after the other, like powerful waves knocking her off her feet. Abandonment, divorce, the demands of raising a child alone . . . Each time she tried to get up again, another wave knocked her back down. Some of the anger and hurt that I've felt towards my mother for years begins to shift slightly as I re-examine her life in this new light.

It takes me a few days to pluck up the courage, but after Simone tells me of Claire's arrest I feel I have to go and see where she was taken.

I have to be brave enough to trace her terrifying journey through the streets to a leafy *arrondissement* on the west side of the city. I ask Thierry to come with me to the Avenue Foch, for moral support.

These days, the former Gestapo offices are highly respectable apartment buildings in one of the most sought-after areas of the city. But in 1943, the elegant road was known by the French as 'The Street of Horrors'. We stand in silence outside the cream stone facade of the buildings. A pigeon flutters on to the grey slate roof of number eighty-four, crooning softly to itself as it nods its way along the guttering.

'Are you okay?' Thierry asks, turning to look at me.

It's only then that I realise I'm crying. It takes me by surprise. I almost never cry. He must think I make a habit of it though, after our trip to Brittany.

He takes my hand and then pulls me to him, kissing my hair as I bury my face in the folds of his jacket and sob.

I cry for all the people who were brought here, for their terror and their pain.

I'm crying for Claire.

I cry for humanity, for a world which can so easily be broken.

I'm crying for my mother.

And – at last – I find I'm crying for myself.

1943

It was several days before the dyer would allow Mireille to return to the apartment above Delavigne Couture. He and his wife hid her in the cellar of a safe house a few streets away from the shop and, despite her protestations that she had to go back to the Rue Cardinale, he insisted that she stay put. 'We have eyes and ears on the streets,' he told her. 'We know that your friends have been taken to the Avenue Foch for questioning. If they are forced to talk, the Gestapo will come back for you as well. You know the rules: the first twenty-four hours are critical. We have to get a warning out to the rest of the network. Even after that, it will be too dangerous for you to be in the apartment while they are still holding your friends. What if they come back to search again and they find you there?'

'But what if Claire and Vivi don't talk? If they are released, I want to be there when they return.'

'We have someone watching so we will know if and when they are released. I know it's hard, but the best thing you can do – for their sakes as well as for your own – is to sit tight here. In a few days we will know, one way or another . . .' His voice trailed off. 'Try to eat something now. Keep your strength up as best you can, eh?'

Those dark, lonely hours were some of the hardest Mireille had ever had to endure. Images of her friends' faces floated before her: Claire's gentle smile; Vivi's eyes, filled with warmth. What was happening to them now? And now? And now? She could hardly bear to think. In her anguish, she lost control and beat her fists against the rough stone walls of the cellar until her knuckles bled. Then, sobbing, she sank to the floor and wept, raw angry sobs, wrenched from her guts, that tore at her throat.

She thought she would go crazy.

As the hours turned into days, she cried out her anger and frustration until all that remained was a cold, hard determination to survive this ordeal, just as she hoped Claire and Vivi were surviving the ordeals of their own.

She'd lost track of time, but at last the dyer opened the cellar door and led her out of the darkness and back up into the grey light of a winter's evening. 'It should be safe, now, for you to return to the *atelier*. Your friends are extremely courageous. They never gave in, even under torture,' he told her. 'They didn't talk.'

Hope leapt in her heart. 'Oh, thank God! Are they alright? Are they coming home?'

He shook his head, his expression grave. 'We have word that they are in bad shape, but they are still alive. They have been released from the Avenue Foch. But they are being taken to a prison, where political prisoners are held. Come now, my child. I will take you home.'

Never had she thought that she would have missed the sewing room, but as she pushed open the door the familiar smell of starched fabric and the sight of the seamstresses' chairs pushed in neatly around the table in the darkened room made her heart turn over with a longing for it all to be as it had been a week ago. She wished that a lamp would cast a pool of light onto one end of the table, making Vivi's copper braid shine as she bent her head to her work. She longed to hear Claire's voice, scolding Vivi as she told her that she was working too late, as usual, and that she should put away whatever it was she was doing and come upstairs for supper.

But the darkness and the silence filled the room, amplifying its emptiness.

She took the next few flights of stairs slowly, putting off for as long as possible the moment when she would unlock the door to the apartment on the fifth floor and step into an emptiness and a silence more terrible than any she'd experienced in the past few days.

She steeled herself, then walked in.

Her own room had been largely untouched – presumably the Gestapo had been too intent on the capture of Claire and Vivienne to bother with anything else – but she was expecting to see the awful reminders of their presence in the other rooms. To Mireille's surprise, though, she realised that someone must have been into the apartment in her absence. Claire and Vivi's rooms were tidy now, the cupboard doors closed, clothes folded and put back into drawers, the chair set to rights. The work of a friend, surely, rather than an enemy?

She caught sight of a soft gleam in the darkness of Claire's room. On the windowsill beside the bed lay the silver locket that Mireille had given her two Christmases ago. Mireille picked it up and ran the chain slowly through her fingers. After a moment's hesitation, she fastened the clasp around her neck. She would wear it for Claire and for Vivi, she decided, until they came home again. She closed the doors to their bedrooms and then walked, slowly, to her own.

She didn't bother to remove her clothes, just kicked off her shoes and pulled the blankets over her shivering body. Lying in the darkness, she remembered something the dyer had said earlier. When he'd come to release her, seeing the expression of relief on her face when he'd told her the news that Claire and Vivi were still alive, he had laid a gentle hand on hers. 'Don't get your hopes up too high, my child,' he'd said, his expression sorrowful. 'Your friends have saved you. And the rest of us, too. But they still may not be able to save themselves.'

She clenched her hand, in defiance, around the locket that hung above her heart. Her still-raw knuckles were covered in scabs which cracked and oozed blood as she curled her fingers into a fist. Claire and Vivi were still alive. They had endured the horrors of torture at the Gestapo's headquarters. Surely, now, nothing else could be as bad? They were still together. Surely they would survive?

~❦~

Claire had continued to hold on tight to Vivi's hand until the car pulled up in front of eighty-four, Avenue Foch. From the outside, it looked like many other buildings in the elegant sixteenth *arrondissement*.

'*Courage*,' Claire whispered, leaning as close to Vivi as she dared. 'I can be strong if you can too.' She wasn't sure whether her friend had heard the words and, if she had, whether they'd registered. Vivi still appeared to be deep in shock, or perhaps stunned by a blow to her head. But after a moment Claire felt a reassuring squeeze of her hand in return.

The car door was flung open and Vivi was dragged out. Then two pairs of hands grabbed Claire and she was manhandled into the building. The bag of clothes she'd packed so hastily was wrenched from her grasp and handed to a grey-uniformed woman who disappeared with it.

'Take them straight to the sixth floor,' one of the men barked, as he removed his cap and gloves. 'Let's see how these dressmakers enjoy a spell in the "kitchen".'

Just like the apartment in the Rue Cardinale, the attic rooms in this building were cramped and sloping with small windows. But that was where any similarity ended. Boards had been nailed across the window-frames and the room that Claire was led into had nothing in it but a single metal-framed chair beneath a bare lightbulb that hung from the ceiling. She heard a door slam shut a little further along the corridor and presumed that Vivi had been bundled into a room similar to this one.

The two men who came to question her were polite at first. 'Please, mademoiselle, take a seat,' one said, patting her shoulder as he ushered her towards the chair. 'We really don't wish to detain you any longer than is necessary. So if you'll just answer our questions then we can let you be on your way. Can I get you anything? A glass of water, perhaps?'

She was aware that his apparent kindness was a ploy to get her to drop her guard. She shook her head, clasping her hands together tightly in her lap to prevent her whole body from trembling.

Their opening questions seemed almost inconsequential, the man's tone pleasantly conversational. How long had she worked for Delavigne Couture? Did she enjoy her work? And how long had her red-headed friend worked there? She refused to speak at all to begin with, shaking her head.

The second man, who had been pacing up and down, turned on his heel abruptly and brought his face close to hers. She could smell the staleness of his breath, and flecks of spit spattered her face as he hissed, 'You are a very attractive young woman, Claire. It would be a shame to spoil such a pretty face. I suggest you start co-operating now. Tell us what your friend – Vivienne, isn't it? – was doing with a shortwave radio in her room. You must have known. And maybe you were working with her, *hein*? Did she give you messages to carry?'

Claire shook her head again, not daring to raise a hand to wipe the drops of spittle from her face. She wondered, briefly, how he knew their names. Someone – Ernst maybe? – must have given them to him.

'Very well.' The man straightened up again. She thought he had turned to walk away from her, so when he spun back round and hit her across the face the blow seemed to come out of nowhere. She cried out then in shock and pain, the sound of her own voice seeming alien to her. She needed to stay strong for Vivi, just as she knew Vivi would stay strong for her. And so she spoke then, determined to regain control of her voice.

Her words were low and trembling, but she managed to say, 'I am Claire Meynardier. Vivienne Giscard is my friend. We are seamstresses in Saint-Germain.' She would hold on to these three simple truths, she told herself. She would say nothing more.

Like waves washing up on the beach, time seemed to advance and retreat and she lost all track of how many hours might have passed. The minutes when they were questioning her felt interminable. But then the lapses of consciousness could have lasted seconds or days.

The pain ebbed and flowed too, sometimes hard-edged and blinding, sometimes enveloping her in darkness. She was sick with tiredness, but they wouldn't let her sleep, questioning, coaxing, shouting until her head spun. And yet, each time she spoke it was to repeat the three truths that she clung on to as she drowned in that sea of pain and time. 'I am Claire Meynardier. Vivienne Giscard is my friend. We are seamstresses in Saint-Germain.' Again and again, through swollen lips, she mumbled the words until, at last, darkness descended.

When she came to, Claire was lying in the corner of the room. Her body was numb with the chill that seeped through the walls and the bare floorboards behind and beneath her but, as she slowly regained consciousness, the numbness was replaced by a burning sensation in her feet. The stiffness of her limbs slowly thawed into a throbbing ache and, as she tried to sit up, a sharp spike of pain shot through her ribcage.

Tentatively, she ran the tip of her tongue over her cracked and swollen lips, and winced. She began to shiver then, uncontrollably.

Her woollen stockings were tangled in a heap beside her and she slowly sat up and began to pull them on over her bloodied feet for warmth. What day was it? How many hours had passed? Where was Vivi and what had they done to her? Her head swam and she lay back down on the floor, curling her bruised and battered body into a ball and tucking her hands into her chest so that they could absorb the faint warmth of her breath. 'I am Claire Meynardier,' she whispered to herself. 'Vivienne Giscard is my friend.'

It was the woman in the grey uniform who opened the door. She looked at Claire without emotion. 'Get up and put on your shoes,' she said. 'It's time to go.'

Claire didn't move, unable to uncurl her aching limbs from the small core of warmth she'd created. Her hands were pressed against her heart and she felt the blood pulsing faintly through her body.

The woman nudged her with the toe of her shoe. 'Get up,' she repeated. 'Or do I have to go and get the men to put you back on your feet?'

Slowly, painfully, Claire sat up then. The woman pushed her shoes towards her and Claire put them on, gasping at the flashes of searing pain as she forced them on to her swollen feet. She couldn't tie the laces, but they were on, at least. She managed to pull herself up using the chair and then shuffled forwards, following the woman to the door.

Each downwards step on the stairs sent more pain stabbing through her feet and up into her calves, but she gripped the handrail and hobbled on, determined not to cry out. At last they reached the ground floor and the woman gestured to her to take a seat on a hard, wooden bench against one wall. Thankfully, she lowered herself on to it. 'May I have some water?' she asked.

Wordlessly, the woman brought her a tin mug and Claire took a few sips, moistening her mouth and washing away the iron taste of blood. Plucking up courage at being granted this small request, Claire said, 'My bag of clothes? May I have it back?' But the woman just shrugged and turned away.

As she sat and waited for whatever was to happen next, she heard two sets of footsteps coming down the stairs. The men carried a stretcher between them and it took Claire a few moments to realise that the huddled bundle of wet rags that lay on it covered a person. And it was only when she saw the tumble of copper hair hanging over the side of the stretcher that she realised who that person was.

Harriet

Outside the building where my grandmother was so brutally tortured, once I've stopped crying – enough to be able to gather my thoughts, at least – I turn away from Thierry and I start to walk. All I know is that I need to be anywhere other than here. How can I ever see the world as a good and kind place to be when I know what obscene cruelty humanity is capable of?

As my feet carry me onwards, the sudden wail of a police siren makes the traffic scatter and a sickening scream of pain and anger fills my head with white noise, blotting out everything else. Without thinking, I begin to run, wildly, panicking. I can hardly see, can't think, can't make sense of my surroundings. Flickering blue lights engulf me and I feel them burning like flames. Stumbling, I blunder off the edge of the pavement and hear a shout, the screeching of car tyres, a blaring horn.

And then Thierry catches me and pulls me back to the safety of the pavement, holding me up as my legs threaten to give way beneath me.

Taking juddering breaths, I look into his face and I see fear written there behind the bewilderment. His eyes are searching mine, asking, *Who is this crazy woman? Why would anyone run into the traffic like that? She is unbalanced, hysterical.*

I can see it in his uncertainty, feel it in the way his touch has become tentative now, not solid and reassuring like it was before.

I've ruined it. I've proven to myself what I've always feared, that I am too damaged to be loved. I'm not strong enough for this. Perhaps Simone was right in the first place: I never should have tried to find out Claire's story. I should have left the questions unasked, let history lie. I was coping, before. On my own. With sudden, breathtaking clarity, I see that I can't inflict the darkness that I carry inside me on Thierry – this man who is standing beside me, tentatively putting a hand on my arm to hold me in case I bolt again. I care about him too much.

'Come,' he says, 'you've had a terrible shock. Let's find a café, get you a cup of English tea?' He smiles, trying to make things right again.

I shake my head. 'I'm sorry, Thierry,' I say. 'I can't.'

'Okay, then I'll take you home.'

But it's there now, between us. Something has shifted. Something has been broken and it cannot be repaired. He leaves me at my door, tries to kiss me, but I turn away pretending to search in my bag for my keys. And when he says goodbye, I can't quite meet his eyes.

I have to let him go.

1943

Mademoiselle Vannier had come upstairs to look for the three girls when none of them turned up for work on Monday morning, and had discovered the apartment in its abandoned state. It was clear that something terrible had happened, but where the girls had gone was a complete mystery. Their absence had been the source of much whispered conjecture amongst the other seamstresses in the days that followed.

And so there were gasps of surprise when Mireille appeared in the sewing room. Without a word, she walked across and took her seat at the table between the two empty chairs belonging to Claire and Vivienne.

The stunned silence gave way to a tirade of questions.

'Where have you been?'

'Where are Claire and Vivi?'

'What happened?'

'They're gone,' she said, bluntly. 'The Gestapo came and took them. No, I don't know why. I don't know where they are now. I don't know anything.'

Mademoiselle Vannier shushed the seamstresses. 'Quiet, now, everyone. That's enough. Leave Mireille in peace and get on with your work.'

Mireille shot her a glance of gratitude as she set her sewing things on the table and, with trembling fingers, began to tack together the pieces of a waistband.

She had scarcely slept and had eaten nothing since her return the night before, unable to get the images of Claire and Vivi's faces out of her head. The dyer had said they were in bad shape. She couldn't bear to think about what they had been through during those four days in the Avenue Foch. But they were alive, she reminded herself. That was all that mattered.

She tried hard to concentrate on her sewing. One stitch, then the next, then the next . . . It helped her to shut out the images of her friends' pain-wracked faces, for a little while at least.

Heads bent over their work, the others shot surreptitious glances at her from beneath their eyelashes. The room was filled with an oppressive silence, heavy with questions unasked and unanswered. Then, without a word, one of the girls slid across from her usual seat into one of the empty chairs next to Mireille. After a moment's hesitation, the girl on the other side followed suit. Scarcely glancing up from her work, Mireille nodded her thanks to them for their gesture of solidarity. And then, blinking the tears from her eyes, she forced herself to sew another stitch and another . . .

Returning upstairs to the silence and the darkness of the apartment was almost as bad as it had been the night before. She made herself heat up a little soup and eat it, wrapping herself in a blanket to keep out the bitter cold. She was just washing up her bowl when a soft tap on the apartment door made her freeze in terror.

But then she heard a familiar voice, softly saying her name, and she breathed again.

Monsieur Leroux accepted her offer of a tisane, and then insisted on making it himself while she stayed in the sitting room, curled up in her blanket. He handed her a cup of lemon balm tea and she cradled it in her hands, letting it warm her.

'Is there any news?' she asked once he'd settled himself in the chair opposite.

His eyes were filled with pain when he raised them to meet hers. 'Nothing more yet. They're being held in the prison at Fresnes.'

She sat up. 'Fresnes? But that's not far. Can we go and see them at least?'

He shook his head. 'Even if they would let anyone visit them, it would be too risky. The intelligence I have is that Claire and Vivi managed to convince the Gestapo that you'd already been picked up. Things are so chaotic these days that they can't easily trace whether or not it's true, so they've stopped looking for you now. If you turn up, you'll be arrested on the spot. And it would make things even worse for the other two.'

'But what will happen to them in prison?'

He shrugged. 'We can't be sure. I have a contact on the inside, so I'm hoping to get some more news soon. Mostly they use Fresnes as a holding place for political prisoners before moving them on to one of the prison camps in Germany. If they are deported it won't be easy to keep track of them. The people who are taken to those places . . . they tend to disappear.'

She studied his face for a moment. Outwardly, he was trying to maintain his usual calm facade. But the shadows beneath his eyes and the lines of pain etched around his mouth betrayed the depth of his anguish. Vivi was clearly more to him than simply another agent in the network that he controlled. Perhaps she really had been his mistress. And perhaps those other rumours about him made more sense now, too. All those women he'd been cultivating – had they had other uses as well? Did he convince some to become agents, persuading them to take on roles within the network as he had done with Vivi? And were others the 'contacts on the inside' he spoke of, the 'grey mice' he'd wined and dined and clothed in couture, feeding him with intelligence from inside the Avenue Foch and the prison at Fresnes? She'd always warmed to him and had trusted him with her life. But now she wondered whether there might be a ruthlessly cold and manipulative side to him as well. Were

Vivi and Claire simply expendable pawns in a horrific game of chess being played out across Europe?

As if reading her thoughts, he said quietly, 'You know, I always believed that the network was more important than any individual within it. But losing Vivienne and Claire has proven me wrong.' For a moment, his whole face crumpled as he tried to stop himself from breaking down. A single, terrible sob wrenched itself out of him, from deep down inside, and he covered his eyes with his hands.

Quickly, Mireille set down her cup and moved across to him. She knelt on the floor at his side and took his hands in hers. His eyes were red-rimmed, and the pain in their depths made her feel ashamed for having doubted him even for a moment. It was clear that he cared as deeply about Claire and Vivi as she did.

'No,' she said. 'You're not wrong. You know as well as I do how determined the two of them were – are – to play their parts. They'd be furious if they thought the network had fallen apart because of them. If . . .' She stopped, then corrected herself. '*When* they come back, do you want to be the one to tell them that we gave up because of them? Of course not! We have to keep going. Because we have to put an end to the terror and the arrests and the disappearances. We have to win.'

As she spoke, Mireille felt the strength of her conviction return, flowing through her veins with a heat that seemed to thaw the icy grip of the winter.

He squeezed her hand, then let go of it in order to fish in his pocket for a handkerchief with which to mop his face. Once he'd regained his composure, he said, 'You're right. Of course, you're right. We can't give up. We have to keep fighting, even if it takes the last breaths in our bodies.'

'Good,' she replied. 'That's agreed then. I'll start my duties again, as soon as you can get the links re-established.'

He shook his head. 'No, Mireille, I'm afraid we can't use you any more, neither as a courier to replace Claire, nor as a *passeuse*. And we certainly can't have another wireless operator located here. As I told you, they'll be on the lookout for you and if you're picked up out there on the streets it'll be the worse for the others, as well as for you with everything you now know.'

Mireille's hand went to the locket around her neck and her fingers tightened into a clenched fist. 'Please, Monsieur Leroux, I have to do something. I can't just sit here while they're out there, enduring . . .' Her words trailed off.

Then she spoke again, more quietly this time but with an undertone of determination. 'One of my friends who lived in this apartment was shot down in cold blood by the Nazis. Now two more have been arrested and tortured and deprived of their liberty. Their rooms stand empty, and I can't bear to look at them. So let me use those three rooms to shelter others who need them. This whole building is deserted when the salon closes and the other seamstresses go home. I'm the only one left. If we run it as a safe house for the network, it will mean that those rooms don't stand empty any more. And it will stop me from going crazy. Because I'll be doing something for people like Vivi and Claire. And then, when they come back to us, when all of this is over, I'll be able to tell them that I was brave like them. I'll be able to look them in the eye and say that, like them, I never gave in.'

Monsieur Leroux raised his gaze to hers. He shook his head again, but this time it was more in admiration than in defeat. 'You know, Mireille,' he said, 'you three young women are some of the bravest people I've ever met. And one day, when all this is over, I hope we will all be reunited in a better world. That really is something worth fighting for.'

⁂

The door slammed shut and Claire's prison cell was plunged into darkness, apart from the letterbox-like slit in the door which allowed a glimmer of light to slip beneath its ill-fitting cover. As her eyes adjusted, she could just make out the narrow bed with its coarse blanket and the bucket in one corner of the room.

She sat down on the hard mattress and covered her face with her hands. Defeat crashed over her like a breaking wave, an overwhelming force that knocked her feet out from beneath her and held her under for a moment so that she felt she could hardly draw breath. Until now, she'd always known Vivi was close by. In the back of the truck that had brought them here, swaying and swerving through the streets, she'd crouched on the floor beside the stretcher and held Vivi's hand. Gently, she'd brushed the hair away from Vivi's face, being careful not to touch the swollen, bruised skin around her eyes and jawline. As she slowly regained consciousness, Vivi had begun to shake uncontrollably and Claire had hushed her and soothed her with those same words that her friend had used to reassure her when her nightmares had woken them both. She repeated them over and over until they became more of a prayer than a statement: 'Hush, now. I'm here. We're together. Everything will be alright.'

Vivi's hair and clothes were damp. Through swollen, broken lips she managed to whisper that they'd filled a bath and held her head under the water repeatedly until she was certain that she would drown. 'But I didn't talk, Claire. They didn't break me. I knew you weren't far away and that kept me strong.' She reached a hand up to touch Claire's blackened eye. 'And you were brave too.'

Claire nodded, unable to speak.

Vivi squeezed her hand, weakly. 'I knew you would be. We will stay brave together.' She closed her eyes then and slept. Claire sat watching over her for the rest of the journey until the truck pulled up with a jerk at the prison gates.

They'd been taken to separate rooms inside the prison. With support, Vivi had managed to stand and then she'd been half-carried by guards into a room where the door was shut firmly behind her. A female guard escorted Claire down a long corridor. She'd hobbled, trying to use only the outer edges of her feet where the pain was just about bearable. Then the guard had made her stand, while she herself sat behind a desk and filled in a pile of paperwork with Claire's details. And finally, without a word, she'd led Claire here, to this darkened cell, in the solitary confinement wing of the prison.

Sitting on her bed in the cramped darkness which filled her nostrils with the stench of mildew and urine, it was some minutes before Claire registered the tapping noise. It seemed to be coming from the wall behind her. At first, she thought it might be rats or mice. Then, as she listened, she realised there was a more regular rhythm to it. Perhaps it was air trapped in the pipes concealed beneath the brickwork, she thought. But the noise persisted.

She raised her head from her hands, to listen more carefully. And then she realised that someone was tapping out a pattern, repeating it over and over again. Three quick taps, and then a fourth with a longer pause, then two more quick taps. And then the same pattern was repeated for a second time, followed by a silence for a few moments before the whole sequence began again. The tapping was muffled by the brick wall, but the repetition was distinct. It had to be a code, spelling something out.

She tapped back on the wall, copying the pattern. The code came back immediately from the next-door cell, repeated more quickly this time. And then she realised that she recognised the first part of it. She'd heard it at the beginning of the radio broadcast that her father and brother had tuned into that evening when they were waiting for the coded BBC message to tell them that the operation was to go ahead to get Fréd to safety. The first four notes of the Beethoven symphony: V for Victory. It was Morse code! And there was another letter added in between. Two quick dots . . .

She tapped the pattern back again, more fluently this time: the letter 'V', then two quick taps, then the letter 'V' again and two more quick taps. There was a flurry of answering knocks, like a round of applause.

It was Vivi! She was there, on the other side of the wall. They were still together, side by side. She wasn't alone.

And now that Claire knew that, somehow the cold and the darkness of her prison cell wasn't so unbearable after all.

❧

Mireille had grown accustomed to the ringing of the doorbell late in the evening, shortly before the hours of the curfew, and to slipping down to open the door and receive the next escapee from the hands of the latest *passeuse* to be recruited by the network. Sometimes there was a single 'guest', other times there might be a couple of people making their perilous journey out of France, grateful to spend a night in the apartment under the roof of 12 Rue Cardinale where they were concealed by a young woman with a mass of dark curls, whose warm brown eyes held a look of sadness in their depths even when she smiled. But one night she opened the door to find Monsieur Leroux standing there.

She pulled him inside and shut the door quickly. 'You have news?' she asked.

'There is news, yes. They have left the prison.'

She gasped. 'Where are they? Can I see them?'

His hazel eyes were clouded with sorrow. 'They've been taken on one of the transports. To a camp in Germany. That's all we know. We have lost them now, I'm afraid.'

'No!' The word was wrenched from Mireille, her pain making it sound shrill in the darkening hallway.

He put an arm around her and hugged her as she cried out for her friends, raging against the cruelty of the world in which they'd all found themselves.

At last she grew quiet, regaining control. 'What do we do now?' she asked.

'Now?' he repeated. His voice was soft at first, but as he continued speaking the words grew stronger and more resolute. 'Now we keep doing what we've been doing. And we do it every single day for as long as we can. Because that's what they would want us to do. There is hope, you know, Mireille. The tide of this war is turning, I'm convinced of it. The Germans suffered a very bitter defeat when the Russians managed to take back Stalingrad in February. Their armies are stretched on all fronts now and the Allies are making headway. You know, even couture is becoming a victim of the war – there's just been an edict in Germany that fashion pictures are to be banned from magazines. So you see, the pressure is having an effect at every level. And that makes it all the more important that we keep our contribution going, because each small act of defiance chips away a little more at the foundations of Hitler's power. Most importantly of all, we have to do it for Vivienne and Claire. Because the sooner there is an end to this war, the greater chance there is that they may still survive it and come back to us.'

She looked at him and saw that his face was drawn with anguish. 'You love her very much, don't you?' she said.

He couldn't speak for a moment. But then he answered her. 'I love both of them, Mireille.'

The next day, she walked to the island in the middle of the river and crept in beneath the branches of the willow tree at its downstream end. Once again, she leaned her head against the tree's rough trunk and let it support her, taking the weight of her worries and her fears for a while. Despite Monsieur Leroux's words of hope yesterday, it felt as if the war would never end. And if it did, would it still be too late for Claire and Vivi . . .?

As the river flowed past, she saw the faces of the people she loved reflected in its depths. Her mother and father; her brother and sister;

baby Blanche; Vivienne; Claire; and the man whose name she still held in her heart, keeping it secret for now. Would she ever be able to say it out loud? Would she ever see him again?

Would there ever be an end to this war?

❧

The journey to the camp was a long one, but Vivi and Claire reassured one another and tried to keep each other's spirits up, helping the other women crowded into the jolting cattle car as best they could. The train seemed to move slowly, like a snake awakening from its winter hibernation, sluggishly uncoiling eastwards, apparently in no great hurry to get them to their destination.

The carriage was filled with an atmosphere of fear and anguish, as cold and clammy as the fog that engulfed the train for much of the day. Many of the women wept uncontrollably. Some were in a bad way physically, the traumas they had suffered taking their toll.

One morning they woke to find the spring sunshine creeping through the slatted sides of the car. But the slight lifting of spirits that Claire felt at the sight of it was short-lived. The rays of light illuminated the face of an elderly woman who had died in her sleep. 'If only the rest of us could be so lucky,' muttered another woman as she helped Claire and Vivienne to cover the body with the old lady's coat and gently move her to one corner of the carriage. The next time the train stopped, later on that day, a guard slid open the door of the cattle truck and told them they could get out to stretch their legs for a few minutes. Noticing the body, he casually pulled it from the corner and dragged it out to lie beside the tracks amongst the bright tangle of fireweed and poppies that had grown up there.

The others stood watching in silence. One or two crossed themselves and muttered prayers for the lost soul.

But then one woman bent down and took the coat from the corpse, draping her own more worn one back over the body. She looked around defiantly. 'Well, it's no use to her now,' she said.

Some of the others turned their backs on her then, but soon the guard shouted at them to get back on board the train and then they were all crammed in together again, with no room for anyone to turn her back on her neighbour, even if she'd had the will to do so.

The time spent in the prison at Fresnes had allowed Claire and Vivi to recover a little – physically, at least – from their treatment at the hands of the Gestapo. Claire could put weight on the soles of her feet again now, the scars from the beatings she'd endured having healed over leaving white wheals of thickened skin, and her toenails were starting to grow back where they'd been wrenched from the nail beds. Vivi's face was healing, although her smile remained lopsided from the damage done to her jaw and the loss of a tooth. She had a cough that rattled in her chest especially in the mornings, having suffered from the dampness of her prison cell after her near-drowning at the Avenue Foch, but she insisted to Claire that she was fine. The two of them, together, kept each other going. Each night, as the train rattled onwards, the two friends would curl up side by side. And in the darkness, when the nightmares and the terror made Claire cry out, as she did in their attic bedrooms, Vivi would take her hand and whisper, 'Hush, now. I'm here. And you're here. We're together. And everything will be alright.'

After several days, the train disgorged its surviving passengers at last, and the women clustered together on the platform of a strange station. The jagged, Gothic script painted on to the wooden signs read 'Flossenbürg'.

Claire blinked in the late spring sunshine, lifting her light-starved face to the faint warmth of its rays. Although she was frightened, dreading whatever unimaginable trials might be coming next, she managed to muster a little inner strength, reminding herself that they had survived this far, that perhaps now the worst was over, and that – most importantly of all – she and Vivi were still together.

The train's cargo – men, women and a few terrified children – was herded into long lines by SS officers and then they were ordered to begin walking. Hungry, thirsty and exhausted, the prisoners stumbled along a dusty road for almost an hour, with any stragglers being ordered back into line at one end or the other of a guard's rifle.

Soon, Claire's feet burned with flames of shooting pain that made her hobble. At one point, she faltered as her legs, which were unaccustomed to bearing her weight for such a long stretch of time after the months spent in a prison cell and cattle car, were seized with searing cramps and felt as if they would give way beneath her. But then Vivi linked an arm through hers and the reassurance of that contact helped Claire walk on.

At last they came to a forbidding-looking gatehouse and passed through a black metal gateway. To either side there stretched a high, razor-wire-capped fence which had guard towers set into it at regular intervals along its length. The muzzle of a machine gun, trained towards the interior of the camp, protruded from each one.

Claire lifted her bowed head to read the inscription set into one of the brick gateposts as they passed by: *Arbeit Macht Frei.* She frowned, trying to puzzle out the meaning. Vivi nudged her. 'It says, work will set you free.'

The sickening irony of the message, as it hung over the heads of the frightened and exhausted prisoners, forced a gulp of astonished hysteria to escape from Claire's mouth. It might almost have been laughter, had it not sounded so strangled and bleak amongst the scared whispers and shuffling footsteps of the crowd, like the involuntary yelp of an animal in pain.

'Hush,' whispered Vivi, as one of the guards craned his neck to try to pinpoint the source of the sound. 'We must try not to draw attention to ourselves. Remember, I'm here. We're together. We will be alright.'

The snaking line was sorted by the guards, who sent the men in one direction and the women in another. There was no sign of the children now, but Claire hadn't seen where they'd been taken. The women were ushered into a long, low building which appeared to be staffed by female guards.

'Line up here,' one said, and gesticulated. 'Single file. Remove your clothes.'

The women looked at one another in astonishment.

'Hurry up! Clothes off.' This time the command was a shout.

Slowly, in numb disbelief, the women began to undress until, at last, they stood shivering, clutching the clothing they'd removed. Then a door opened and, one by one, they were led into the next room.

'Leave your clothes here, on the floor.' The guard's tone was as harsh as her words.

Ashamed, humiliated, exposed, Claire was made to stand before one of several desks that were arranged along the walls of the inner room. She felt like a heifer being assessed at a cattle market as rough hands examined her, taking measurements, listening to her chest, checking her teeth and eyes. She glanced across to where Vivi was enduring similar treatment, trying not to cough as the stethoscope chilled the skin on her back.

'What was your job?' asked the woman seated behind the desk.

'I am a seamstress,' Claire replied and she heard Vivi give the same information at the next desk along. Notes were made on a form which was then put on to one of several piles of papers. The woman behind the desk nodded to a guard and Claire and Vivi were led out into the next room. As they went, Claire noticed that some of the women were being ushered in a different direction, for no apparent reason. Some sort of arbitrary sorting process seemed to be being carried out by the guards.

It became apparent where those women had been taken when they appeared a few minutes later, their heads newly shaved, looking even more shockingly naked as they rejoined the other women in the next room along. Claire and Vivi exchanged glances, unsure whether it might be a blessing or a curse to have been allowed to keep their hair.

They were each handed a pile of folded clothing. The underwear was stretched and worn so thin the fabric was translucent in places. And when they shook out the other coarse cotton garments, woven in blue and white stripes, they found they'd been given a loose-fitting over-shirt and a pair of trousers.

'Don't put them on yet,' ordered the guard as one of the bare-headed women began to pull on the shirt she'd been given to cover herself up. 'Here, take these.' The guard then handed them strips of white fabric, two for each prisoner, upon which an identification number had been stamped in indelible ink. Consulting a list that had been handed to her by one of the women who'd been sitting behind a desk in the previous room, she also gave each of them a triangle of coloured fabric. Claire noticed that hers and Vivi's were red, but some of the other women were given triangles of yellow or black or blue material. And several were handed two triangles, usually a yellow one along with one of the other colours.

'Next door.' The guard pointed. The line of women shuffled forwards. And there, Claire and Vivi found themselves in more familiar territory. Women, dressed in the same blue and white striped clothing and wearing white headscarves, sat behind sewing machines, which whirred busily as they stitched the identity numbers and triangles on to the shirts and trousers of the newest arrivals at the camp. The sewing was rough and ready, stitched with coarsely spun thread and executed as quickly as possible, and then the uniforms were handed back.

In the room next door was a heap of shoes. The guard pointed at them. 'Find a pair that fits.'

The women picked through the shoes, looking for their own, but most had to give up and make do with what they could find. Claire managed to grab a pair of boots, slightly larger than her usual size. They went on more easily than her old shoes, which she couldn't see on the pile. But when she put her weight on them, she discovered that the ends immediately began to chafe against the raw ends of her toes, still vulnerable where the newly emerging nails had not yet covered the tender skin.

Carrying their piles of clothing, the women were finally led into a long, tiled shower room. Even though the water was barely lukewarm, Claire felt a little better once she'd scrubbed herself with a bar of hard soap. There were no towels, but the women were finally allowed to put on their newly issued uniforms.

'What do you think?' Claire tried to muster a little defiant courage, as she gave a twirl mimicking the models in the salon at Delavigne Couture. 'This season's style.'

Vivi smiled back at her. 'You know what I think?' she replied. 'I think you and I need to get jobs in that sewing room.'

Harriet

I've been avoiding Thierry's phone calls and messages, sending brief replies only when I have to, saying that I'm too busy to meet up or go out. The truth is, that day when we went to the Avenue Foch and I had a full-on panic attack has left me shaken. Just when I'd started to feel I had some sort of roots, some sense of connection to my family, I've discovered that it comes at a price. The price of knowing how Claire suffered and seeing how that trauma was, inevitably, passed on to my mother. It seems inescapable. A life sentence. And if it's true, if it's built into my DNA, then how could I ever contemplate inflicting it on the people I love, passing it on to children of my own, perpetuating the pain and the loneliness in another generation?

If I thought that knowing my family history would empower me then I was sorely mistaken. What I've learned of Claire's story so far has left me feeling trapped. That was the risk I took, coming to Paris, searching for the girls in the photo. I thought I had the courage to find out who I really am. But now I am afraid that it's done more harm than good.

At the same time, there's a sense that I've come too far to stop. I need to follow Claire's story to the end. I can only hope that there'll be some shreds of redemption in it, for me as well as for her.

Simone has continued to tell me our grandmothers' stories, but each new instalment comes very sporadically. There are parts of the story that she herself hasn't known until now. She says she has asked Mireille to fill in the gaps, but it takes time for her letters to arrive. I wonder whether remembering these things and writing them down is painful for her.

Simone and I are both so busy at work that it's hard to find the time to talk at all really. That suits me just fine: I'm not ready to tell her about ending my relationship with Thierry. Would she be sorry or pleased? I'm not sure whether she's heard anything, from him or from other mutual friends, but in any case she doesn't bring it up. Disappointingly, we've been told that neither of us will be included on the trip to Nice for the eco-cosmetic launch, but Florence and two of the account managers are going and there's still lots to do to help them prepare.

On top of everything else, the Haute Couture Autumn/Winter Shows are running this week, too. It's the first week of July and the city seems far too hot and muggy to enjoy looking at heavy woollens and stiff tailoring so I can't seem to summon up much enthusiasm, even when Simone and I are given tickets to the Chanel event on the Tuesday evening. We take our seats in the Grand Palais, several rows back from the celebrities and fashion editors, and watch the models stride down the catwalk in Karl Lagerfeld's embellished tweed creations. The collection is exquisite: each item has been carefully structured to flatter the female form and the designs are both clever and quirky. But I am distracted by the floor show around us. As a backdrop to the show, the designer has brought the dressmakers from the *ateliers* along, to illustrate the fact that it has taken a small army of workers to make each of the finished garments that we are applauding. I watch, fascinated, as they ignore the action on the catwalk and continue to work on half-finished versions of the same garments that the models are wearing. To me, these modern-day seamstresses provide a direct connection to Claire, Mireille and Vivi and many of the traditional techniques that my grandmother would have used are still employed today.

Instead of the show being a welcome distraction, though, it only serves to remind me of the terrible ordeal that Claire and Vivi went through, sent from the city where they were tortured and imprisoned to the Nazi work camps in Germany. I feel the panic rising in my chest, squeezing the breath from my lungs. Suddenly the heat and the opulence of the Grand Palais become too much to bear and I pick up my bag, making my excuses as I slip away from the show early, hurrying back to the seclusion of my attic room across the river.

That night, I lie in my bed and wonder if I'm having some sort of a breakdown. I gaze at the photograph on the chest of drawers beside me. 'Help me,' I whisper.

Claire, Mireille and Vivienne smile back at me, reaching out across the years to comfort me. Three such different characters. And I remind myself that if Mireille and Vivi hadn't helped Claire to keep going then I wouldn't be here today.

'You need to keep going too!' I imagine I hear Mireille saying decisively, her dark curls bouncing.

'It's only when you know the whole truth that you will understand,' Vivi's calm eyes seem to be telling me.

And beside them Claire smiles her gentle smile, telling me that, even though she never knew me, she loves me. She is here with me. She will never leave.

1943

Paris was descending into chaos. As the war ground on and the Germans suffered more and more losses, the round-ups and deportations became more frequent, more random and more brutal. Most of the time, Mireille only left the *atelier* to go and get food, eking out the rations she was able to find for her 'guests' with the extra bits and pieces she was able to obtain on the black market which were paid for with money given to her by Monsieur Leroux. The two separate strands of her work, during the days and the nights as well, kept her busy. But whenever she could find the time, she would walk to the willow tree on the end of the island in the Seine and take refuge beneath its graceful arms.

One July day, as she sat watching the river flowing by and wondering what the ones she loved were doing at that moment, a smell of burning hung in the air. A plume of smoke smudged the sky over the Tuileries gardens and, loath to go back to the empty apartment just yet, she went to see what was happening.

A crowd had gathered in the park where she had taken Claire to meet Monsieur Leroux almost eighteen months ago. It felt like a lifetime had passed since that day. It had been winter then, but now it was high summer and the close, muggy air pressed in on Mireille, making little rivers of sweat trickle down the back of her neck.

As she drew closer to the Musée de l'Orangerie, she realised that soldiers were carrying framed pictures out of the gallery. She slipped into the crowd so that she wouldn't be spotted. Appalled, she watched as one of the framed canvases was lifted high into the air and then thrown on to the bonfire which raged on one of the grass *parterres*. 'What are they doing?' she asked a man standing next to her, who was watching the scene in grim silence.

'They have deemed these works of art to be "degenerate".' The man spoke with a quiet scorn. 'Art threatens the Nazi regime by depicting the truth of subjects they find abhorrent, apparently. And so they are burning them. I have seen, with my own eyes, a Picasso thrown on to that fire. Anything they don't like, anything that doesn't fit with their picture of the ideal world, they destroy.' He shook his head and his eyes burned with a passion born of fury. She noticed that his unkempt beard contained tiny droplets of paint and realised that he must be an artist. 'First they burnt books, now they are burning paintings, and they burn people, too, in those prison camps of theirs, I've heard tell. Remember this day, young lady; you are witnessing a holocaust of humanity. Remember it, and tell your children and your grandchildren so that they never let it happen again.'

As another painting was hurled on to the pyre, she turned away and hurried home. But when she got back to the apartment, she couldn't rid herself of the smell of the smoke that clung to her clothes and hair. And in spite of the heat of the July evening, she shivered as she remembered the man's words: '*They burn people, too, in those prison camps of theirs.*' For the millionth time, she prayed to any god who was left to listen that Claire and Vivi might still be alive and that they might be kept safe. *Please. Let them come home one day soon.*

~❊~

As Claire began to get her bearings, she discovered that the camp at Flossenbürg was just one of many in the area, built to provide slave labour for the German war effort. The rough barracks, in which the prisoners were housed, occupied one sector of the central site. Factories had been established in the vicinity, manufacturing textiles, munitions and even Messerschmitt aircraft, making the most of the steady stream of prisoners for their workforce, who arrived on trains like the one that had brought them there. She picked up these snippets of information from one of the girls in the bunk above the one that Claire and Vivi shared, who had spent a few months in the much larger camp at Dachau. There, she told them, she had worked in the brothel supplied for SS personnel. 'They would talk among themselves while they waited outside the cubicle, as if we weren't capable of understanding what they said while we were lying on our backs,' she said, scornfully.

'It must have been horrendous for you, being subjected to that,' Claire had said.

'Oh, it's not so bad once you get used to it. You get better food over there. Until you get ill and your hair and teeth fall out, that is.' She opened her mouth to display her gaping, bloodless gums. 'That's when they send you back here and you have to go and work in the factories again.' She'd looked at Claire appraisingly. 'They'd like you over there. A true Aryan, with your colouring, would be very popular. And you were one of the ones who didn't have your head shaved when they processed you. That means you could be on the list.'

Claire had shivered and pulled her headscarf down a little lower over her forehead to cover her hairline. The girl's eyes had a deadened, soulless look to them, a look which was shared by many of the inmates who'd been in the camps for a while.

Each day, after the morning roll call when they were forced to stand for an hour or more in the central square outside the barracks, Claire and Vivi would follow the guard who was in charge of the workers in the textile factory. They would file silently past the end of the alley on one side of the camp which led to the squat brick building whose tall chimney belched thick grey smoke into the sky day and night. Everyone knew what it was for. Sometimes they would hear stories of bodies piled up outside, a tangled heap of naked limbs and faded blue and white striped clothing, a scene from the inner circles of hell.

Some of the men who worked in the aircraft factory wore the blue triangles of voluntary labourers. Although, as Vivi remarked, 'voluntary' wasn't a very accurate word to describe people who'd been ordered to leave their homes and come and work like slaves, under the command of an enemy power. Claire often thought of her brothers, Jean-Paul and Théo. Had they worked somewhere like this? Were they here, perhaps, somewhere amongst the sea of sunken-faced inmates in one of the satellite camps? If so, Jean-Paul would wear a blue triangle on his clothing and Théo the red triangle, like hers and Vivi's, worn by political prisoners and prisoners of war.

It was Vivi who'd worked out the code that the triangles represented, through talking to the other women in the barracks. Yellow ones were worn by Jews, and sometimes a red inverted triangle was overlain by a yellow one the opposite way up, indicating a dual categorisation. Green triangles were worn by convicted criminals, who were often put in charge of work parties as they were prison-toughened which made them ruthless overseers, or *kapos* as they were known in the camp, prepared to mete out punishments to their fellow inmates. Black was for those classed as mentally ill, or as gypsies, vagrants and addicts.

Claire had been deeply shocked at seeing her camp-mates labelled in this crude and shameful manner, just as she, herself, was labelled. But as the months went by, she'd almost grown accustomed to it and scarcely registered the triangles of coloured material any more.

Vivi had managed to get them work in the textile factory by talking to the senior, the woman who oversaw their particular hut. Claire had heard her asking how they could get jobs in the sewing room at the reception centre that they'd passed through when they'd entered the camp.

'Those are jobs for privileged workers,' the woman had replied. 'You can't just walk into them. Everyone wants to work in such easy conditions sitting at a sewing machine in the warmth.'

'But we are experienced seamstresses,' Vivi had protested. 'We can work fast and accurately, and we know how to fix those sewing machines when the bobbins get tangled or the needles jam.'

The woman looked her up and down. 'That's as may be, but you still can't walk into one of those jobs so easily. Since you and your friend claim to have such talents, though, I'll speak to the *kapo* who's in charge of allocating workers to the textile factory. Perhaps they can put your special experience to good use there.' Her tone was cutting, but she kept her word and two days later Claire and Vivi were ordered to join the line of textile workers.

The factory floor had been a shock to Claire at first, but slowly she'd grown used to the noise and the unremitting workload. Vivi had seemed more at home from the start, and Claire remembered what she'd said about working in the spinning mills in Lille before the war.

The factory made the shirts and trousers for camp inmates as well as manufacturing clothing for the German military. Claire was set to work stitching grey army trousers. Vivi made socks for the soldiers, setting up the machinery and keeping it running at its maximum capacity all day long. Glancing up from her work, every now and then, Claire would notice how Vivi would talk to the other workers, and especially to the factory foreman who allocated the jobs, and how everyone warmed to her friendly manner and easy competence.

As the summer wore on, conditions became more and more unbearable in the barracks. The stench of the nearby latrine block mingled with the smell of sickness and decay which hung heavy on the air in the oppressive hut. The overcrowded bunks crawled with fleas and lice, which feasted on the wasted bodies of the prisoners. Infected bites became festering sores, and every morning the hut's senior would select a couple of the more able women to carry the bodies of fever-ridden inmates to the hospital block. Some mornings, for some of the women, it was too late: their corpses would be removed, wordlessly and unceremoniously, by the prisoners whose job it was to pull a handcart to the crematorium where the chimney cast its pall of grey smoke over the camp from dawn until dusk each day.

In the textile factory, the noise and the heat were merciless. One day, when the foreman's back was turned, Claire managed to smuggle a pair of scissors from her workbench back to the hut. That evening, she cut off her hair. As the pale strands fell to the floor around her feet, she experienced a searing pang of shame. She remembered pinning up the blonde lengths in front of the mirror in her room, wearing the midnight blue gown with the silver beads, preparing to go and meet Ernst on that New Year's Eve so long ago. Her need to feel loved, to enjoy the sense of luxury and plenty that she'd so craved, had been her downfall, bringing her here, in the end, to this living hell. She hacked viciously at her hair and angry tears ran down her face.

Then Vivi appeared at her side and took the scissors from her. 'Hush,' she said. 'I'm here. We're still together.' She wrapped her arms around Claire's shaking shoulders and whispered in her ear, 'Don't cry. You know the ones who cry are the ones who have given up. We won't ever give up, you and I.'

Then Vivi had handed back the scissors and said, 'Cut my hair off, too.' She'd turned to face the rest of the hut, summoning up a smile. 'Who else would like to join us? It's cooler, and it'll make it much easier to comb out the lice.' A queue of women had formed of those who still had their hair, and afterwards they helped one another to clean their shorn heads. The differentiation between those who'd had their heads shaved and those who hadn't was erased. And to Claire, it seemed that the stench and the degradation seemed a little less pervasive that evening, displaced by a sense of camaraderie that had flickered into life.

1944

The city froze that January. It was one of the coldest Mireille could remember, and now that supplies of food and coal were at their lowest ebb she felt that her body and her mind had frozen as well. She sleep-walked through her days in the sewing room, wrapped in a blanket as she tried to stitch together the pieces of the few items that were still being ordered. Many of the girls had left the *atelier*. Some – the Jewish girls and one or two others – had simply disappeared, as Claire and Vivi had done. Others had decided to go back and struggle to survive with their families in the more rural areas, where at least there was a chance to grow a little food.

The temptation to go home was strong, but Mireille knew she couldn't leave Paris, even if she had been able to get a pass to travel. Applying for one would draw attention to herself. In any case, she had to stay, for the sake of the fugitives that she sheltered in the attic rooms in the Rue Cardinale and for the sake of her friends, Claire and Vivi. She had no idea whether or not they were still alive, but she knew she had to keep going, keep hoping that one day they would return.

She left the apartment as seldom as possible, and curled up in her blankets when the air raid sirens sounded and she heard the distant roar of the bombers overhead. She often wondered whether 'Fréd' was in one of the planes and tried to give herself courage by imagining that he was, that he knew she was there and that he was guiding his bombs away from Saint-Germain, keeping her safe.

Monsieur Leroux brought her news, occasionally, of the war beyond her country's borders. The German forces were stretched thinner than ever now, and the privations that they'd inflicted on the countries they'd occupied were biting them too. The Allies were stronger than ever, making advances. Surely, he said, if the tide continued to turn like this, the war couldn't go on much longer . . .

She tried hard to hold on to his words, even though when she studied his face it was gaunt and twisted with anguish, belying his underlying sense of desperation.

She had often mulled over what he'd said that day when he'd come to tell her that Vivi and Claire had left the prison and been taken to a camp in the east. '*I love them both, Mireille.*' What had he meant by that? What was his relationship with Vivi, and what were his feelings for Claire? Could he love them both, equally?

One evening, after she'd settled the family of refugees that she was sheltering for the night in their bedrooms, she joined him where he sat at the table in the sitting room.

For a moment they were both silent. And then she said, 'I wonder what they are doing now.' There was no need for her to say their names; they both knew who she was referring to.

'I tell myself every day that they are doing what we are doing. Staying alive, keeping going, waiting for the day we can be together again. I think we have to tell ourselves that. It's what gives us a reason to carry on.'

She tried to read the expression in his eyes, but the depth of his pain obscured everything else. 'Vivi . . .' she began, but stopped, unable to find the right words to ask him what she wanted to know.

He studied her face for a moment. And then he said, his voice breaking with emotion, 'Vivi is my sister.'

All at once it made sense. Their closeness. The way they smiled at each other. But also the way she'd seen him looking at Claire, sometimes. He really did love them both. But in very different ways. The pain in his eyes made sense now, too.

He'd lost his sister as well as the woman he was falling in love with. And he blamed himself.

∾⁂∾

The cold would have killed the women in the hut, its icy fingers freezing the blood in their veins, had there not been so many of them crammed on to each bunk. In winter, the fleas and lice bit less, which meant there were fewer deaths from typhus, but influenza and pneumonia stepped into the breach to continue the brutal, remorseless harvest of lives through the camp. Weakened by near-starvation and despair, few of the camp's inmates had the resources to put up much of a fight.

One evening, when they arrived back from the factory, the hut senior drew Vivi and Claire aside. 'They are asking for more women who can sew, to work in the reception centre. There are so many more people to process these days, they've brought in extra sewing machines. I've put your names on the list.'

'Thank you,' said Vivi. Over the months they'd spent in the camp, she'd told Claire to bring back any odds and ends from the factory whenever she could, to give to the senior, as Vivi herself did too, cementing them into her good books. Everything had value – a handful of buttons, a needle and thread, some scraps of material. At last the gifts had paid off, buying the two of them their places in the relative warmth and safety of the reception centre.

And so the next morning, instead of trudging along the snow-packed track to the factory, they walked a few hundred yards to the huddle of buildings beside the gates to the camp. As they went, Claire blew on her hands, trying to stop her fingers from freezing. 'I wonder who'll take over our jobs in the factory,' she mused aloud.

Vivi began to speak, but the cold air caught in her lungs, making her whole body convulse as she coughed. When she found her voice again, she said, 'Well, I hope whoever takes over my machine doesn't discover that I set it to make the toes and heels of the socks thinner instead of reinforcing them. I reckon there'll be quite a few German soldiers with very sore feet by now. That's been my most recent contribution to the war effort!' For a moment, her hazel eyes flashed with a little of their old spark, and Claire couldn't help laughing. The sound was like music in the frozen air, a sound so unusual that it made the prisoners walking a few yards ahead of them turn and stare. In the nearest guard tower, the barrel of a machine gun swung in their direction and Claire quickly stifled her mouth with her hand.

Vivi coughed again, and her breath turned into little clouds above her head which froze into droplets of ice, weaving themselves into her halo of short, russet curls. A ray of low winter sunshine illuminated her for a moment and Claire was struck by how beautiful her friend looked in that moment, as out of place in the drab surroundings of the camp as a ruby nestling in a heap of rags.

∾✴჌

Mireille could sense that the German grip on Paris had begun to weaken. There were fewer soldiers on leave, these days, sitting at the cafés and restaurants along the Boulevard Saint-Germain, and more and more military convoys leaving the city, heading northwards.

Monsieur Leroux arrived at the apartment one evening in June, carrying a large box. He set it down on the table in the sitting room with a flourish. '*Voilà!* A present for you, Mireille.' She opened the box to find a wireless radio set.

A year ago she might have felt a qualm of fear at having such a thing under her roof, but now it represented a small freedom.

Once he had plugged it in and positioned the aerial correctly, a voice filled the room. At first she could scarcely grasp what the announcer was saying.

'What does he mean?' she asked Monsieur Leroux. 'What is this "Operation Overlord"?'

His eyes shone with a look of hope which had been absent for such a very long time. 'The Allies have landed on the beaches of Normandy, Mireille. This is it. The big push! They are fighting on French soil.'

Every evening after that, she would hurry back upstairs from the sewing room once the working day was over and switch on the radio to listen to the latest news from the BBC and the Free French broadcaster, Radiodiffusion Nationale. The voices filled the room with bulletins announcing the latest advances as, town by town, the Allies clawed France back from German control. And as she listened, those same voices seemed to fill her heart with fresh hope. She began to let herself believe, again, that there would be an end to the war; that she would be able to see her family soon; that Claire and Vivi would come home; and that maybe – just maybe – out there somewhere the young Free French airman, whose name she whispered at night in the silence of her darkened room, was fighting his way back to free the city where she sat waiting, in limbo, for her life to begin again.

Slowly but surely a new tone of defiance crept into the voices coming through the radio, until, at last, the tide turned.

It was a hot August afternoon and Mademoiselle Vannier had sent the few remaining seamstresses home early. There was so little work these days and only one team remained, working on the increasingly sporadic orders that came in. More often than not, the salon downstairs remained closed, the blinds drawn over the plate glass windows embellished with the name Delavigne Couture.

Mireille flung open the windows of the apartment to try and encourage a breath of early evening air to cool the overheated attic rooms, and then she turned on the radio. As she poured herself a glass of water in the kitchen, the announcer's words drew her back to listen more closely.

'Let us put an end to these convoys,' the voice urged. 'Yesterday another thousand or more men and women were sent east. And today we say "Enough!" Enough of our countrymen have disappeared to the German work camps. It's time for them to be allowed to come home now. Citizens of Paris, it's time to put an end to this. The Métro workers, the *gendarmes* and the police have come out on strike. We call on all other citizens to join them in a wider act of resistance. Rise up now and let us take back our city!'

As if in response to the call to arms, she heard the sound of gunfire from the direction of the river, followed by the dull thud of an explosion somewhere further to the north. There were shouts on the street below, and the sound of running feet seemed to replicate the throbbing of her pounding heart.

She felt an overwhelming urge to be part of it, whatever it was that was happening out there . . . Without stopping to think, she ran down the metal stairs and out on to the Rue Cardinale. The tall buildings hemmed her in on the narrow street and so, instinctively, she turned and headed for the river's more open vistas.

A group of young men marched briskly towards the Pont Neuf, carrying whatever arms they'd managed to procure from who-knew-where. More men emerged from the cellars and the attics of the buildings along the quayside, waiters and clerks and policemen: Resistance fighters all.

Mireille hesitated in the shade of a plane tree, unsure which way to go. At the end of the bridge, men and women were setting up barricades, dragging anything they could find to pile up across the road. Two men began cutting down one of the trees that flanked the entrance to the bridge, hacking desperately into it with axes.

Mireille ran to help a group that was levering up paving stones, adding them to the growing defences. Her hands bled as she clawed at the mortar holding a slab in place, prising a corner loose until the stone was freed and she could stagger to the barricade with it.

'Look out!' a man shouted, as the tree began to topple, and she leapt clear as it fell.

Just then, a German armoured car swept towards them across the bridge, spitting machine-gun fire. Bullets ricocheted off the stonework as the Résistants returned fire, and the man dragged Mireille down to crouch behind the fallen tree as a bullet embedded itself into the trunk beside her. The armoured car swerved and then careened off along the *quai* in the opposite direction. The man grabbed her arm and pulled her to her feet. 'Go home, miss,' he said. 'It's not safe out here on the streets. The city is a battleground now. Get yourself back inside.' At the far end of the bridge, a German tank lumbered into view, its gun barrel swinging menacingly towards the barricades. 'Hurry! Go now, while you can.' He pushed her towards the Rue Dauphine and she ran, stumbling, towards the shelter of the narrow streets of the *rive gauche*. As she fled, she glanced back over her shoulder at the tank as it advanced on the barricades, where one of the fighters lay, at the end of the bridge, in a pool of bright blood.

Back in the apartment, the radio was still filling the empty rooms with its tirade, urging the citizens to retake the city. She flung herself down on to the chair, gasping for breath, and sat listening late into the night to the voices from afar and the closer patter of gunfire, as the battle for Paris raged on.

～❦～

In the camp, they were used to 'selections' being made almost every day. Prisoners were marched away or herded into buses to be transported to and from the many other satellite camps that dotted the region. Some came back to report where they'd been, but others never returned.

At roll call one morning, when the other prisoners marched off to the factories for the day, Claire and Vivi were ordered to remain behind, along with a number of other women. Claire risked a glance at the others left standing on the dusty square in front of the huts. One or two looked afraid, not knowing where they might be sent next and what fate awaited them there. But most just stood with their eyes cast downwards, scarcely able to care. Vivi caught her eye and smiled, encouragingly.

'Eyes forward,' snapped the guard.

The women stood, swaying in the summer sun that beat down on their shaven heads protected only by thin cotton headscarves, until at last they were ordered to begin walking. The bedraggled, starving line of women filed out through the gates of the camp and followed the guards to the train station, where a line of trucks was drawn up alongside the platform.

'Please God, not again,' Claire prayed, remembering the long, slow journey that had brought them to Flossenbürg in the first place. A guard pulled open the heavy sliding door of one of the trucks and at first Claire couldn't make sense of what she saw. Slowly, squinting against the strong sunlight, in the darkness inside the wooden carriage she made out a tangled heap of blue and white striped cloth and pale limbs. Dark eyes gazed up at her, sunk into skull-like faces. And then she realised that these were women. The stench of death made her cover her nose and mouth, as the guard hastily pulled the door shut again.

'Next carriage,' shouted an SS officer, waving them further down the platform. In silence, the women climbed into the empty cattle truck that awaited them. The wooden door rolled closed, shutting out the light, and a few minutes later the train lurched forward.

The battle for Paris raged through the streets of the city for four days. Mireille listened to the radio broadcasts as reports came in that the Resistance fighters had occupied the Grand Palais and were coming under fire from German troops. Skirmishes were breaking out all across the city but, at the same time, columns of German vehicles had been seen moving down the Champs-Élysées, retreating eastwards.

The next night, the pitch of the broadcasts changed again, becoming even more frenzied. 'Take heart, citizens of Paris!' cried the announcer, 'the Second French Armoured Division is on its way. A vanguard is at the Porte d'Italie right now. Rise up and fight to take back your country!'

From the road below came the sound of running feet and volleys of shots.

But then she heard something else. She pushed her feet into her shoes and ran downstairs, hurrying towards the river again for the first time since she'd helped build the barricades on the Pont Neuf. She joined a growing flood of people taking to the streets of their city and, one by one, they added their voices to the song.

'*La Marseillaise*' rang through the streets as French and Spanish troops, in American tanks and trucks, opened fire on the German fortifications.

~✿~

When they'd boarded the train at Flossenbürg, Claire and Vivi hadn't known where they were being taken, or how long the journey would last. But after just a few hours' jolting progress, the train jerked to a halt.

The women lifted their bowed heads at the sound of shouted commands and then they heard the cattle-car doors being pulled back. At last their own carriage was opened and they helped one another down, blinking in the evening sunshine. They turned their faces away from the piles of bodies that were being unloaded from further up the train and stacked beside the railway tracks. Male prisoners in the ubiquitous striped uniforms were loading the corpses on to handcarts and wheeling them away.

Those who were still alive were ordered into lines and herded alongside the train to a high, white gatehouse. As they walked, one of the other women fell into step alongside Claire and Vivi.

'Are you the ones from Flossenbürg?' she asked, keeping her voice low so it wouldn't be heard beneath the sound of shuffling feet. 'I saw the name when we stopped at the station.'

Claire nodded.

'And you?' asked Vivi. 'Where have you come from?'

'Further north,' replied the woman. 'A place called Belsen. I'm hoping this camp will be a bit better. It certainly can't be any worse.'

'Do you know where we are?'

'I heard one of the guards say we were being sent to Dachau. Away from the bombing in the north. They're building new factories here, to replace the ones that have been destroyed. So they need more workers.'

'Silence!' roared a guard. 'Keep moving there!'

As they filed through the archway of the gatehouse, Claire lifted her eyes to read the now-familiar words set into the iron gates: *Arbeit Macht Frei*. This time, she read them in silence.

The women were led to barracks far bigger than the ones in the camp at Flossenbürg. Row upon row of them stretched away into the distance. It seemed to Claire that Dachau was as big as a town. In the centre of the camp, behind a cluster of trees, a tall chimney rose into the August sky, staining the blue with a cloud of grey smoke. It was a sight she recognised from the previous camp and she shuddered, knowing that this must be where the handcarts of corpses were being taken for disposal.

Vivi tugged at her sleeve. 'Come on,' she said. 'Let's find a bunk before they're all taken.'

After they'd queued for meagre rations of watery soup and a small hunk of hard black bread, they went back inside and their new hut senior called for the women's attention. She consulted a clip board, telling each group where they had been allocated to work the next day. She looked at the numbers sewn on to Claire and Vivi's jackets and consulted her list. 'You two, report to the reception centre. You'll be in the sewing room. Do you know what you're doing?'

They both nodded.

'Very well. Finish your food and get some sleep. It's an early start in the morning.'

In the crowded bunk that they shared, top-to-tail, with two other women, Claire whispered to Vivi, 'We'll be alright in the reception centre here, won't we? Just like we were before. Thank goodness for our sewing experience. It might just save our lives.'

Vivi brought her hand to her mouth, her body juddering as she tried to suppress her cough. When she could speak again she whispered, 'We'll be alright. Get some sleep now, Claire. It's been a long day.'

～✤～

Claire grew used to the rhythm of work in the sewing room at the Dachau reception centre. All day long, a continual stream of new prisoners was admitted and the sewing machines whirred as the workers attached the numbers and coloured triangles to the blue and white striped uniforms, one of each on the shirt just above the heart and one of each on the right leg of the trousers. It tore at her soul to have become a part of the grim machine processing each new inmate with ruthless efficiency and she felt a sense of guilt as she passed back each completed item to its recipient, meeting eyes filled with fear and despair. She tried to encourage them at first, with a kindly word or two, but the guard who oversaw the sewing room had shouted at her to stop talking and concentrate on her work. So now she had to make do with a faint smile instead.

She knew she was lucky, though. With only a short walk to the reception centre each day, she and Vivi conserved what little energy they were able to glean from the scant rations that formed the prisoners' diet in the camp, and Claire felt a little stronger than she had done when she'd worked in the textile factory at Flossenbürg. At the end of the day, as they made their way back to the barracks, beneath the watchful eyes of the guards in the towers around the camp perimeter, she noticed that Vivi's cough seemed a little better too, although maybe that was just because it was summer now. She knew as well, from what the other women in their hut said, that her work was a little easier than jobs in the factories and the surroundings were less harsh.

They'd been prisoners in these camps for more than a year, she realised, and for a moment a sense of desolation threatened to overwhelm her. Would they ever see Paris again? She glanced across to where Vivi sat at her sewing machine, her head bent over her work. As if sensing she was being watched, Vivi looked up and shot Claire a smile and a nod, reassuring her. *We are together*, Claire told herself, repeating the mantra that had kept her going through so many times of despair. *Everything will be alright.*

All at once, the guard, who had been leaning against the wall watching the women work, strode across to where Vivi sat and yanked her to her feet, hitting her hard around her head. The line of prisoners shrank back and one woman screamed at the sudden violence of the gesture.

Claire watched, horrified, as several yellow triangles fluttered to the floor from Vivi's lap, scattering like the wings of broken butterflies on to the bare boards at her feet. The guard shouted, and two of her colleagues came running in from the room next door.

'Traitor! French whore!' the guard screamed. She reached down and scooped together the triangles of yellow cloth. 'How many of these have you exchanged for blue ones? Don't deny it! I've been watching you. I saw you do it. And you've been leaving off the yellow ones when there are two to be sewn on, as well. I can have you shot for this.' She glanced around at the terrified seamstresses and prisoners who had all frozen in their places. 'Let this be a lesson to you all. Don't you dare think you can disobey orders.'

In the stillness, the sound of Claire's chair scraping on the floorboards as she stood up made everyone turn to stare at her. Vivi's face was white and a trickle of blood ran from her bottom lip, but she looked pleadingly at Claire and shook her head, almost imperceptibly, wordlessly begging her to stay where she was.

'You too?' snarled the guard. 'Are you also a traitor? Or do you simply want to volunteer for hard labour alongside your friend here?'

Claire opened her mouth to reply, but just then Vivi called out, 'No! Leave her. It was me, on my own. No one else knew.'

'Take her away,' snapped the guard. 'And you,' she spat at Claire, 'sit back down and get on with your work. I'll be watching you, so don't think you can try any such clever tricks, either.'

'Please . . .' said Claire.

'Silence!' roared the guard and she pulled her revolver from its holster. 'I will shoot the next person who opens her mouth. Now, are you going to get on with your work or do I have to clear the whole lot of you seamstresses out of here and allocate your cushy jobs to others who won't be so ungrateful?'

Slowly, numbly, Claire sank back down into her seat and bent her head over her sewing machine, her tears falling on to the blue and white striped shirt on the table in front of her, as Vivi was frog-marched out of the reception centre.

⁎

Claire was frantic. No one knew where Vivi had been taken. The senior in the barracks just shrugged when Claire begged her to try to find out.

'She shouldn't have been so stupid as to try to trick the guards. Pulling that stunt, hiding the yellow triangles to try to save prisoners. After she was so lucky to have that job, as well.' She shook her head. 'She's probably in the crematorium by now.'

It must have been about two weeks later – Claire had lost track of time, and another prisoner had taken Vivi's place in the shared bunk – when Vivi reappeared in the barracks one evening. She was thinner than ever and her cough had returned. Her clothes hung like rags from her frame and she walked with a stoop, seeming to have crumpled in on herself. Claire ran to her, and helped her to the bed, making the grumbling woman who'd taken Vivi's place move to another bunk. She fetched some soup and tried to give it to Vivi, but Vivi's hands shook so badly that she couldn't hold the bowl without spilling it. 'Here,' Claire soothed her, 'let me.' Little by little she spooned the watery brew of potato peelings and cabbage into Vivi's mouth.

Later, when she'd regained her strength enough to speak, Vivi told Claire that she'd been put in solitary confinement for two weeks. She'd lain alone in the darkness, listening to the moans and cries from the neighbouring cells, and kept herself going by repeating over and over the words that she and Claire had whispered to each other so often: *I'm here. We're still together. Everything will be alright.* 'As long as I knew you were okay, I could bear it,' she said.

Claire had helped Vivi to lie down. 'You'll get better now,' she said. 'I'll look after you. Will you go back to work in the factory, do you think?'

Vivi shook her head. 'They've told me to join the labour detail tomorrow morning after roll call.'

'No!' Claire's eyes widened in horror. 'You haven't got the strength to do that work. It will kill you.'

'That's exactly what they're hoping. When the guards took me from the sewing room, one of them pushed me up against the wall of the reception centre and put his pistol to my head. But then, just as he was about to pull the trigger his colleague stopped him. "A bullet is too good for a French whore like her," I heard him say. "We can get some more work out of her – let her die a slower death."' She stopped, struggling for breath as painful coughs seized her body.

'Hush,' Claire urged her, 'don't try to talk. Rest and get your strength back.'

Vivi continued, as though her friend hadn't spoken. 'But I don't intend giving them that satisfaction, Claire. Now I'm back with you, I'll be stronger. We'll keep each other going, you and I, won't we? Just as we have always done?' Vivi smiled at her, but even in the darkening hut as night fell, Claire could see that her eyes were deep pools of sadness.

❧

Claire couldn't bear to remain at her job in the reception centre, sewing the numbers and triangles on the uniforms of new prisoners. After another month, she plucked up her courage and spoke to the senior in the hut, asking to be transferred to work with Vivi.

The woman regarded her with surprise. 'Do you know what you are asking? Your friend has been allocated to the women's heavy labour detail, by order of the camp's Kommandant. It's a wonder she is still alive. It's only because the summer has been kind that any of those poor souls have survived. But winter's on its way now. It will decimate them.'

'Please,' Claire said firmly. 'I want to be transferred. There are plenty of others who are desperate to have a job in the sewing room. Let me be with Vivi.'

'Very well. But don't come and ask me for your comfortable job back when the snow begins to fall and you're expected to spend ten hours a day shovelling the roads clear. I hope you know what you're doing.'

Claire did indeed realise that it was very likely that neither she nor Vivi would survive the winter working with the cohort of prisoners assigned to hard labour duties. But as she'd watched the work take its toll on Vivi she'd had time to think about what it would mean if Vivi were no longer here. And she knew she wouldn't be able to live with herself if she had to spend those long, dark nights in that crowded bunk without her friend there to whisper, 'I'm here. We're together. Everything will be alright.'

Claire had no choice. She would rather die with Vivi than live on without her.

1945

The city had been liberated and Paris returned to French governance, but Delavigne Couture had closed its doors for the final time. Mademoiselle Vannier announced to the seamstresses on the first floor one morning that there would be no more work coming in once they'd finished the commissions they were working on. She told the girls, though, that Monsieur Delavigne had asked around on behalf of his workers and there was an offer from a larger couture house which still had plenty of work coming in. Anyone who wanted to could begin there the following week.

Later that same day, she had a quiet word with Mireille, telling her that the building would be put up for sale, eventually, but that she could stay where she was for the time being, as it would be good not to leave the place completely deserted while things were still so unsettled in the aftermath of the city's liberation. 'I hope you will be coming with me to work at Monsieur Lelong's? You are one of our best seamstresses, Mireille. I know you will be welcomed there.'

Mireille considered for a moment. She longed to go home and see her family, but the war continued to rage across Europe, and there were still skirmishes on French soil as the last of the German troops moved to consolidate their final defence of the eastern border. Travel was risky and the railways were largely destroyed where Resistance fighters had sabotaged the lines to prevent the efficient movement of German troops.

It was probably safer for her to stay where she was for now . . . and if she was completely honest with herself, there were other reasons why she was reluctant to leave. She waited, daily, for news from Monsieur Leroux of Vivi and Claire. And then, what if the airman came back to look for her . . .?

And so she agreed. She would work for the new couture house and stay put in Paris for the time being.

~❧~

Lucien Lelong's couture house had survived the war and was now thriving, thanks to a designer with a reputation for brilliance whom he'd employed.

Mireille's knees shook when she was introduced to this same designer, a Monsieur Dior. He was working on some new looks to mark a new beginning, he explained to the team from Maison Delavigne, as they were being given a tour of the *atelier* on their first day. 'I am pleased to welcome you to Lelong. Maison Delavigne's seamstresses have a reputation for perfection,' he said. 'And I expect nothing less.'

Mireille enjoyed her work with her new employers. It was still hard to come by some fabrics, but Monsieur Dior made the most of what was now becoming available. His ideas included softer outlines and subtle embellishments, and there was a little more fullness in the skirts of the gowns Mireille stitched. The *atelier* hummed with the sound of sewing machines and a sense of busyness that had long been absent at Delavigne Couture. Monsieur Dior's reputation was growing rapidly and wealthy clients from around the world had begun to demand Parisian couture once again.

She couldn't help thinking how much Claire and Vivi would enjoy working here, using their skills to breathe life into Monsieur Dior's stunning evening gowns, as they painstakingly worked on their intricate beadwork. She wished they were here now, sitting at the sewing table beside her, exchanging an occasional smile when they looked up from their work, pausing to stretch cramped fingers and aching necks.

When would the war finally end? Much of France had been reclaimed now, but the Germans had consolidated their remaining forces in the Vosges Mountains in the east. The radio broadcasts that she listened to avidly announced that, despite last-ditch attempts by Hitler's troops, the Allies were fighting their way across Belgium into Germany now. As she listened to the news each night, she wondered when she would hear the news she really longed for: news of her friends.

Monsieur Leroux still worked unceasingly to try to find them, through his contacts in the army and in the Red Cross. Surely he would track down Vivi and Claire soon, she told herself. Only then would she be at peace.

⌘

In Germany, the winter had been another cruel one. At first, when Claire had joined Vivi on the hard labour detail, they'd pulled a heavy roller over the roads that had been built to link the new, underground factories that were being constructed in an attempt to protect production against Allied bombs. Wagon-loads of rubble arrived by train on the siding that had been built alongside the camp – rubble cleared from cities which had been targeted in bombing raids. The starving, skeletal prisoners were ordered to ferry it, barrowload by barrowload, to the road site. Harnessed like horses between the handles of the roller, Claire and Vivi had to throw themselves forward to get it to move at all and then, for hours on end, they trudged over the rough mixture of clinker and rubble, crushing it and flattening out the surface.

Then the snow had begun to fall and the women had been set to work clearing it with shovels to keep the roadways open so that the prisoners could walk to the factories each day. It was hot work, which made sweat soak their striped jackets, rotting the fabric until the seams frayed. But at the same time their fingers froze around the handles of their heavy shovels, bleeding and turning black at the tips where frostbite nipped them.

As the ground froze and the snow continued to fall, the factories at Dachau had been commanded to increase their productivity. Like the crematorium, the munitions factory ran day and night. One day the *kapo* in charge of their work party told Claire and Vivi that they had been reassigned to work the night shifts there.

Their new job involved dipping metal shell casings in an acid bath to clean and toughen them before they were packed with explosives. The acid splashed and burned their arms, eating into what little skin still covered their jutting bones. Exhausted, they fell into their bunk each morning, just as it was vacated by its night-time occupants, pulling dirty, ragged blankets around themselves and huddling together for warmth. And each time they did so, they would whisper the words to each other that kept them alive, before falling into an uneasy, pain-wracked half-sleep. When she woke towards evening, Claire would lie listening to the labouring of Vivi's breath, the faint rattle of her lungs mingling with the sound of the wind as it scoured the walls of the hut, and she would quietly pull the edge of her blanket over her friend, trying to will back her strength and protect her from the life-sapping harshness of the reality that surrounded them.

When they were roused from their bunk by the day shift workers who'd returned for the evening, the block senior made Vivi and Claire carry out the bodies of those who hadn't made it to another night shift. They would add them to the piles on the wooden carts which did the rounds of the camp each morning and each evening, delivering stacks of corpses to the crematorium.

At last, the day came when the sun climbed a little higher above the razor wire surrounding the electrified perimeter of the camp, and patches of bare mud began to show through the snow covering the ground. As they trudged to their shift in the munitions factory one evening, Claire whispered to Vivi that they had done it: they'd survived the Dachau winter. Surely there wouldn't be another one, she told her friend – the war would end and they'd be free by the time the next snows fell on the camp. Vivi had smiled and nodded but couldn't speak, as a coughing fit seized her and convulsed her bones, rattling them like the bare branches of the trees outside the gates of the camp that shook and shivered in the wind.

New prisoners continued to arrive at Dachau, in greater numbers than ever. Some of the trains that pulled up alongside the camp pulled open-topped trucks filled with rubble and coal and raw materials for the factories. But others drew long chains of those wooden-sided cattle-cars, and when the guards drew back the bolts that fastened the sliding doors another human cargo was discharged. In the barracks, the new arrivals would tell of the head-high piles of dead bodies, which had to be unloaded from the train and stacked beside the tracks. Some of the prisoners said they had been brought to Dachau from other camps which were being evacuated as the Allies advanced. Wherever they came from, they all had stories to tell of torture and murder and starvation and slave labour. And every one of those camps seemed to have a tall chimney at its centre which breathed the stench of death into the skies over Europe.

The new arrivals also brought with them fresh outbreaks of lice and fleas and disease that spread quickly in the already squalid barracks. The women did their best to help each other, cleaning one another's heads, offering water and tending the sick as best they could. But survival was becoming an impossible challenge. As the population grew, dysentery filled the barracks with its sickening stench and the milder winds of spring brought with them a resurgence of the deadly kiss of typhus.

It was April. Still cold enough to cause a frost to form on the roofs of the barracks overnight and to freeze Claire's hands and feet as she and Vivi walked back to their block after another night shift in the arma-ments factory. Every bone in her body ached with cold, exhaustion and hunger, the Holy Trinity of the concentration camp. The sky beyond the watchtower glowed red as another dawn broke over Dachau, but the column of grey smoke rising from the tall brick chimney in the centre of the camp stained the beauty of the sunrise with its grim pall.

Vivi's cough was dry and painful-sounding as she lowered herself wearily on to the bunk. Claire brought her a tin cup filled with water, but Vivi had already sunk into a deep sleep by the time she came back from the tap, so she set it carefully beneath the bed for later. She drew the edge of her blanket over her friend's wasted, angular body, noticing a rash of dark bites on her chest where the blue and white striped over-shirt hung loose from the concavity beneath her collarbones.

Later that day, as Claire drifted in and out of a troubled slumber, a sudden commotion in the hut forced her fully awake.

Some of the women who were supposed to be out working the day shift had returned to the barracks and the noise of their boots hurrying back and forth across the floorboards made the hut walls reverberate.

'If you have a blanket, bring it with you,' shouted the block senior. She strode the length of the long room, shaking awake the exhausted inmates who'd worked the night shift and telling them to get up. 'Hurry. You will be leaving shortly. Assemble on the square as quickly as possible.'

Claire gently tapped Vivi's arm, but there was no immediate response. She nudged her more firmly and Vivi coughed, that dry, rasping sound that was so painful to hear. Then Claire realised that her friend's body was burning. She sat up, as best she could in the confined bunk, and drew back the collar of Vivi's shirt. And she saw what she'd been dreading: the dark rash had spread to cover Vivi's chest. It was a sight that she was familiar with from trying to help other women in the block. It was the sign of typhus.

As the hut emptied, the block senior hurried over to the corner where Claire was trying to get her friend to take a sip of water from the tin mug. Vivi's eyes were glazed with the fever that was blazing within her wasted body. 'Get up! Be quick! You need to be on the square now for a roll call.'

'She can't . . .' Claire said, turning frantically to the senior. 'She's ill. Look at her.'

After a cursory glance, the senior snapped, 'Well, you'll have to leave her then. Those who are too sick to go will be left here for the guards to deal with.'

'Go?' Claire asked. 'Go where?'

'The Allies are advancing. They'll be here any day. My orders are to evacuate the camp. We're to march west, to the mountains. Bring what you can and get outside now.'

Claire shook her head. 'I won't leave her,' she said.

The senior had already started to walk away. She turned to glare at Claire. 'In that case,' she snapped, 'you can stay for all I care. You two have been nothing but trouble from the very start. But I'm warning you, the camp is being destroyed. The SS are disposing of anyone left behind, the sick and the dying. If you stay, you will die with her.'

Claire's voice was quiet, but determined. 'I won't leave her,' she repeated.

The block senior shrugged. Then she turned on her heel and left the hut, slamming the door behind her.

Claire lay back down next to Vivi and tried to cool her fever by wetting a corner of her shirt and gently stroking it over her burning forehead.

'I'm here,' she whispered. 'We're together. Everything will be alright.'

The sounds from beyond the hut walls were muffled: running footsteps gathering in the square, then silence for what seemed like hours while the headcount took place, she assumed, and then the sound of shuffling feet as a few thousand prisoners began their long march out through the metal gates, beneath that grotesque slogan, towards the

Vosges Mountains where the beleaguered German forces were trying to consolidate one of their final strongholds.

As dusk dimmed the light that filtered through the grimy windows of the hut, the camp beyond fell silent. Claire continued to bathe Vivi's forehead and to sponge down her skin, which seemed as fragile as tissue paper and so hot it might burst into flames. Her friend muttered and coughed and groaned, as the pain and the fever consumed her. All through the long darkness of the night, Claire kept trying to get her to drink a little water and continued to whisper reassurances – 'I'm still here. We're together. I won't leave you, Vivi.' – until at last she, too, fell into a troubled sleep.

At daybreak, Claire woke to find Vivi's eyes on her. They were still glazed with the fever, but she was awake. Claire smoothed the halo of sweat-soaked hair back from Vivi's face, praying that it was a sign that the fever was breaking and that she might pull through.

The sound of heavy boots running past the door of the hut startled Claire. Was this it? Were these the guards, coming to dispose of the sick and the dying as the senior had predicted?

But the footsteps faded away round the end of the barracks. And then suddenly a rattle of gunfire sounded, close by. A shouted command made Claire sit up. The voice wasn't German; it was American.

'Vivi,' she whispered, 'they're here! The Americans. We've made it.' But Vivi seemed to have sunk back into unconsciousness, each gasping breath making her chest rattle.

'I'm going to get help, Vivi,' Claire told her. 'They'll have medicine. Hold on, I'll be back very soon.'

She staggered to the door and pushed it open, blinking in the April sunlight. Her legs felt so weak that she could scarcely stand, but she knew she needed to go and find someone who could help Vivi. Every minute counted. Holding on to the walls of the hut for support, she made her way to the open space of the square in front of the rows of barracks.

From force of habit, she glanced up nervously at the nearest watch-tower in the fence that enclosed the camp. But instead of the silhouette of a Nazi soldier with a machine gun trained on the camp interior, an empty square of sky was framed beyond the abandoned tower. Leaning against the side of a hut for support, she stumbled towards the central square.

It was the smell that hit her first. Overlying the background stink of death and decay, the usual wisp of acrid, grey smoke still hung in the air above the brick chimney behind her. But as she neared the square a more pungent stench filled her nostrils. As she rounded the corner of the last hut, she choked as a thick pall of smoke enveloped her, eddying around her on a gust of breeze. As it cleared, she could make out a smouldering heap of what looked like railway sleepers in the middle of the parade ground. A charred hand reached from the top of the pile, pointing towards a heaven that she no longer believed could exist, as her numbed senses told her that this was a hastily assembled funeral pyre. The crematorium was too slow: the camp staff had tried to burn as many bodies as possible before the camp was liberated, in an attempt to destroy the evidence of what had gone on there.

Lined up on the parade ground, where once they had forced the prisoners to stand for hours on end in all weathers as headcounts were made or punishments meted out, were some of those same camp guards. American troops, wearing rounded helmets and khaki uniforms, held them at gunpoint. A prisoner staggered on to the square, his legs barely able to hold him up, and launched himself forward, trying to attack one of the SS guards. He screamed as he did so, uttering inarticulate, agonised cries, giving voice to the outrage that the guards' inhuman treatment of so many innocent people for so many years warranted. His weakness made his attack ineffectual, though, and two of the American soldiers caught him and held him off the SS personnel, gently helping him away.

Relinquishing the support of the hut wall, Claire stumbled across to where a soldier wearing a white armband emblazoned with a red cross was stooping over the body of a collapsed prisoner. '*S'il vous plaît*' – she clutched at his sleeve – 'my friend. You have to help her. Please.'

The medic straightened up, realising that the prisoner on the ground was beyond help. She tugged on the sleeve of his jacket again. 'Please, come with me.'

His voice was kind, even though she couldn't understand the words he said. He tried to make her sit down but she found the strength to resist, to pull him towards the hut. Realising her intent, he went with her, following her in through the door and over to the corner of the bunk that she and Vivi shared.

Claire knelt down and seized her friend's hand. 'Vivi, help is here!' she cried.

But there was no answering squeeze of her fingers, no flutter of eyelids opening to display a pair of clear hazel eyes.

And then she realised that the rattle of Vivi's breathing had fallen silent and the blue and white striped shirt hung in motionless folds over her heart.

A heart that had been so filled with courage and strength.

A heart that beat no more.

The medic laid a tender hand on Claire's emaciated shoulders as she knelt by the wooden bed.

She sobbed into the soft halo of Vivi's copper-coloured hair, lit by a shaft of sunlight which crept through the dirty windows to illuminate the two women huddled together in the empty hut.

Harriet

I'd never even heard of Flossenbürg, so I go online to research it. I'm horrified to find that there were hundreds of so-called work camps like it scattered across Nazi-occupied Europe, from France in the west to Russia in the east. The numbers are horrendous, a grotesque record of what happened in the concentration camps. I discover that Claire and Vivi were just two of the literally millions of people who were imprisoned, enslaved and killed. Disease, malnutrition and exhaustion caused the deaths of many; still more were murdered by firing squads or in the gas chambers of the extermination camps like Auschwitz, Buchenwald and Bergen-Belsen. Dachau, where Claire and Vivi ended up, was one of the biggest and longest-established camps.

My research is interrupted by a tap on my bedroom door. 'Come in,' I call.

Simone pushes the door open, tentatively. 'Harriet,' she says, 'come out with me this evening. A group of us are going to watch the Bastille Night fireworks on the Champ de Mars. It's always spectacular.'

I shut my laptop and rub my neck to release the tension. The things I've just read have made my head throb. 'That's really kind, but I think I'll stay in.'

Instead of retreating, Simone takes a step forward, coming closer. 'Harriet . . .' She hesitates, choosing her words carefully. 'I heard about you and Thierry. I'm sorry. Really I am. You were good together.'

I smile and shrug. 'Yeah. I'm sorry too. I'm just not in the right place at the moment, I guess. But actually I don't think I've ever been very good at relationships.'

She sits down on my bed and shakes her head emphatically, her curls bouncing. 'That's not true. You are one of the best-liked people in the office. You've been a good friend to me. And you are a good grand-daughter to Claire, you know, continuing the search for her story. She'd be so proud of you. But you need a night off. It will be a good distraction. Please, come out with me. After all, it's France's biggest night of the year! Thierry won't be there, by the way, if that's what's stopping you,' she adds. 'He's working at a gig tonight.'

Her dark eyes glow with such genuine friendship that I can't refuse her. 'Okay, then. Just give me ten minutes to change,' I say.

꧁꧂

The streets are filled with a river of people making their way towards the Champ de Mars. The grassy slopes that flank the wide sweep of space in front of the Eiffel Tower are already almost completely covered with spectators as we approach. But Simone is an old hand at this and she quickly spots her group of friends who've spread a blanket out to keep enough room for us to join them. The sky is just beginning to darken and there's a buzz of anticipation in the air as the tower's metal frame is lit in stripes of blue, white and red and the music starts. The fireworks will only begin at eleven, creating a spectacular end to the national holiday, but they are preceded by a concert. I settle back, leaning on my elbows, and let the sights and sounds wash over me. Simone was right, it is good to be out. And I might not have another chance to see this again. I wonder where I will be this time next year, when my internship will be a thing of the past.

The crowds are good-natured, everyone out to enjoy themselves, and there's a great deal of friendly banter. Suddenly, though, something changes. I can't put my finger on it, at first; it's subtle, an atmospheric shift. The light show continues on the Eiffel Tower and the music plays on, but the sounds of the crowd become muted, somehow; I glance around, the all-too-familiar sensation of anxiety gripping the pit of my stomach. Around us, people are checking their phones. Ringtones are drowned out by the music, but more and more people appear to be listening to messages, or making calls. I turn and look towards Simone, who sits just behind me. She has taken her phone out of her pocket and is studying it. The smile has gone from her face.

I reach out and tap her ankle to get her attention. 'What is it?' I ask.

She shuffles down a little so that she's sitting next to me. 'There's been an attack. In Nice. Reports are just coming in. No one seems to be quite sure what's happened. But it sounds bad.'

Our eyes meet in the darkness and I know we're both thinking the same thing. 'Florence? And the others? They're still there, aren't they?' As far as I can remember, the product launch was scheduled to end two days ago but the team had planned to stay on to pack up and enjoy the Bastille Day holiday there.

Simone nods, busily composing a text. 'I'm just sending them a message now.' She bites her lip, pressing send and then anxiously checking for a reply.

After a couple of minutes, her phone pings and I watch her face, which is still creased into a frown, as she scans the screen. 'They're okay,' she says. 'They're stuck in a bar just off the beachfront and there's been some sort of incident. The police have sealed off the city centre, apparently. But they're all safe.' She and I both breathe again.

We try to concentrate on the show as the sky lights up with fireworks. But there's an air of tension and distracted preoccupation all around us. As soon as the last sparks fade against the black of the sky, we begin to make our way home. Simone checks the news reports that repeatedly light up the screen of her phone and she relays them to me as we walk. 'A truck has hit a number of bystanders on the Promenade des Anglais. They're saying there are some injuries, perhaps some deaths. It sounds bad.'

Subdued, we climb the stairs to the apartment on the fifth floor and retreat to our rooms in silence.

❧

The next morning I wake early. Simone is already up, watching the television in the sitting room. She glances up as I join her on the sofa and I can see she's been crying. As the news reports continue, I understand why. A terrorist drove a truck down the main road along the Nice beachfront last night. The promenade had been blocked off for the Bastille Night festivities and it was crammed with holidaymakers. But the lorry had been driven into the crowds, deliberately targeting people on the pavement, carving out a swathe of destruction and devastation. The early morning reports estimate that over eighty people have been killed and more than four hundred injured, some critically.

'Is there any more word from Florence and the others?' I ask, when I can speak.

Simone nods. 'They are at their hotel, packing up to leave. They'll be back later.'

We sit in silence for a moment, feeling thankful that the people we know are safe, but unable to get out of our minds the thought of so many others whose lives have been brutally ended or changed for ever.

Feeling sickened, I pull on a jacket and head out to get some fresh air. The early-morning city is quiet after the noisy celebrations of last night which have been forgotten now, overtaken by this latest terror attack on French soil. Without planning where I'm going, I head towards the river. I cross the road and stand for a moment, leaning on the wall opposite the Île de la Cité. At first I hardly see the landscape before me. A kaleidoscope of nightmarish images plays in my mind, of a truck careening down a crowded street, and of the concentration camps that I'd researched yesterday. What is this world where human beings can be the perpetrators of such inhumanity against their own kind? I'm trying hard not to let the rising panic overwhelm me and I press my hands against the wall, taking deep breaths.

As my breathing quietens, I realise that I'm looking at the downstream end of the island. And then I notice it: Mireille's willow tree. It's still there, on the point at the very tip, its branches trailing their green fingers in the flow of the Seine. I cross the bridge and find the narrow stairs that lead down to where the boat trips depart from the island. The cobbled quay skirts a small public garden and I follow it to the tree. In the middle of the city, I am in an oasis of solitude. The noises of the first of the rush-hour traffic on either side of the river are muted by the veil of leaves and the quiet sounds of the river lapping at the stones that reinforce the banks of the island. Just as Mireille found sanctuary here all those years before, I sit with my back against the trunk of the tree, leaning my head against its reassuring solidity, and my mind calms enough to be able to think more clearly. Setting aside the horror of the terror attack in Nice for now, I mull over what I've learned about my grandmother, longing for her to ground me and reassure me.

It was a miracle that Claire survived. I realise that if Vivi hadn't been there to encourage her and support her, she never would have made it. Vivi's determination to keep going – and not only that, but to keep trying to find ways to sabotage the Nazi war effort – speaks of an awe-inspiring strength of character. The concentration camp system was set up to be totally dehumanising for the inmates. But it couldn't break Vivienne's spirit: she never lost her humanity right up to the very end.

When that end came, though, Claire was left alone. Not only did she have to bear the guilt of having been the cause of Vivi's arrest in the first place, but she also had to carry the guilt of survival with her for the rest of her life, alongside the scars left by those traumatic eighteen months in the camps. She went on to marry and to have a child. I've worked out that my mother was born when her own mother was almost forty . . . it must have taken many years for Claire's broken mind and body to heal enough for her to be able to sustain a pregnancy. And so Felicity was named for the happiness that she represented to her parents – a miraculous child born to a woman who had survived so much.

Now that I am able to understand it better, I have come to see my mother's death in a new light. Her final act may have been to take her own life by swallowing a handful of pills and a half-bottle of brandy, but I know that what killed her was the fragility that she had inherited. Born in peacetime, she was still a child who had to carry the legacy of war and it was a legacy that bestowed upon her burdens of her own: the burden of embodying happiness; the burden of those trauma-induced genetic changes that were passed on to her; the hard-wired fear of abandonment. These were the factors that created the perfect storm of despair and hopelessness that overwhelmed her and finally led her to commit suicide.

It helps me to know this, to be able to understand so much more about my mother's life and death. But it terrifies me as well. How can I escape the same fate? In a world that seems filled with fear and panic, what can I do to stop the cycle repeating itself? Do I carry that same fragility in my own genetic make-up? Am I helpless, or is it possible for me to retake control of my life?

I realise that I can't find the answers to all these questions on my own. Perhaps I shouldn't be such a stubborn, independent Breton or Brit. It's time to be brave enough to ask for help.

And so it is, sitting within the sheltering arms of Mireille's tree, that I summon up the courage to make an appointment with a counsellor. If it is easier for me to express myself in a foreign language, maybe it will help me talk freely, at last, about the burdens of my own.

1945

'Mireille, there is great news!' Monsieur Leroux seized her and hugged her when she opened the door in response to his pounding. 'They've found Claire in one of the work camps! I tracked her down through the Red Cross. She is alive. She's been ill, and they've been caring for her in the camp hospital, but now she is well enough to be evacuated. I'm going out there, to bring her back to a hospital here in Paris where she can continue her recuperation. And I'll try to find Vivi too. Claire will have news of her, surely. If Claire has survived then there's hope that Vivi has as well. You know how strong she is! Perhaps Claire will be able to tell us where she is.'

Mireille's heart felt as if it would burst with the mixture of emotions that bubbled up at the sight of his joyful face. 'Where is Claire?' she asked.

'A camp called Dachau. Near Munich. I'm leaving today. As soon as I know more, I'll let you know. They're coming home to us at last, Mireille, I feel certain.'

～❦～

Claire's eyes fluttered open as sunlight streamed through the windows of her hospital room. Her hands looked as though they belonged to someone else where they lay against the clean whiteness of the turned-down sheet. At the end of her skeletal arms, their skin reddened and scarred with acid burns, her knuckles were swollen knobs of bone, her finger-tips cracked and hardened. It was hard to believe these hands had ever carefully pieced together offcuts of midnight blue crêpe de Chine with stitches so tiny they couldn't be seen, and held delicate silver beads in place as she sewed them around the neckline, creating her own constel-lation of tiny stars in a night sky.

She was still weak from the fever that had overwhelmed her the day after she'd watched Vivi's body being laid in a hastily dug mass grave, alongside so many others. Even though it was April, the grip of winter had seemed loath to leave Dachau that day and it had snowed, lining the grave with ermine and drawing a soft, white shroud over the piles of corpses that lay stacked beside the muddy trench.

Typhus had swept through the camp and even after its liberation the few thousand remaining prisoners who had been too sick or weak to set off on the death march to the mountains with their fellow inmates, continued to die in their hundreds, in spite of the ministrations of the international Red Cross and the US army doctors. Claire was one of the lucky ones. When the fever had seized her in its brutal grip, she'd been treated promptly and had been well cared for in the makeshift hospital.

And yet, as her strength slowly began to trickle back into her veins, she wished she had died with Vivi. Instead of a liberation, it felt like a lifetime's sentence: she would live with the knowledge of having been unable to save her friend. And she knew that her life would be filled, every day, with the guilt. It was her fault Vivi had been captured; Vivi had looked after her and protected her, but she hadn't been able to do the same. She hadn't even been there when Vivi had taken her last breath.

She had wanted to lie down beside Vivi's body in the snow-lined grave and sleep for ever.

A nurse, taking the pulse of a patient in the bed opposite, noticed that Claire was awake. 'Here,' she said, 'let me help you sit up a little.'

She plumped the pillow and said, 'Drink this.' Claire obeyed, too weak to protest even though the tonic tasted bitter and made her want to retch.

She drifted in and out of sleep and each time she woke she opened her eyes expecting to see Vivi's smile, dreaming that she would hear her whisper that Claire wasn't alone, that they were together, that everything would be alright. But she saw only the clean, white sheets that covered the broken husk of her body and an empty chair next to her hospital bed, and the only voices she heard were those of the nurses as they went about their duties. And she would drift off to sleep again, thinking – hoping – that perhaps this time she wouldn't wake up . . .

The next time she awoke there was someone sitting in the chair. The figure bent towards her, and for a moment her breath caught in a gasp as she looked into Vivi's clear, hazel eyes.

But then, as she focused, she realised it wasn't Vivi.

It was a man, who reached for her hand and held on tight, as if he would never let it go.

Harriet

The office at Agence Guillemet is once again a frenetic hive of activity. The usually quiet hum becomes a crescendo of ever-more-frantic conversations as Paris Fashion Week approaches and the pressure mounts on the account managers to handle last-minute crises (models going AWOL, a shipment of shoes stuck in French customs, requests for radio and press interviews . . .). Simone and I are run off our feet, helping get everything ready and keeping the coffees coming. We work all through the weekend and barely stop to grab a sandwich for lunch on the Monday, the day before the official launch of Fashion Week. My year-long internship is up, but Florence has asked me to stay on for an extra few weeks to help with the busiest time of the year. I've put off thinking about what I'll do next. I'd love to stay on in Paris, but I haven't had a chance to talk to Florence about the possibility of a full-time position at Agence Guillemet. I know it must be a long shot, though, or she'd have suggested it before now. Maybe I'll have to go back to London and try to get a job there. Every time I think about leaving Paris, I feel a wrench of sadness, as if the tentative roots I've put down here are about to be wrenched up as I start somewhere new all over again. The pattern of my life – the constant upheavals, the packing and unpacking, the next move to another place where I don't really have any sense of belonging – seems inexorable and inescapable.

I try not to think about that today, though. Work is the perfect displacement activity so I immerse myself in it. I'm just finishing up, putting the final touches to some goody bags filled with our client's eco-cosmetics that will be handed out to guests at one of the catwalk shows, when Florence comes through reception. 'You're working late, Harriet.' She smiles. 'And thank you, those look wonderful.' She fishes in her handbag (a classic Mulberry, naturally) and brings out a couple of white cards. 'Here,' she says. 'I have two extra of these. I think you and Simone more than deserve them. I'll see you there.'

She gives a little wave as she sweeps out of the door, calling, '*Bon courage!*' as she heads home to prepare for the biggest week of the year in the fashion capital of the world.

I examine the cards. Embossed across the top is a logo that is instantly recognisable.

I run up the stairs to the apartment, taking them two at a time, and am so out of breath by the time I get to the fifth floor that I can scarcely get the words out to tell Simone that we have invitations to the *Vogue* party. And it's being held at the Palais Galliera. So now I know exactly how Cinderella felt when she was told that she'd be going to the ball.

⁂

As we join the procession of the glamorously famous climbing the steps of the museum, I'm so excited I can hardly breathe. In the background, the Eiffel Tower flashes as if clad in silver lamé and then sparkles as if covered in sequins. It's been the headline of all the papers, a light show commissioned especially for Fashion Week. There's a sense of magic in the air, which is heightened by the sight of the museum building as we approach, lit so that the pure white of the stonework appears ethereal against the black of the night.

Inside, the hall and main gallery are filled with people dressed in a dazzling range of outfits, from the avant-garde of those who are trying hard to grab the attention of the movers and shakers in the fashion world to the classically understated of those who have no need to try at all. Cameras flash and a film crew circulates, capturing the glittering array of guests. Music pumps from hidden speakers and both the temperature and the volume of conversation in the room soar. Clutching our glasses of champagne, Simone and I weave our way through the crowd, nudging each other as we recognise models, actors and fashion editors. Florence catches sight of us and waves us over to where she is in conversation with a man whom she introduces as one of the directors of Paris *Vogue*. She is generous in including us, but we are aware, too, that this is a business event for her and so we soon drift away, leaving her to her high-level networking. Simone bumps into a client of the agency who she's met before and I leave them to chat as I circle the room. I can hardly believe this is the same place that I've come to for refuge, seeking out the peace and reassurance of the history it contains. It's the perfect setting for this glamorous party, of course, but a little bit of me resents the invasion. How many of the people here have even noticed the exhibits, I wonder.

Setting down my empty glass, I slip through into an adjacent room which is almost empty. Everyone wants to be where the action is, hoping to be snapped in one of the photographs that will appear in *Vogue* magazines from New York and London to Delhi and Sydney. So it's easy to find a little peace and quiet away from the hubbub in a room where a series of Belle Époque evening gowns are displayed in glass cases.

As I stand looking at a beautiful crystal-encrusted satin creation which would overshadow any of the party outfits in the next room, a voice says, 'Hello.'

I turn to see the woman with the silver-white hair. Tonight, instead of her tailored jacket she is wearing a black dress which is cut to drape elegantly around her neat figure. It looks deceptively simple, but I think that Mireille and Claire would have appreciated the technical complexity of the design, made to flatter and flow, balancing the monotone severity of the garment with a series of tucks that give the dress its structure.

'Good evening,' I reply.

'It's certainly busy through there.' The woman smiles, tilting her head towards the main exhibition hall.

'I know. It's a fantastic party. I just wanted to get a breath of air.'

'I understand.' She turns to face the dress in the display case. 'Beautiful, isn't it? You enjoy the history of these pieces, don't you? I've seen you here before, *n'est-ce pas?* Usually you are writing in your notebook. Are you a journalist?'

I tell her about my internship at Agence Guillemet, which will soon be coming to an end, and that I've been piecing together the story of my grandmother – the one I mentioned to her that day when we met in the Lanvin exhibition, who worked in couture during the war years.

She nods. 'It's a good thing to do, writing it down. The strands of history can be so tangled and complex, can't they? Here at the museum, we attempt to tease out some of those strands, letting the clothes tell their stories. And stories are so important, aren't they? I always believe we tell them in order to make sense of the chaos of our lives.'

'You work here, then? At the Palais Galliera?'

She digs into the clutch bag she carries and hands me a card. She is Sophie Rousseau – manager of early twentieth century collections.

'Thank you, Madame Rousseau. My name is Harriet. Harriet Shaw.'

She shakes my hand formally. 'It's nice to meet you, Harriet. And I've enjoyed our conversations. Get in touch when you're next coming in. If I have the time, I'll take you to see some of the gowns we have from the 1940s in our archives in the basement here.'

'I will. Thank you.'

She appraises me with her warm grey-green eyes. And then she says, 'I don't know if it would interest you, but there's a huge development project planned for the museum, to create a new, larger exhibition space in part of the basement. We will be taking on some additional staff shortly to begin planning for it. The museum will be closed for a while, but when we reopen we'll be able to display many more of the items that are kept hidden away in the archives. Send me your CV if you like and I'll pass it on. When you've finished your grandmother's story, there are plenty more to help tell here.'

'A job? Here at the Palais Galliera? It would be beyond my wildest dreams!' I exclaim. 'I'd love to send you my CV.' I tuck her card carefully into my handbag.

'Well now, it's probably time to return to the *mêlée*, don't you think? *Allons-y!* But I'll look forward to seeing you again soon, Harriet. Enjoy the rest of your evening.'

I float through the remainder of the party, trying – and failing – to keep my feet on the ground as I imagine myself working in these very rooms. Perhaps it's the champagne giving me courage, but I'm beginning to dare to dream of a life for myself in Paris.

1945

Each weekend, Mireille made the trip to visit Claire at the American Hospital in Neuilly, bringing with her news from the world outside: a world no longer at war. She would tuck her arm into Claire's and take her outside to walk slowly along the paths between manicured lawns and beds full of bright flowers, letting the summer sun coax a little colour back into her cheeks. When Claire grew tired, they would sit on a bench beneath the trees and Mireille would entertain her friend with stories from the Lelong couture house, describing the latest designs created by Monsieur Dior and adding snippets of gossip about the clients who came for their fittings.

At first, it seemed that Claire was reluctant to return to the world that she'd been taken from, almost as if she didn't want to be there. But slowly, week by week with help and care, Mireille watched her friend return to life. And very gently, when she sensed the time was right, she began to prompt Claire to talk about the things that had happened to her and to Vivi. Some of the memories were still too painful to bring out into the light of those Paris summer days, but Claire talked about working in the textile factory and the sewing room in the camp's reception centre, and she remembered how Vivi had never stopped finding ways to resist, in spite of the beatings and the torture, the starvation and the cold. When others around them had been deprived of the last scraps of their humanity, Vivi had refused to relinquish hers. It was those memories, more than anything else, that helped Claire to begin to heal.

Mireille was cycling back from Neuilly one Sunday evening when she reached the Pont Neuf. She dismounted and propped her bike against the wall, then slipped down the steps on to the island in the middle of the Seine. The willow tree was still there, on the point at the end of the Île de la Cité, a survivor of the battle to liberate Paris. She crept in beneath its branches to sit for a while, and think of home and watch the river flow past. She heard the sound of footsteps hastening along the cobbles of the quayside behind her, but thought nothing of it, assuming it would be one of the boatmen going about his business, returning to his vessel in the golden light of the summer's evening.

The footsteps stopped. Then she heard a voice, softly calling her name.

She scrambled to her feet, steadying herself against the solid trunk of the tree. And there, parting the languid greenery and ducking his head beneath the willow's branches was a man in a French army uniform. He set down his heavy kit bag and as he reached her side he put out a hand, tentatively, to touch her face, as if making sure she was real, not some vision from a long-lost dream, standing there beside the river as it turned to gold in the evening light.

'I was coming to find you in the Rue Cardinale. I saw you from the bridge. At least, I thought it was you, with those curls, so I had to come and check,' he said. 'Mireille Martin. How I have missed you.'

And she lifted her hand to cover his and spoke the name that she'd kept a secret for so long, the name of the man she'd fallen in love with.

'Philippe Thibault. How I have missed you, too.'

❦

When they'd made the journey from Dachau to the hospital in Paris, it had felt like a dream to Claire. How could it have taken so long for the train that she and Vivi had travelled on to reach the camps when the Red Cross ambulance taking her back was just one long day's drive? She had been that close, all along, and yet she had been worlds away from her home in the city.

It had taken a few days to arrange the transport and during that time Monsieur Leroux had scarcely left her bedside. Although now she knew he wasn't 'Monsieur Leroux' at all.

The first thing he'd asked, as he sat holding her hand, was whether she knew where Vivi was. She'd looked at him in numbed silence at first, still seeing shadows of her friend's eyes in his. Her head felt heavy and sore in the aftermath of the fever, and she was confused by the sight of him here at Dachau, struggling to understand what she was seeing and hearing. The sound of Vivi's name, spoken aloud by him, was a shock.

Her lips were dry and cracked and he had to lean close to make out her reply. 'I couldn't save her,' she whispered. 'I tried. She saved me, but I couldn't save her.' Then the tears began to fall, soaking the parched, drawn skin of her face like rain falling after a drought, and he gathered her frail body into his arms and held her as she cried.

In the days that followed, while they waited for her to be strong enough to make the journey back to Paris and he made the arrangements with the American Hospital, he was a constant presence at her bedside. He fed her the nutritious soup, which was all her starved body could digest at first, a few spoonfuls at a time, filling her shrunken stomach. He made sure she drank the bitter-tasting tonic and he gently massaged ointment into her hands and feet, soothing and mending the broken, scarred skin. He refused to leave, even when night fell, and she would awaken from her nightmares to find him there, holding her hand, soothing her as Vivi had done before. 'Hush now. I'm here. You're alright.'

She couldn't talk, yet, about what had happened at the Gestapo headquarters in the Avenue Foch, nor on the train journey to Dachau, nor at the camp. Instead, he talked and she listened in amazement – sometimes wondering whether she'd dreamed what he'd told her about himself and about Vivi.

The first thing was his name. Laurence Redman. ('Everyone calls me Larry, though,' he'd told her). Not Monsieur Leroux, after all, although the French was a direct translation from the English.

And the second thing was that Vivi was his sister.

They had grown up in the north of England, not in Lille, although their mother was French and Lille had been her home town. Their English father owned a textile factory and that was how Vivi had known so much about the machinery in the factory in Dachau. 'She used to follow Dad around, asking endless questions, wanting to know how everything worked. She always loved sewing,' he told Claire. 'When she was little, she used to make dresses for her dolls. Then she progressed to making her own clothes. She worked at the local theatre, too, making costumes – she loved all those rich fabrics and trimmings. And it turned out she was a talented actress as well.

'When war broke out, I was selected to train with the Special Operations Executive,' he continued. 'So when she came to me and told me that she wanted to join too, to do something to help the French, I knew she would be the perfect fit. We're both fluent in French because our mother always spoke it at home, and our knowledge of textiles and fashion were exactly what the SOE were looking for to set up a network based in Paris, where the couture industry provided the perfect cover.'

He stopped then, unable to continue for a minute as he remembered his beautiful, lively sister. 'I tried to dissuade her,' he said at last. 'But you know how she was – so stubborn, so determined. And those, too, were characteristics that made her perfect for her role. She was just what they were looking for. She did the training and passed with flying colours. And so they gave her one of the most dangerous roles going. Wireless operator for the network, camouflaged by her role as a seamstress in the heart of Paris. I didn't know whether to be proud of her or frightened for her, my little sister.'

When he broke down, burying his head in his hands, Claire reached out and stroked his hair. Gathering her strength, she spoke then. 'You and I, we both carry the weight of our guilt. We both played a part in her fate. But, listening to you, I now understand that nothing we could have done would have stopped her. She was determined to fight for France, for what was right. It's who she was. She would always have put herself in the way of danger, stood up against what she knew to be wrong. She had real courage. She was a soldier.'

They wept together, their tears mingling, comforting one another, and while the grief cracked open her heart, hurting almost as much as Claire's physical scars, she knew that the tears and the pain would allow something new to grow from it. With him – Larry – at her side, together they could find a way to live again.

He told her one other thing too. Vivi's real name. She wasn't called Vivienne.

She was called Harriet.

Harriet

So now, at last, I know who I am.

I am Harriet. Named for my great-aunt who died in Dachau on the day it was liberated. Harriet, who chose the name Vivienne because she loved life. Harriet, who was warm and friendly and oh so brave. Brave enough to turn towards danger when freedom was threatened; brave enough to volunteer to put herself right in the heart of the war, in one of the most dangerous roles there was. When the average life expectancy of a wireless operator in the Resistance was six weeks, she survived for four years.

I am Harriet – and although she died before I was born, I know that I am loved by my grandmother Claire, who grew to find a courage within herself that she hadn't known was there. Claire lost her own mother, and history repeated itself – as it has a horrible tendency to do – when I lost mine. I've read that the currents of trauma run deep in families. They can be inherited, passed down the generations from one to the next, ruining lives as they go. Perhaps that's what happened to my mother. But I won't let it happen to me. Now that I understand where that trauma came from, I can see it for what it is. And by finding the courage to turn and face it, I have the opportunity to stop it in its tracks.

What gives me even more hope is that during my sessions with the counsellor she has told me that new research has found that the effects of inherited trauma can be reversed. Our brains and our bodies have the capacity to heal, to build resilience that will help us to counteract the vulnerabilities that inherited trauma predisposes us to. She's given me some books to read which say that to be able to do this, the mind has to reframe and release the trauma so that the brain can reset itself.

I realise that the story of Claire and Vivi (who was really Harriet) has allowed this to happen for me. I know now that I can heal the past damage that I've carried with me all my life so far. More than that, I realise that I can decide to set down the weight of it at the side of the path that is my life and to walk on without it.

Now that I know the whole story of my grandmother, I sit in stunned silence, thoughts whirling in my head. I touch the charms on the bracelet passed down to me by my grandmother and my mother: the thimble, the tiny pair of scissors, the Eiffel Tower. I understand the significance of each one now.

I came to Paris feeling rootless, without a family of my own. I was looking for something, although I didn't know what it would be. A photograph brought me here. I reach over and pick it up, in its frame, and I imagine I can hear the echoes of the girls' laughter as they stand on the corner of the street, outside Delavigne Couture, dressed in their Sunday finery as they set off, one May morning in Paris, to visit the Louvre.

Because of them, Simone and I are here now. Not just here working for Agence Guillemet and living in the apartment under the eaves of the building in the Rue Cardinale; they are the reason that we are here at all. What if Mireille hadn't gone to save Claire on the night that Billancourt was bombed? What if Vivi – my great-aunt Harriet – hadn't protected and helped Claire to survive the terrible ordeals of torture at the hands of the Gestapo, solitary confinement in Fresnes prison, and almost two years in the hell of Dachau concentration camp?

I wouldn't be alive if it weren't for them. I owe them my life, too.

When that photograph was taken, those three young women – full of hopes and dreams – had their lives ahead of them. It seems to me that they epitomise a love for life. They weren't to know, on that May morning, just how far that love was going to be tested.

And then I think of my mother. How deep do depression and despair have to drag a person until, at last, they reach a place where they can't bear to go on? Claire and Vivi showed how much the human spirit can endure: brutality, cruelty, inhumanity – all of these can be borne. It is the loss of those you love that is unbearable.

All of a sudden, I realise that through hearing the stories of my grandmother Claire and my great-aunt Harriet, I have finally come to understand what it was that killed my mother. It was grief. No matter what it might say on the death certificate, I understand, now, that she died of a broken heart.

My history has set me free. The past has given me a future. Perhaps it is a future that involves staying on in my dream job at the Palais Galliera, because Sophie Rousseau has passed my CV on to the director of the museum and I've been invited to attend an interview. It's a daunting prospect. I want this job so much it hurts. But I will give the interview my all and accept the outcome, whatever it may be, because I'm not scared to live my life any more, whatever it may bring.

I understand, too, that I have been scared to love, because the stakes seemed just too high. I've seen what the price of love can be and I decided that it was too high to risk having to pay. So I've always protected myself from it. I haven't dared to risk loving my father, my step-family, my friends. And Thierry. I have kept my heart locked away to protect it. But now I have been shown the truth. Claire and Vivi are not just faces in a photograph any more, they are a part of me. I owe it to them to tap into the legacy of courage that runs through my veins. They have given me the gift of life. Until now, I have allowed the legacy of trauma to imprison my spirit. But through hearing their story, I know that I am strong enough to turn away from it. I won't let the darkness win. I will turn my face towards the light. And, just maybe, I'll be able to love as open-heartedly as they did.

As I reach for my phone, the charms on my bracelet clink against each other, making a sound like a faint, triumphant round of applause. There's a message I need to send and I don't want to waste another moment before I do so.

I scroll through my contacts and I select Thierry's number.

~⁂~

Thierry's apartment is a tiny studio in the Marais. It's only one room, but the magical thing about it is that it opens on to a narrow balcony where there's just enough space for two chairs, side by side. We've sat here for hours, and I've talked more than I think I've ever done before. We've agreed to take it slowly – neither of us wants to get hurt and I know that my pulling away from him before has left him cautious. But he's prepared to give it another go, and I sense that this time the connection is stronger than ever, on both sides of the relationship.

As Thierry goes inside to fetch glasses and a bottle of wine, my phone rings. Loath to spoil the peace of the moment, I'm about to switch it off when I see that the caller is Sophie Rousseau, from the Palais Galliera.

'Hello?' I say, tentatively.

Her voice is warm as she tells me that she wanted to be the first to congratulate me: I've got the job.

When Thierry returns, I am on my feet, looking out across the city. Darkness is falling and the lights of the city begin to twinkle, sequins on a black velvet robe. They call it the City of Light. And now I can also call it my home.

~⁂~

We go out that weekend to celebrate, meeting Simone and the rest of the crowd in the same basement bar where Thierry and I first met.

There's music and friendship and many, many drinks to toast my new career. And Thierry and I hold hands under the table, not wanting to let go for a moment now that we've found each other.

At the end of the evening, we decide to walk back to the apartment in the Rue Cardinale with Simone. We say goodnight to the others and the three of us begin to wander slowly homewards. Simone hangs back a little, giving me and Thierry space to walk on ahead. I love the feeling of being close to him, his arm wrapped around my waist. I turn to glance back and see Simone is rooting in her handbag for something. She pulls out a pair of earphones and waves them at me triumphantly, then begins to walk again, still a few yards back, listening to her music.

I hear the faint wail of sirens behind us and turn to see the flicker of blue lights in the distance. They are approaching fast, speeding along the street as they chase a white van, herding it towards us. Simone, still wired to her music, is oblivious and she smiles at me enquiringly. Thinking I am waiting for her to catch up, she good-naturedly waves her hands, shooing me on ahead. But the van is speeding towards her, the driver losing control. The lights of the police car are gaining on it, engulfing the white sides of the van in their blue flames as it draws alongside, trying to force the driver to pull over. Time seems to stand still as the van swerves and mounts the pavement behind Simone.

Without thinking, I run.

I run towards the blue lights, towards Simone, who has stopped, frozen, as the lights envelop her too, silhouetting her against the white metalwork which will throw her high into the air when it hits her, crumpling her body into a broken, huddled mass.

I reach her a split second before the van does, my momentum carrying me on as, with all my strength, I push her out of the way.

I hear a scream and a noise like a whip cracking.

And then all the lights go out at once and there is darkness.

My father is reading me a bedtime story. It's *Little Women*, I realise, one of my all-time favourite books. I listen to the rise and fall of his voice, chapter after chapter, telling the story of Meg, Jo, Beth and Amy. I'm dreaming, of course, but it's such a comforting dream that I don't want to open my eyes and make it come to an end. And so I keep them closed, so that I can stay just like this, resting in a time of innocence from years gone by.

Something keeps trying to pull me out of the dream, though. A nagging thought that I can't quite grasp, just out of reach. It's telling me to open my eyes, saying that, while that part of my past was filled with kindness and love, I have a present and a future that are filled with even more love. Another voice – not my father's – tells me that it's time to wake up and live.

When I open my eyes at last, the soft light of an autumn afternoon turns tumbling brown leaves into spun gold outside the windows of an unfamiliar room. My head feels strangely heavy and constricted, as if my scalp is too tight. Very carefully, I turn it a fraction, first one way and then the other. To the left, my father sits in a chair at my bedside, intent on the book he holds in his hands as he continues to recite the March family's story. To my right is Thierry. His head is bowed, as if he's praying as he listens to the words my father is reading. He is holding my hand, carefully avoiding the tube which runs from my arm to a drip stand beside the bed.

Experimentally – because everything seems very far away and disconnected and I'm not sure I can feel my fingers – I give Thierry's hand a gentle squeeze. He doesn't respond. So I try again.

This time he lifts his head. And when his eyes meet mine, a smile like a sunrise spreads slowly across his face, as if all his prayers just came true.

❧

My hospital room is filled with flowers. A vase of bright sunflowers from Simone sits on the windowsill, alongside roses from Florence and my colleagues at the Agence Guillemet and a bunch of sweet-smelling white freesias from Sophie Rousseau at the Palais Galliera.

The biggest bouquet of all is from my stepmother and sisters and it was delivered with a card sending their love and urging me to come home. 'They're longing to see you,' Dad says. 'As soon as half term arrives, they're coming over. We're all so proud of you, Harriet. And the girls never stop talking about how cool it is having a big sister who's made a career for herself in French fashion.'

'It'll be fun showing them round the museum,' I say – and I find that I mean it. I actually quite miss them.

I've been asleep for five days, apparently, in a medically induced coma. And my father has sat at my bedside on every single one of those days and read from the book my stepmother put into his hastily packed suitcase. '*Take this to her,*' he tells me she said. '*It was always Harriet's favourite.*'

Thierry visits often and the nurses have all fallen in love with him, they tell me. 'Not that he ever notices us. When you were in the coma, he wouldn't leave your side,' they say. 'Such a romantic!'

My mind is a blank when it comes to remembering the accident, so Thierry fills in the missing parts of the jigsaw for me. 'The police were chasing a suspect. And the tip-off they'd been given was right – they found bomb-making materials in the back of the van. The driver was part of a terrorist cell. There've been several arrests.'

He takes my hand, and strokes it, carefully avoiding the tape covering the needle which connects me to the drip at my bedside. 'You pushed Simone to safety – without a doubt, you saved her life. The van would have flattened her. But when you ran towards her, the wing mirror caught your head, a real crack, it knocked you out cold. I thought you were dead. Those were some of the worst moments of my life. The police wouldn't let me hold you – you had a severe head injury and they were worried that your neck might be damaged too, so we couldn't move you. At last the ambulance arrived and they brought you here.

They did a scan and then operated straight away, to relieve the pressure on your brain. You were put into a coma to allow the swelling to go down. It was touch and go, they said. They told me to call your father and ask him to come as quickly as he could. Simone and I were beside ourselves. She was in shock at the time too, of course. She's been here every day as well, but they only allow two people in at a time.'

Thierry phones Simone to let her know that I've woken up and she demands to speak to me. We don't have much of a conversation, what with my drowsiness and her crying as she thanks me, over and over, for saving her life. But through her tears, she promises she'll be in first thing tomorrow morning.

I feel exhausted. My head is still heavy, my brain thick with drugs and concussive shock, so Dad kisses me on the forehead, just below the line of the crepe bandage, and heads back to his hotel for the night. After he's gone, Thierry kicks off his boots and climbs on to the bed beside me, gently wrapping me in his arms.

'I have something for you,' he says. He reaches into his pocket and brings out my charm bracelet. 'They had to take this off you before you went into the scanner and the nurse gave it to me for safe-keeping. I know how much it means to you.'

'Thank you. Can you help me put it on, please?'

He fastens the catch. And then he fishes something else out of his pocket. A little square box. He helps me to open it and inside is a tiny golden heart, engraved with the letter 'H'.

'I thought maybe your bracelet might have room for one more charm,' he says.

Smiling, I rest my throbbing head on his shoulder, which feels more comfortable than any pillow. And then, still holding the little box, I drift off into another deep, deep sleep.

Simone arrives as I'm finishing my breakfast the next morning. It's a plastic-wrapped croissant and a cup of coffee but, given that it's the first proper food I've eaten in almost a week, it tastes pretty good to me and certainly a lot more satisfying than an intravenous drip.

After she's hugged me so hard that I can hardly breathe, Simone wrinkles up her nose at the remnants on my tray. 'Ugh, that looks inedible,' she says, picking it up and moving it to an empty table at the bed opposite mine. She fishes in her handbag and draws out a punnet of sweetly perfumed strawberries, a freshly made drink from the juice bar around the corner from the apartment in the Rue Jacob, a box of macaroons from Ladurée and two bars of Côte d'Or chocolate.

'Here,' she says, handing me the juice, 'drink this first. You need your vitamins. And then you can eat the rest.'

The juice is slightly sludgy khaki colour, but whatever is in it tastes absolutely delicious.

Simone kicks off her shoes and props her feet on my bed and we spend a happy hour or so eating chocolate and chatting. She fills me in on the news from Agence Guillemet and tells me that everyone sends their love.

A nurse comes to shoo her out at last, saying that I need to rest, and Simone gathers up her things. Then she hugs me again, a gesture of solidarity, and sisterhood, and friendship. And, as she stands up and heads for the door, she pauses, turning back to say, 'By the way, my whole family are demanding that I come home and that I bring you with me. They all want to meet you. To thank you in person for saving me. Especially my grandmother, Mireille. She says she wants to tell you more about Claire . . . about what happened afterwards. And she has something for you.'

My father comes in at lunchtime, bringing me some little savoury pastries from a *charcuterie* that he passed on the way to the hospital from his hotel. We share them as he tells me how excited my sisters are to be coming to visit at the end of October. My stepmother's already booked the Eurostar tickets. 'They miss you, you know, Harriet. They're looking forward to spending some time with you. We all are.'

He takes my hand in his and holds it tightly. 'I owe you an apology,' he says.

'What for?' I ask, genuinely taken aback.

'For not handling anything very well when you most needed me to. I'm so sorry, I could see how badly you were grieving when Felicity . . . well, when she died. I was so consumed by my own sense of guilt, of having failed you, that I just couldn't find the words that needed to be said to help you get through it. I should have reassured you, kept you with us instead of sending you away to boarding school. I thought it was the right thing to do at the time, giving you your space, not forcing a new family and a new home on you. But now I think it was probably the last thing you needed. We should have stuck together and muddled through. Worked things out a bit better. I should have been there for you.'

I give his hand a squeeze. 'It's okay, Dad. I think we were all trying to make the best of a horrific situation. I know you wanted what was best for me – I just don't think any of us knew what that was, though. I can see, now, how hard it was for you as well. For all of us. But we've come through it. Older and wiser, eh? And I think we're all ready for a new beginning.'

I can see now, with the benefit of hindsight and a large pinch of perspective, that it really was tough for him as well as for me. It must have been hard for my stepmother, too, but now I realise how hard she tried to care for me and to make me a part of the new family into which I'd been catapulted.

Dad gently touches the charms on the bracelet around my wrist. 'Felicity always loved that bracelet, wore it all the time. It was her link to her own mother. It's good to see you wearing it too. She would have been happy to know you've carried on the tradition.'

Then his eyes fill with tears and I pull him closer so that we can hug each other. He strokes my hair, like he used to do when I was a little girl and, through his tears, he smiles. 'I couldn't bear to lose you, you know, Harriet. It would have been too much. I love you and I'm so proud that you're my daughter.'

After he's gone, I reflect on what I've learnt about the paradox of love: when the price of losing it is too high a risk to take, we draw back and protect ourselves from that loss, even though that means we stop ourselves from loving wholeheartedly. After Mum died, I think Dad and I were protecting ourselves from ever feeling that way again. But maybe now, at last, we can both put the burden of our grief aside and walk on, together. Bringing comfort to one another.

The father and daughter who were left behind.

Harriet

Staying in south-west France with Simone's family is like being swept into a fast-flowing river of noise and love and laughter. Her parents envelop me in hugs that last almost as long as those they bestow on their daughter. Her mother, Josiane, weeps tears of joy and relief over us both and thanks me over and over again for saving Simone's life. Her father, Florian, is a man of few words, a stonemason like his father before him, who works in the family firm with his three brothers. But he, too, enfolds me in a bear-hug which speaks volumes and leaves me gasping for breath.

Simone's older sisters are a little shy at first, but quickly relax over the supper that gathers us all around a long table outside under an arched trellis hung with jasmine and fairy lights. At first the evening is filled with laughter and chatter as the family catches up with local news. Later, though, we talk more sombrely about the accident and how lucky we both were.

By the time I fall into bed in the Thibaults' spare room, I scarcely have time to turn out the light before I sink into one of the deepest sleeps I've ever enjoyed.

Next morning, I join Simone at the breakfast table. She's been up a while already, I can tell, eager to spend time with her family, and has picked a bunch of autumn flowers to take to her *mamie*, Mireille. The fresh bread which Josiane puts on my plate is the perfect combination of soft and crusty, and I slather it with white butter and a generous helping of amber apricot jam. It tastes better than any creation from the finest of patisseries in Paris ever could.

As Simone and I walk up the hill to the little cottage where Mireille lives, we're accompanied by half a dozen swifts who swoop and soar overhead, filling the perfect blue dome of the sky above us with their complex, never-ending dance. This far south the season is slower in turning, the last days of summer lingering longer here than in Paris. The sun warms my back, but at the same time there's a mellow softness to the light and a sense that the swifts are flexing their wings, preparing to make their long journey south for the winter.

We turn into a lane and pass the end of a driveway lined with tall oak trees. A large black cat, which has been dozing in the shade, gets to its feet as we draw near and stretches luxuriantly. Simone bends down to scratch behind his ears and he purrs loudly, butting her hand rapturously with his broad head. 'Hello, Lafitte,' she says. 'Where are my little cousins today?' She explains that one of her uncles – another of Mireille's stonemason sons – lives in the house with his English wife and their children, and that the old cat is very much a part of the family.

We carry on up the lane, escorted by the cat as far as Mireille's house. He watches as we turn in at the gate and then, tail held high, makes his way back down the lane to his lookout post under the oaks once more.

Mireille's cottage is surrounded by vineyards hung with grapes which, Simone tells me, will be harvested in a few weeks' time. Bright geraniums blaze in pots at every window. Simone knocks and then pushes the front door open, calling, '*Coucou!*'

'Come in!' The voice that replies is cracked and softened with age. 'I'm in the kitchen.'

Although she will shortly be celebrating her one hundredth birthday, I would still recognise Mireille from the photograph of the three girls on the Rue Cardinale. Her hair is pure white now, but a few unruly curls still make their escape from the bun at the nape of her neck, refusing to be constrained. Her deep brown eyes are still bright, her gaze birdlike as she smiles up at us. She's sitting in an old armchair which dwarfs her diminutive figure, and has a bowl of peas on her lap which she's been shelling into a colander, her claw-like fingers still deft in their work despite being gnarled with arthritis. I picture those same fingers in years gone by, flying over fine fabrics, a needle flashing as it laid down one tiny stitch after another.

She sets aside the bowl, smoothing down the apron she wears, and hauls herself to her feet, embracing her granddaughter. 'Simone, *ma chérie*,' she murmurs, cupping her face between those gnarled hands, letting her know how much she is treasured.

Then she turns to look at me. '*Harriette*.' She pronounces my name as though it were French. 'Here at last.' She nods, as if listening to internal voices that we cannot hear. 'You have a lot of your grandmother in you. But your eyes are those of your grandfather. And, of course, your great-aunt too.' She pulls me close, with a surprising amount of strength for such a diminutive and elderly lady, peering into my face as if she is reading all that is written there. Her bright eyes seem to pierce to the very core of my being. She nods again, apparently approving of what she has seen there.

Then she clasps me in an embrace that is tender and loving, and for a moment I am overcome with the feeling that there are three people holding me, not just one. It is as if she is the keeper of their spirits: Claire and Vivi are here, holding me as well.

'Bring the tea things,' she says to Simone, gesturing towards a tray. 'We will sit in the garden.'

She takes my arm and I help her outside. To one side there's a neat bed of vegetables, the well-worked soil as dark as chocolate, nourishing a rich treasure trove of ruby tomatoes, emerald green courgettes and the amethyst and silver thistle-like heads of artichokes. Pea plants scramble up a bamboo wigwam, the last of the summer stems clinging on with their thread-like fingers. We make our way to the shade of a lime tree whose leaves are just beginning to be edged with gold, and sit down on a bench beside a little tin table.

Mireille reaches for a thick, leather-bound photo album which sits on the table, moving it to make space for Simone to set down the tea tray. 'As you can see I like a proper pot of tea, in the English style.' Mireille smiles. 'I had an English neighbour who taught me to appreciate such things.' She gestures towards the sprawling stone house that we passed on our way here, where Simone's cousins live, just visible beyond the oak trees that surround it. 'My friend is gone now, alas. But her niece is married to my second-youngest son and they live in the house these days, so happily I can still visit for tea sometimes. It's funny, isn't it, how the strands of our lives interweave themselves in unexpected ways?' She tilts her head to one side, her bright eyes shooting me another piercing glance.

'Fate is a strangely complicated thing, is it not?' she continues. 'But I have lived so long now that very little surprises me. When Simone told me that Claire's granddaughter was sharing the apartment with her in the Rue Cardinale, I had a premonition that you would come here one day. Although I had no idea that you would do so having saved my granddaughter's life. And so we come full circle, *n'est-ce pas?* If I hadn't gone to save Claire that night when Billancourt was bombed, you would not have been there to save my Simone all these years later. So it seems that fate still has a few surprises up its sleeve, even for someone of my advanced age. Which is just as it should be.' She chuckles and pats my hand.

'Pour the tea for us, Simone. And I will show Harriet the pictures of her beautiful grandmother.'

She heaves the album on to her lap and begins to turn the pages until she comes to the pictures she's looking for. It takes me a moment to understand what I'm looking at. There's a bride, in a beautiful dress whose full skirt emphasises her tiny waist. Her dark curls are tied back loosely and woven with starry flowers. The lines of the dress are breathtaking. It's a perfect example of Dior's New Look, the style that made him world-famous in the post-war years.

And then I look at the figure standing next to the bride: her maid of honour. Her white-blonde hair is caught up in a smooth chignon and she holds a posy of pale flowers which match the bride's more lavish bouquet. There's something fragile about her, something almost other-worldly. But it's her dress that makes me gasp. It's midnight blue, cut on the bias, draping softly over the thin lines of the young woman's body. And just visible where the light catches them, I can make out a scattering of tiny silver beads along the neckline which sits beneath the sharp wings of her collarbones.

'Wasn't she beautiful?' Mireille turns the page, showing me more photographs from her wedding day. 'Your grandmother Claire . . . and that's Larry, your grandfather, of course. A very handsome couple they made. Do you recognise the dress, Harriet?'

I nod, unable to speak, my eyes shining with tears of joy and sadness. 'It's the one she made,' I whisper at last. 'The one pieced together from scraps.'

'When I moved out of the apartment in the Rue Cardinale, I found the dress in Claire's wardrobe. I packed it up and brought it home with me. I told her I had it but when she came for my wedding she didn't want to look at it at first, wanted to tear it to pieces and throw it away. She said it was a reminder of her vanity and naivety, and she'd prefer to forget. But I told her she was wrong to think that way. That it was a triumph. A thing of beauty that she'd created from those off-cuts, a manifestation of the way she managed to create something so beautiful in a time of hardship and danger. I made her promise not to throw it away and asked her to wear it to be my maid of honour. That way, from then on it would also be associated with something joyous. I wanted to turn it into an emblem of survival and of the triumph of good over evil, you see.'

'It's so beautiful,' I agree. 'And so is your wedding dress, Mireille. Did Monsieur Dior design it for you?'

She laughs. 'He did. Well spotted. You really do have an eye for fashion, just as Simone told me. Can you guess what it is made from?'

I peer closely at the photograph. The fabric is a creamy white, so fine that it looks almost translucent. 'From the way the skirt falls in those folds, I'd guess it was silk.' I look up at her. 'But where did you get such fine material so soon after the war?'

'My husband, of course.' Her eyes twinkle with amusement. 'When Philippe came to find me in Paris at the end of the war, he had with him a large kit bag. There were almost no personal belongings in it. But it did contain one large army-issue parachute. This time, he hadn't buried it in a turnip field. He kept his promise to me and saved it for me to make something from. As it turned out, what I made was my wedding dress!'

As I hand the photo album back to her, she catches sight of the gold charm bracelet on my wrist. 'But how wonderful to see this being worn still!' she exclaims. 'I gave it to Claire on my wedding day as a gift for being my maid of honour and my friend. Knowing that she was going to make a new life in England, with Larry, I wanted her to take a little bit of France with her. It had just the one charm on it – *la Tour Eiffel*. She wrote and told me that your grandfather gave her a charm each year on their wedding anniversary.'

She peers closely at the bracelet, separating the charms with the tip of her gnarled finger so that she can see them more clearly: the bobbin of thread, the scissors, the shoe, the tiny thimble. When she comes to the heart that Thierry gave me, she pauses. 'This one looks brand new.' She smiles.

'It is,' I say. 'Perhaps Thierry and I will keep the tradition going. Or maybe start a new one of our own.'

We sit for over an hour, sipping tea and poring over the album of photographs. At last, Mireille sets the book aside. 'It's nearly time for you to go home for lunch,' she says to Simone. 'But before you do, help me to my feet. There is something else I want to show Harriet.'

Back inside the cottage, she leads the way down the hall to a formal sitting room. The shutters have been closed to keep out the bright sunlight and she instructs us to open them. Two long, ghostly shapes hang from a shelf on one wall and Mireille shuffles over to them. They are sheets, covering two garments on coat-hangers and, very carefully, she begins to un-pin the first one. Simone moves to help her and, as I watch, the Dior wedding dress emerges from its wrappings. In real life it's even more beautiful than it was in the photograph. The bodice of the dress is embroidered with cream flowers and the centre of each is picked out with a tiny seed pearl. Mireille gently runs the tip of her bent forefinger over the tiny stitches. 'Claire's work,' she says. 'I made my dress and she did the embroidery for me. She was always the best at that.'

Then she turns to the second draped sheet. 'And this is for you, Harriet.' She undoes the pins that hold the sheet in place and as it falls to the floor it reveals an evening gown of midnight blue crêpe de Chine, whose neckline sparkles where the sunshine that floods the room catches the constellation of tiny silver beads scattered across it. It's only when you look closely that you can see that the body of the dress has been pieced together from offcuts and scraps, with stitches so tiny and perfect that they are almost invisible.

'Claire's dress,' I gasp.

Mireille nods. 'When she left after my wedding, to start her new life in England with Larry, she decided that she didn't want to take the dress with her. "It belongs in France," she told me. And so I kept it, all these years. I didn't know it at the time, but I kept it so that when her granddaughter finally came back, she would have this piece of her grandmother's life. And through it, she would understand a little bit more of who she was and where she came from. Take it with you, Harriet. It's time its story was told now.'

Carefully, I take the dress down from its hanger and the fine silk whispers as I let the folds of deep blue fabric run through my hands. Simone helps me to wrap it in tissue paper to preserve it for the journey back to its original home in Paris.

As we say our goodbyes, Mireille reaches into the pocket of her apron. 'I have one more thing to give you, Harriet,' she says.

She pulls out a silver locket which hangs on a fine chain. She hands it to me, saying, 'Go ahead, open it.'

Even before I prise open the catch, stiff with age, I know what I will find within. And, sure enough, when the two halves open, the faces of Claire and Vivienne-who-was-really-Harriet smile up at me from the palm of my hand.

2017

The exhibition is finally ready now. As I leave the gallery and go to join my colleagues for a celebratory drink at the bar around the corner, I turn out the lights. But just as I'm about to press the last switch, I hesitate.

In the centre of the darkened gallery the display case is still illuminated, the light catching the tiny silver beads scattered along the neckline of the midnight blue dress. From a distance, you might think it's been cut from one single piece of fabric. It's only when you look more closely that you can see the truth.

I understand it a little better now; the truth about my grandmother and my great-aunt; the truth about my own mother; the truth about myself.

This extraordinary dress – this piece of living history – has helped to tell the stories of Claire and my great-aunt Harriet. They were ordinary people, but the extraordinary times that they lived in saw them step up to become extraordinary too. No matter how tough it got, no matter how dark the night, they never gave in.

And their stories have helped to illuminate the truth about my mother. At last the fog of anger and pain that have enveloped my feelings for her for all these years have dissipated, letting compassion shine through. She was the daughter that Claire and Larry had, late in life once Claire's broken body had finally healed enough to bear a child.

They named her Felicity for the joy she brought them, and they had poured into her all their hopes. But perhaps she had carried the burden of their guilt and grief as well. Was it something that was inherited through the genes? Or was it passed on to her in other ways that were subtly invasive, ways that Claire couldn't prevent? The night fears, the trauma, the knowledge that human beings are capable of being so inhuman? Were they all still there, beneath Claire's scarred skin, those deeper scars that could never be healed? And did my mother pick up on that, on some subconscious level?

I realise, too, that in spite of everything else they went through, my grandmother and great-aunt never had to endure being abandoned through their darkest days and nights: they were there to comfort and reassure one another, come what may. Perhaps that, therefore, is the most powerful feeling of all, the feeling that you are not alone in the world. And perhaps, when my mother found herself abandoned, by her parents who had died and by the husband who left her alone with the daughter that should have bound them together, she didn't have the resilience to carry on. It was abandonment that broke her heart.

I'm sure that Claire was only trying to protect her own child, my mother, by not telling her about what had happened in the war. All my mother had known was that it was something terrible, shameful, somehow, something never to be mentioned by either of her parents in case the healing scars were reopened. And she had known her aunt Harriet's name. I wonder what she had known of Harriet's story. Had Claire ever talked about the guilt? Was Felicity aware that both her parents felt responsible for the suffering and death of the friend and sister they loved so much? And was naming me after my great-aunt Harriet an attempt by my mother to put the past to rights?

I wish my mother had known the whole story. Perhaps she would have understood, then. Perhaps she wouldn't have felt so alone. She would have felt, as I do, that no matter how dark the night became she could make it through. Because she would have known that Harriet and Claire were a part of her, as they are a part of me.

I think of the three girls in the photograph who brought me here to tell their story. Their faces are even more familiar to me now because I can see that they live on. In Mireille's face, her dark eyes sparkle with the same humour and kindness as the eyes of my friend Simone – the friend who is alive today because her grandmother saved my grandmother all those years before.

In my grandmother Claire, I see the loving gentleness that is reflected in the photograph of my mother, holding me in her arms as a tiny baby.

And then there is my great-aunt, for whom I am named. Harriet, who took the name Vivienne because she was so full of life. I know I have a little of her courage. I know, if I am called upon, I will stand up, as she did, and turn to face danger. I won't run away. I will fight for what is most important. For life.

I open the locket that I wear around my neck and I look at the photographs of my grandmother Claire and my great-aunt Harriet that are held safely within.

The light in their eyes shines, even in the darkness of the shadows that partially obscure their faces in the small black and white photos. Just as the silver beads still shine on the neckline of the dress as I turn out the last of the lights in the gallery and the display case is plunged into darkness.

And as I close the doors of the exhibition hall behind me, I sense that they are here with me, Claire and Vivi, reaching out across the years to take my hand and to whisper, *'Hush now. We are together. Everything will be alright.'*

AUTHOR'S NOTE

The research I carried out for some sections of *The Dressmaker's Gift* was harrowing in the extreme, but I felt it was important to persevere in order to do justice to telling the stories of some of the very brave women who worked for the Resistance and suffered in Nazi concentration camps during World War Two. Reading their stories led me to dedicate this book to them.

As ever, I have tried to stay as true to the facts as possible. I would like to acknowledge some of the sources of information that I used here:

Anne Sebba's brilliant book, *Les Parisiennes: How the Women of Paris Lived, Loved and Died in the 1940s*, provided insights into life in Paris throughout the war years.

Sarah Helm's brave and insightful book, *If This is a Woman: Inside Ravensbrück: Hitler's Concentration Camp for Women*, is an essential reminder of the atrocities that were carried out by the Nazis and of the courage of the women who were incarcerated in the camps.

Referenced in a *New York Times* article by Eric Lichtblau – 'The Holocaust Just Got More Shocking' (1 March 2013) – a research project at the United States Holocaust Memorial Museum documented all the ghettos, slave labour sites, concentration camps and killing factories that the Nazis set up throughout Europe. What they found shocked even scholars steeped in the history of the Holocaust. The researchers catalogued some 42,500 Nazi ghettos and camps throughout Europe, spanning German-controlled areas from France to Russia and Germany itself, during Hitler's reign of brutality from 1933 to 1945. They estimate that fifteen to twenty million people died or were imprisoned in the sites.

The United States Holocaust Memorial Museum Encyclopedia of Camps and Ghettos, 1933–45: https://encyclopedia.ushmm.org/

Palais Galliera – the Museum of French Fashion: 10, Avenue Pierre 1er de Serbie, 75016 Paris. www.palaisgalliera.paris.fr/en/

Research into inherited trauma has been a topic of debate for some years. An article in the UK *Guardian* newspaper (21 August 2015) cites a study at New York's Mount Sinai Hospital: 'Study of Holocaust survivors finds trauma passed on to children's genes'. However, some scientists remain sceptical about the idea of genetically inherited trauma and the nature versus nurture debate continues to run on this issue. Either way, what is heartening though is that with the right help and support it is possible to rebuild resilience and counteract the effects of trauma. The Trauma Recovery and Empowerment Model is widely used by mental health practitioners as a basis for rehabilitation. A counsellor or family doctor can help with access to support in this area.

If you have been affected by any of the issues touched on in this book then I hope you will talk to friends and family. More support is available, too, from the medical profession and from the Samaritans in times of crisis:

UK: www.samaritans.org

USA: www.samaritansusa.org and www.suicidepreventionlifeline.org

ACKNOWLEDGMENTS

A massive thank you goes out to the many members of the team who help my books see the light of day: to all at the Madeleine Milburn Agency – Maddy, Giles, Hayley, Georgia, Liane-Louise and Alice; to the Lake Union team at Amazon Publishing, especially Sammia, Laura, Bekah and Nicole; and to the editors who have helped polish my manuscript – Mike Jones, Laura Gerrard, Becca Allen and Silvia Crompton.

Special thanks to my friend and fellow author Ann Lindsay, who so generously shared with me her experiences of working in Paris in a couture house immediately after the war and who gave me a wealth of information and detail which helped bring Claire, Vivi and Mireille's world to life. Any errors or embroidery of the facts are my responsibility alone.

The Birnam Writers' Group provided support, encouragement and constructive observations: Drew Campbell, Tim Turnbull, Fiona Ritchie, Lesley Wilson, Jane Archer and Mary MacDougall; and Frazer Williams at The Birnam Reader Bookshop provided the perfect meeting space and delicious cakes.

As ever, another big, heartfelt thank you goes out to all the friends and family who encourage me and provide love, gin and hugs, especially Alastair, James and Willow.

And, finally, I am so grateful to all my readers for their support and I would like to thank you personally for reading my books. If you have enjoyed *The Dressmaker's Gift*, I should be very grateful if you would consider writing a review. I love getting feedback, and I know reviews have played a big part in helping other readers to discover my work.

Merci, et à bientôt,

Fiona

ABOUT THE AUTHOR

Fiona Valpy spent seven years living in France, having moved there from the UK in 2007. She and her family renovated an old, rambling farmhouse in the Bordeaux winelands, during which time she developed new-found skills in cement-mixing, interior decorating and wine-tasting.

All of these inspirations, along with a love for the place, the people and their history, have found their way into the books she's written, which have been translated into French, Dutch, German, Norwegian, Italian, Czech, Turkish, Lithuanian and Slovenian.

Fiona now lives in Scotland, but enjoys regular visits to France in search of the sun.